To the Top of
Greenfield Street

Praise for
To the Top of Greenfield Street

"Ryan Standley's To the Top of Greenfield Street had me realizing once again why the genre is one of my all-time favorites. Eric's transformational time spent on Greenfield Street is **breathtaking**... Peopled with characters who are complex, **unforgettable**, and very true-to-life. I was wrapped up in his story from the first pages until the last and **loved every minute** I spent on Greenfield Street... the **best coming-of-age novel** I've read this year, and I'm looking forward to future works by this author. It's **most highly recommended**."

- Jack Magnus for *Readers' Favorite*

"A **well-crafted** and emotionally **compelling** coming of age tale...Standley's debut is an endearingly emotional journey of a teenager reconciling himself to his new surroundings after a tragedy forces him to move to a new town. Standley's portrayal of Eric and his other teen characters showcases his **profound understanding** of usual teenage apprehensions and struggles. The novel's chief appeal lies in Eric's **well-articulated** resilience despite his insecure demeanor. **Swift narrative**, deeply realized characterization, and tight plotting make this coming of age story **irresistible**."

- *The Prairies Book Review*

"**Compelling** realistic YA fiction! Well-drawn characters and **tight chapters** propel this coming of age story. **Highly recommended** for readers interested in **realistic** YA fiction... At its heart, this book is about home --losing a home, creating a new one, and learning to become more at home in one's self. **A great debut!**"

- Todd Mitchell, bestselling author of *The Traitor King*

"Tapping into the rich and sometimes painful vein of childhood nostalgia, To the Top of Greenfield Street by Ryan Standley is **a deep dive into the teenage psyche**... An entertaining, relatable, and **heartfelt** story. The narrative voice captures the struggles of youth, but also peppers in humor and sarcasm, emotional descriptions, and meaningful moments of **growth and revelation**."

- *SPR Editorial Review*

To the Top of
Greenfield Street

A novel

Ryan Standley

♡

For B.D.S.

Copyright © 2020 by Ryan P Standley

Summary: After tragedy strikes, Eric Daniels (15) moves to a small town, lands his first kiss, and is betrayed by a jealous friend.

Published by Ryan P Standley at Found My Heart. Printed in USA

Cover designed by Ryan P Standley with Canva

Follow the author on Twitter and Instagram @RyanPStandley

Library of Congress Control Number: 2020914676
ISBN 978-0-578-74129-1 (pb)   ISBN 978-0-578-78606-3 (hc)

JUNE
1993

Chapter 1: Fattie and Hairy

A ray of sunlight blazes through my eyelids and wakes me up. I'm in a basement, lying on a musty plaid couch, still wearing my t-shirt and jean shorts from last night. My hair is longer than ever, and I sweep the bangs off my forehead. I squint in the sun and its intense glare reminds me of the fire.

Pulsing light poured upward, into the darkness that night, as millions of glittery orange sparks flew miles into the sky. Amongst a crowd of neighbors lined up behind yellow tape, Dad and I stood there, our jaws dropped, frozen in shock, and watched our house burn.

The house fire sounded like a waterfall. Or like a bathtub faucet cranked to full blast. The heat hit like an oven. Beads of sweat rolled off Dad's face and I saw the flame's reflection on his skin. Fire burst into rooms and splashed around like a stormy orange sea with breathtaking power.

The next day Dad and I sifted through the debris. Baseball cards, comic books, and my Chicago Bulls 3-Peat pennant were ashes. My bike was charred black and the tires completely melted off. The Nintendo looked like a pile of burnt marshmallows and reeked of chemical death.

Somewhere in the ruins, Dilly was cremated. He was a stuffed animal (and I am 15) but that little duck was always there for me. His fuzzy yellow body was shaped like a teddy bear, and his orange beak looked like two plump lips. I stopped snuggling him years ago but still stared at him sometimes, especially on the bad days.

I'd always been a fat boy. I had a flabby neck roll like a baby. It trapped sweat and stunk. I had to look up and scrub every time I showered. Black sweat residue collected everywhere, just awful.

Most kids loved picking on fatties. Dumb kids, smart kids, pretty girls, even friends I thought were nice, could insult me at any moment. They waited for me to mess up, with "fattie" ready in their back pocket. Some kids felt compelled to prod me. Their pointer finger slowly approached my gut and no matter how much I flexed, stretched, or sucked it in, they found mushiness, and it killed me.

Last month school let out, thank god. Summer was my chance to escape and maybe fix myself. I played basketball every day like MJ. Free throws, rebounds, and layups for hours until sweat soaked through my shirt and shorts. I didn't eat ice cream, chips, or french fries. I felt lighter on my feet, and not so out of breath. Maybe the girls would notice me now. Maybe the guys would throw me a pass. Then the fire destroyed my momentum. Dad and I have lived off fast food, cable TV, and I haven't shot a basket in weeks.

At first, Dad thought he could find a local job. He rented the cheapest hotel room in town and rifled through the classifieds. As money ran out he called every friend he ever met. Then last night we hopped in his pickup truck, left Iowa, and drove here.

The Garcia House. Manny, Patti, and Nate. Freeport, Illinois. They offered us a room and gave Dad some work. He left early, and I'm still lying here on the couch like a turd.

"Eric Daniels! It's way past noon. Are you sleeping, still?"

That's Nate, I think. His voice sounds deep.

"Yeah, I'm up!" I yell.

"Be right down!" he replies.

I raise the blinds and open the basement window. Hot air and light flood the room. Now I recognize these old couches, this room. Nate and I had sleepovers here. Several. We ate caramel corn, drank pop, and watched movies on this ancient TV. We were so little back then that we both fit on one couch. Behind the couches, there's a pool table and the Garcia bar. I remember when Manny and Dad built it. The marble countertop still looks shiny and smooth.

I imagine Mom, Dad, Manny, and Patti, sucking down beers and laughing so loud. Manny sat behind the bar, Dad stood at the side, and the girls chatted at the corner. Mom leaned forward, cigarette dangling off her fingers, its smoke floating past her permed hair and tinted prescription glasses. Was Mom still around back then? Of course, she was.

Nate's footsteps clamor down the stairs. The basement door swings open and a tall, lanky kid stands beside the pool table. It's shocking to see Nate all grown up. His bony shoulders look way too wide for his thin frame. Nate has bushy eyebrows and thick chin stubble for a 15-year-old. He barely has a forehead. His thick brown hair is buzzed short except for one odd-looking half-inch-wide bang that dangles past his chin. Nate catches my eye, tucks the bang behind his ear, and nervously scratches his brow. His yellow t-shirt reads 'Bite Me' in bold black letters. His orange plaid shorts clash with his green Nikes. His legs are covered with gobs of even more hair.

"How you been, buddy?" Nate asks, "You're not as fat as I remember."

Okay. Um. I'll take that as a compliment, I guess.

Nate pulls the bang from behind his ear and sucks on it. He realizes what he's doing, and tucks the bang away. Then he turns and runs upstairs.

"I can tell you like donuts," Nate yells, "Come on up!"

Nate leads me to the kitchen, where the sun reflects off the linoleum floor. Glossy black cupboards contrast with the white Formica countertops, and the wooden kitchen table rests on wobbly chrome legs.

Nate hands me a white cardboard box stamped with 'Donuts Plus' in purple ink. Two chocolate long johns are left, and I stuff one in my mouth. It's super sweet and the cream filling tastes like banana. I lick the icing off my fingers and follow Nate outside onto the back porch.

The wooden deck stands five feet above the ground and the far edge of the floorboards forms a crescent. I remember an above-ground swimming pool stood here once. We played Marco Polo, I got an ear infection and nearly drowned. I hate swimming. Anything that involves taking off my shirt is not good.

A lawnmower fires up somewhere nearby. Nate's yard could use a good mow. The grass is long and wet and the blades bend nearly in half. A giant puddle rests between a crabapple tree and a rundown shed in the back of his yard. Good sized lawn though, as big as a basketball court.

I smack a fly off my leg and notice Nate staring at me. He squints and nods slightly like he's thinking of what to say. I try to imagine him as a child. He's always had those heavy eyebrows, and his light brown eyes feel familiar. For a moment his eyes swell with an idea. Then his lips purse and he lets out a dramatic sigh.

"Fire sucks, huh dude?" Nate says.

I nod. Duh. Stupid question. But I guess he's just trying to start a conversation. I wonder how much he knows. Does he want to know? I'm not sure what to tell him.

"How long are you staying for, bud?" he asks, changing the subject, and twirling his bang around his pinky finger. "All summer, or what?"

I shrug. How should I know? I just got here.

"Well," Nate winks at me, "I know something that's sure to cheer up your sorry ass. Come on."

Nate leads me around the house to the front yard. We follow the sidewalk up to the top of Greenfield Street and then go down the hill on the other side. The street ends in a cul-de-sac with larger homes and manicured landscaping. I'm not used to all these beautiful lawns. My neighborhood in Iowa was downtown, all cement, and alleyways.

Nate gestures with his chin towards a light blue house with a shiny black BMW in the driveway. The home is colossal, with two floors, a dormered attic, copper downspouts, and a brick entryway. Big money here. Even the mailbox on the curb looks expensive.

"Shh," Nate whispers, "Listen."

A crow caws and a dog barks in the distance. A truck engine barrels down a freeway somewhere nearby. Sweat rolls down my back. I smell hot, dirty water evaporating off the asphalt.

"Hear that?" Nate grins and it's a genuine smile this time. His eyes sparkle and a wide gap shows between his two front teeth. His thick eyebrows bob up and down. "Oh boy!" he nods, "It's them."

I hear them. Of course, I do. It's an unmistakable sound, and it makes me more nervous than anything in the world.

Chapter 2: Jet Setting

Nate and I are listening to girls giggling nearby. Multiple girls. And judging by Nate's obvious excitement, they must be cute. I also hear a faint, rhythmic squeak. What the hell is that?

Nate pumps his eyebrows again and tiptoes through the grass to the back of the house. I'm not sure I want to, but I follow him. I don't have much choice.

Most of the backyard is taken up by towering oak trees, with a giant trampoline on the lawn, and two teenage girls bouncing away. Nate and I hide behind a bush before they see us. Their faces hide behind long hair that flies every which way. They chat about some boy named Greg. The brunette does a backflip like it's no big deal. They're doing pirouettes and toe touches, and then the blonde drops an elbow like she's Hulk Hogan. Watch out.

Nate whispers, "That's Melissa, with the brown hair. This is her house. And the blonde, that's Jen. I wish she was my girlfriend. I love her, dude. Seriously. I'm obsessed."

"This'll be fun," Nate winks, "Watch this."

Nate sneaks up close to the house, finds the garden hose, and turns the faucet. He clicks the nozzle setting to 'Jet,' jumps into the yard, and opens fire.

Cold water cuts through the hot air and shrill screams of panic ring in my ears. Melissa and Jen are instantly soaked to the core, and the trampoline surface turns slick as grease. Their arms flail for balance as they slip onto their butts, and fall onto the lawn. Nate can't stop laughing as he continues to douse them.

"Nathan Garcia, I'm gonna kill you!" Melissa yells.

Melissa lunges at Nate, stuffs her hand across the nozzle, and a heavy mist shoots in every direction. Then with ninja speed, she elbows Nate in the chest. He recoils, loses his grip and Melissa claims the hose. She fires directly into Nate's face, flushing his open mouth with water. Then she grins, points lower, and soaks his entire crotch. She knows she's won now and wants Jen to see. Melissa glances around the yard for her and instead spots me hiding in the bushes.

"Who are you?" Melissa asks, shocked to see an unknown face.

"That's my friend. Eric," Nate says, "He's from Iowa."

"Oh," Melissa smiles, "Welcome to Freeport, bitch."

Melissa squeezes the trigger and a jet of frigid water splashes against my chest.

I'm instantly soaked and too stupid to run. Instead, I turn around, and my butt gets a thorough soaking. I can't stand the cold and I yelp like an injured puppy. I tuck my body into a ball and grab my knees. What am I doing on the ground? Now I'm all muddy. The water pelts the back of my neck. I feel like I'm gonna cry. Then the water stops, thank god. I look to see if she's laughing but she's not. Melissa watches Jen, who reappears from the woods.

Jen sneaks behind Nate with two giant handfuls of nasty brown leaves. She reaches up and drops the mulch down the back of Nate's 'Bite Me' t-shirt. Nate immediately arches his back and cringes as the dry debris glues itself to his soaking wet shoulders.

"What the hell?" Nate yells, "Gross!"

Nate has trouble peeling off his shirt since it's so wet. He finally gets it off and flaps it in the air like a dirty rug. Leaves and sticks fly everywhere, except for the ones still stuck to his skin. He's a skinny kid, with zero muscle tone.

"Serves you right!" Jen laughs and high-fives Melissa.

"Hey Nate," Melissa calls, "Let me help you wash off."

The hose fires again and splatters against Nate's back. But Nate's used to the water temperature by now and he rubs his back like he's washing in the shower.

Melissa tosses the hose onto the ground and sweeps the long hair off her face and neck. Jen does the same. Nate watches Jen's every move very closely.

I have some manners so I look away. But for some reason, Melissa moves into my view. Does she want me to watch? Melissa catches my eye and smiles. She bends at the waist and wipes dried grass trimmings off of her ankles.

"I am like, soooo soaked, Nate," Melissa coos, "You big jerk."

"Oh, please, Melissa," Jen rolls her eyes, "You know you wanted it."

"It did feel good," Melissa giggles and throws me another look.

I can't handle this. My face is flushed. I'm out of my element here. Girls never talk to me. Ever. I take a deep breath and stare at the trampoline.

"You want to bounce?" Jen asks. "I wouldn't try now, it's still pretty wet."

Jen's blue eyes shoot me like lasers. "Do I know you?" she asks.

"Nah," Nate says, "Eric is my oldest friend. I mean, he's 15 too, but I've known him for a super long time. We used to hang out in grade school. Right, Eric?"

I nod.

"He's gonna stay at my house for a while," Nate continues, "Him and his dad. They lost everything. Whole house burned down."

"Oh no!" Melissa gasps, "That's so sad! You poor thing!"

"Damn," Jen says, "But Freeport sucks. Why would you come here?"

Jen's eyes drill me again. She's like a TV reporter, like, she really wants some answers. Meaningful answers too, not some yes-no stuff.

"Uh," I stammer, "I had nowhere else to go."

My voice sounds stupid. They must know I suck. I'm a fattie. They surely realize this now. I'll get shunned soon, I can feel it. Nate grins at me like I'm an idiot, but Melissa has sympathetic eyes. Jen seems undecided.

"So your dad is here?" Jen says, "But where's your mom?"

Oh, god. Please don't ask about her. The fire is enough already. We just met for christ's sake.

"Where's your mom?" Jen persists.

"She left. Years ago," Nate answers for me, "Just ran off. Never to be seen again. Right, Eric?"

Thanks a lot, Nate. A simple "gone" would have worked. I should have answered myself.

A window opens, and I smell pasta boiling. The comforting aroma of hot carbs distracts everyone, and I'm no longer the center of attention. Is it suppertime already? I slept in way too late. A voice I assume is Melissa's mom calls the girls inside to eat.

"We're having a sleepover here tonight," Jen says, "You guys wanna stop by? Like maybe 11?"

"Yes!" Melissa whispers, "We can sneak out. My parents will be asleep by then."

What? Girls at night? Until now, I'd never spoken to a girl past 3 PM.

"Nice," Nate nods casually, "See ya then." This guy still has his shirt off. He holds 'Bite Me' over his shoulder like it's a sport coat at Prom. Does this stuff happen to him every day? What kind of magical town is this?

Chapter 3: The Sneak Out

"Eric? Eric, is that you?"

Nate leads me down Greenfield Street, back from Melissa's, and I see an older woman, with shoulder-length red hair standing at the end of Nate's driveway. Her billowy white blouse flutters in the breeze. That must be Patti, Nate's mom.

"Eric! Come here! You got so tall! Come on, give your old pal Patti a hug!"

Patti is just as I remember, with happy green eyes and upturned wrinkles from years of laughter. Her long red press-on fingernails hold an extra thin cigarette. Her arms reach high for a hug as I near.

"Wait, nope!" she drops her arms, "You guys are soaked. And filthy! I'll hug ya later. What the hell were you boys doing? Eric, your clothes are ruined. I'm definitely going shopping for you."

"Oh no," I smile, "That's fine--"

"You better let me, 'cause I'm gonna. What do you have, two outfits? That won't do," Patti winks. "My God, Eric, you look like a whole new person. You could have gone on a crime spree before you grew up. Nobody would recognize you now. So tall, transformed like a butterfly. Got your mom's pretty blonde hair, huh? That mother of yours. Donna, Donna, Donna. Best friend for years and then fell off the planet. I've tried calling her, you know. I miss her. Seeing you brings it all back. All the memories. Good times," Patti sighs, "Nate, you have some extra clothes Eric can borrow. Help this boy out. Poor thing."

"You boys hungry?" Patti continues, "That's the only reason you came home, right? Don't worry, I ordered pizza. God, it's hot out, isn't it? They had the AC cranked at the bank, and now I'm dying here. Manny is too damn stubborn to buy central air, and he said he'd install my new pool weeks ago. Driving me nuts."

Patti talks so much, so fast, it's ridiculous. Happens a lot when adults speak. Some old people could blabber all day.

Nate seems numb to Patti's voice and walks right by her. I smile politely and follow Nate to the back porch. Nate drapes his wet t-shirt over a sunny chair but I keep mine on. He doesn't want to see my fat rolls. Nobody does.

"Jen's pretty! Right? And so smart!" Nate grins, "She's perfect, dude. She's going to Harvard. You know that? She swears that she is. And I believe it. Who else says that when they're 15?"

I hear Dad's truck and smile as it pulls into Nate's driveway. Soon the sliding glass door opens and he sees me. Dad looks like hell, all sweaty, gross, and covered in dirt. Kinda like me. Gray stubble covers his chin and bags swell under his eyes. He's out of breath. What happened? He plops onto a patio chair and pops open a can of beer. Dad takes a long sip and a smile covers his face.

"Looks like you had fun today, Eric," Dad says, "You're soaked. Playing in a sprinkler or something? Hot enough for it." Dad wipes the sweat off his forehead, reaches into his pocket, and lights a Marlboro. He exhales a cloud of white, and his smile gets wider. "Long drive last night. Man, I'm beat."

The sliding door opens again and Manny, Nate's dad, steps onto the porch. He's a short, solid, barrel-chested man, with a thick, black beard and giant hands. Manny looks much heavier than I remember, especially around his neck. I've noticed many dads gather some serious neck fat.

Manny takes a long look at me and smiles. "Look at you, Eric! Ya grew up! Nice to see you again, kid. How are ya?" Not expecting an answer, Manny slaps Dad on the back and chuckles, "You still alive, Mike? Huh? You gonna survive this gig?" His high-pitched laugh sounds like Nate's.

"Oh, I'm fine," Dad nods, "I barely slept is all. I need a mattress. You seen that garage sale down the block? You seen any mattresses there?"

"Don't get a pissed-on mattress," Manny says, "That's gross. Go to Kmart. They're cheap there. I'm paying you, aren't I?"

"Barely," Dad grins.

"Son of a bitch!" Manny laughs, "I just bought us beers!"

Patti chimes in from the doorway, "Buy him a mattress, Manny! Be nice."

The doorbell rings and Patti pays the pizza delivery boy. Nate and I chow down on a meat-lovers' and breadsticks while Dad and Manny drink another Bud.

18

Manny tells us about an extra room downstairs, behind the bar, with a bathroom. He says Dad and I can set up some mattresses there and "move on in." We all go downstairs and check it out. With no windows, the room feels like a cave, but it's at least ten degrees cooler. Dad sneezes a few times. He thanks Manny and says he'll buy the mattresses tomorrow. For tonight though, it's back to the plaid couches, and Dad's so tired he passes out in a minute.

By 9:30, the sun is long gone and so are both dads. Patti watches the local news and falls asleep by 10:45. There's no sneaking out of here. It's more like walking away. A light breeze breaks the heat, and Nate and I head to Melissa's.

The whole walk I'm nervous as hell. I'm such a rookie with social stuff, especially girls. They never spoke to me before. I don't know what to do. I'll follow Nate's lead. I watch him closely. He's kinda frowny and bored like it's no big deal. I take a deep breath. No big deal, Eric, no big deal.

We get to Melissa's house and walk around back. A dim light flickers in a basement window. Nate peeks inside. The TV plays an old rerun of *Bewitched*.

"That show is so annoying," Nate says, "There's no way they're watching that garbage."

The back door squeaks open and Jen stands alone in the doorway.

"Melissa's sleeping," she whispers, "Forget her. Let's go, boys."

Chapter 4: Bright Blue Vomit

Jen leads us back up Greenfield Street and down Alamo Drive. The homes are all dark and very quiet, but the light from one house fills the street. A little white house with black shutters has a big backyard. It's a sturdy one-story home, like many on this street, and similar to Nate's. "Jen's house," Nate whispers. Several rusty, bumper-stickered cars are parked here. I hear music and voices, and see shadows of several kids. The smell of beer and cigarettes drifts to the curb.

"This is awesome, Eric," Nate grins, "Your first Freeport party! Already."

More like my first party anywhere ever. But I'm not telling anybody that.

"Damn it, Rachel," Jen says to herself, "I knew it." Jen walks up the driveway like she's on a mission. She looks pissed.

A sweet, blue smoke fills the garage, and a circle of kids pass around a small glass pipe. What in the hell is that? Drugs? Oh my god. I'm at a drug party? That's not good. Nate doesn't look surprised or worried, so I try to stay calm. There's a couple in the corner sharing a pint of whiskey, straight up. Jesus. Two big dudes smoke cigarettes and compare tattoos. Either of them could whoop my butt so fast. This crowd is way older. I'm an imposter. It's obvious. I don't party. I feel watched. I really want to leave.

One dude is slurring drunk and has a heavy accent. He wears thick glasses and a girl's plastic headband in his long blonde hair. His white t-shirt has a bright blue stain right across the chest. A cigarette dangles off his lips. Here he comes. Great.

"Jenny, my love, how are you?" the drunk belches, "Looking for your sis? Rach's out back."

"Thanks, Declan," Jen says, "You doing okay there, bud?"

"But of course!" Declan smiles as Jen disappears through a door.

Declan giggles at Nate, "Nathan my boy! How are ya? How have you been? I have a question. I do. And it needs ever so dearly to be answered."

"What?" Nate smiles.

"What the fuck is wrong with you, mate? When are you gonna slice off this blasted hair bang turd piece of shit dangling thing? You do know you look like an idiot. How are the girls gonna make love to you with that...that...hair sausage hanging across your face?"

Nate is still smiling. This Declan guy must be friendly. His accent is definitely Irish.

"Well? Won't you introduce me to your lovely friend here, Nathan? Where are your bloody manners? Excuse me! Where are mine? You guys need some beer, right? Liquor? Weed? What do you want?" Declan clumsily bows to us like a king's servant. "What can I provide you for, good sirs? I am Declan. It's a pleasure to corrupt you."

Declan sports a wide grin and holds out a sweaty right hand. This dude is a seasoned partier. He must see right through me. I've never partied. This sucks. I have to bluff him. I impersonate Nate and act as cool as possible, which looks a lot like being bored.

"That's Eric," Nate says.

"Eric, huh? Eric," Declan squints at me, taking a close look, swaying from side to side like a snake charmer. "Eric... Eric. Is. Very. Serious." Declan scowls, "Are you feeling very serious tonight, Eric? Nate, is he very serious? Or bored? Overwhelmed? No, he looks very serious. Very nice to meet you, Eric. Seriously."

"Let's go find Jen," Nate smiles.

"Have it your way," Declan says, "Maybe we can share a drink later, okay, boys?" he winks, "A pleasure to meet you."

I eagerly follow Nate inside the house, which is packed, and the music is loud. Some girls sit on the couch and talk, while another group plays cards at the dining room table. Their game involves drinking, cussing, and yelling. So obnoxious. Empty plastic cups and beer cans are everywhere. Nate leads me through the living room and opens a sliding glass door to the back porch.

A 20-gallon red plastic tub rests near the doorway. A few orange slices and several ice cubes float in a bright blue liquid. Near the patio table, a blonde girl stands and talks to Jen. The girl looks just like her, but slightly taller, with shorter hair and a dimpled chin. Definitely sisters, and arguing like it too.

"Jenny?! What the hell?"

"Mom is so gonna kill you, Rachel."

"She doesn't give a shit! She's with Andy again."

"But this party is way too big. How many people did you invite?"

"Shut up!" Rachel grabs Jen's wrist and moves the argument into the backyard.

Jen's conversation may take a while. Great. I don't want to go back inside the stuffy house, or the garage with that Declan dude. Overwhelmed? He totally knows. But am I overwhelmed? That's not the right word. I'm annoyed. This party sucks. Do all parties suck? They must.

"Nate," I ask, "Should we head back home?"

"No way, dude. You kidding me? We just got here. Jen won't be long."

Wonderful. Nate sits down on the porch steps. I take a breath and sit beside him. Our backs face the party. I want to leave. What is Nate thinking? Does he actually like being here? He looks happy. He can't stop smiling.

"Hey, little bros!" a long-haired guy yells from behind us, "Try the Smurf Piss! It's delicious! A two buck cup gets you all fucked up!"

"No money, bro!" Nate smiles, "Thanks, though."

The Smurf Piss guy returns to his conversation at the patio table. I listen in. The movie *The Shining* gets compared to *A Clockwork Orange*. Then the group argues music. Nirvana versus The Beatles. Their opinions are extreme and they cuss so much. I'm getting dumb just listening. Where is Jen?

Footsteps approach us. My heart skips, and I imagine a giant, muscled monster beating the crap out of me. I want to run. I could leave Nate here. I could find his house. It's not that far away. But I'm too chicken to move.

The mystery footsteps race right by. A skinny dude in a white tank top and ripped jeans vomits all over the bushes. He's hacking and spitting up bright blue vomit. The Smurf piss did the trick.

I hear more footsteps and expect a parade of barfing people. Instead, I see familiar red flip flops.

"Gross," Jen says, "That dude is retching. Will he live? My god. Let's get out of here."

Sounds good to me. Finally, a voice of reason.

Jen pumps her eyebrows and jingles a set of car keys in the air.

"Sweet!" Nate grins, "Time for a joyride?"

"You know it," Jen says, "You ready for this, Eric?"

"Huh?" Ready for what? This is not fun either. Jen can drive? She's 15! These kids are bad news. I want to go home. Right now. I've never ridden in a car with anyone younger than 40.

Chapter 5: The Donut Monster

Jen leads us down the street to a rusty white Chevy Cavalier. The windows are rolled down and the doors are unlocked. She hops in and sits behind the wheel. Nate sits shotgun, and I climb in the back. I can't believe I'm agreeing to this. It's the dumbest thing I've ever done. I buckle my seatbelt and take a deep breath. What am I doing? Why don't I run away? I'm an idiot. I'm literally strapping myself to this vehicle. This steel death box full of juvenile delinquents.

Jen buckles up and starts the engine. I must be radiating anxiety. Am I sweating? Jen turns to me and winks.

"I'm sixteen in September, Eric," Jen says, "I already took driver's ed. Aced it. Relax, okay? Jesus."

"Where are we headed?" Nate asks.

Jen shrugs and cranks up the radio.

A Madonna song plays and Nate changes the station. "This song is overplayed," he explains, and all pop music is "repulsive." Nate finds a classic rock station and turns it up. Queen plays 'We Are the Champions' and Nate sings along. He's not hitting half the notes. Why is he singing?

Is Jen deaf or what? She doesn't react to Nate at all. Tunes him out completely. She's focusing all her energy on the road. That's a good thing.

A traffic light glows green and she turns left. She stays on the same street for miles and we pass a JCPenney, a Kmart, and several fast-food restaurants. Then we pass the edge of town.

A cornfield gives way to a cemetery, then a wide stream, a bridge, and a railroad track. Soon we pass a brown wooden sign that reads 'Krape Park.'

"Back entrance," Nate announces. He points out the playground, tennis courts, sledding hill, and football field. An antique totem pole near the front entrance looks familiar. I think I fed ducks at this park once. There's an antique carousel, boat docks, and a quiet stream that shimmers in the moonlight.

"Five-O," Nate points to a cop car parked on the roadside. Oh god. Not the police. If the cop sees us he'll know we're too young to drive. I see the cop's face behind the wheel. He's looking down, possibly asleep. Thank goodness he didn't see us. I take a breath.

"I'm hungry," Jen says, "Let's eat, huh?"

Jen passes the totem pole again and exits the park. We drive to a corner strip mall. I instantly recognize the restaurant name from this morning, 'Donuts Plus.'

"Oh, hell yeah!" Nate laughs, "This place is the best!" He hops out of the car and runs to the door. I'm right beside him, while Jen lags behind.

The yellow table tops match the yellow checkered floor tiles and the yellow nicotine-stained walls. In some impossible way, the smell of sweet dough overpowers the Marlboros. A half-dozen truckers inside drink coffee, smoke cigs, and stare at newspapers. There's no store employee in sight. The glass display case is full of fresh long-johns, twists, bear claws, jellies, and more. My mouth waters. There's a silver call bell on the counter, and I reach out to ring it. But Jen swoops up from behind me and grabs my hand.

"Don't," she says, "Trust me. I can't eat here anymore. Neither should you guys."

"What?!" Nate exclaims, "Why?"

Jen shakes her head, "Check it out."

Nate and I follow Jen to another door, several feet from the entrance. The Donuts Plus employee entrance gapes open. A single bulb hangs from a wire and blinks like a strobe in a horror movie. An old frail woman in a threadbare tank top stands alone in the kitchen. Her thin gray hair is soaked in grease, swept close across her balding skull. A cigarette dangles from her lips, with an inch-long ash that's just waiting to fall.

The woman holds a plain yeast donut in her bare hand. In her other hand, she holds a glop of vanilla icing. She slaps the icing onto the donut, places it on a tray, and grabs another.

"No spatula?" Nate whispers to himself.

The frosting is running low in her enormous 10-gallon cardboard drum and she reaches way down inside for another handful. She stands up straight and smears another roll. Sweat drips everywhere. Her cigarette ash has gone missing.

Then she coughs so loud, like she's dying, hacking directly onto her hand. She scratches her ass. Then she grabs another donut and frosts it up.

"Oh, fuck," Nate mutters.

A wave of laughter hits me. Jen laughs too, then Nate, louder than ever. We all huddle together, just cracking up. Nate whoops with joy and startles the poor woman. Now her entire cigarette drops into the frosting bucket. She cusses as she fishes for the butt. She looks up at us and smiles. Oh, no! More frightening! Five teeth in her entire smile.

"Run!" Nate laughs, "The beast has spotted us! Run for your lives!"

We hop back in the car but we're still laughing. I have a hard time catching my breath. I'm crying. I haven't laughed like that in a while. Jen giggles so much that she can't even put the key in the ignition.

"We just ate those donuts today," I say.

"No!" Jen laughs.

"Yes, we sure did!" Nate howls, "Their secret recipe! No wonder they're so yummy!"

"So gross!" Jen laughs.

"What next?" Nate sighs, "Oh boy. That'll be hard to beat."

The laughter dies down and Jen drives us to Cub Foods. The huge 24-hour grocery store is still open even though the parking lot is completely empty. After we walk inside, Jen admits she's lost her appetite. I agree. Nate has a new plan.

"Okay, Harvard nerd," Nate grins, "Time for some math."

"Ooh, fun!" Jen smiles. She is not joking.

We find the tissue aisle, and Jen studies the prices of the toilet paper. Single-ply, multi-ply, perfumed, and quilted. Within seconds she calculates the price per roll and per sheet and decides that Scott's brand is the best deal.

"Nope," Nate says, "See? Told you math sucks. You want a shorter roll because if that big boy gets stuck on a branch, you're screwed."

"But it won't get stuck because it's heavier," Jen argues.

After a brief debate, they choose the generic brand. I have no money, but Jen and Nate insist that's not a problem. They pitch in five bucks each. Jen adds up how many 4-packs we can afford, and I help carry.

I'll have to add TP-ing houses to the repertoire. These Freeport kids like breaking the rules. Jen insists there's nothing else to do, and for some reason, I believe her. I'm not as nervous anymore. These kids are growing on me. We throw the tissue into the trunk and head home.

Then two blocks from the grocery store, blue lights flash behind us. Are you kidding me? Police? I knew it. I knew these kids were trouble. Am I gonna get arrested now? This can't be happening.

Chapter 6: Only Three Things To Do

"Cops!" Nate exclaims, "Oh, shit!"

"I know, okay? Relax!" Jen says. She takes a breath, "You too, Eric. Jesus. Are you alright? My god. Breathe. Act like you're asleep or something."

I close my eyes but they pop right back open. I realize I'm chewing on the neck of my t-shirt. It's all sweaty too. I spit it out. Breathe, breathe. I close my eyes again. Nope. Doesn't work. They open. The cop's lights are so shiny. He's closing in on us.

Jen applies her blinker and pulls to the side of the road. Nate takes several deep breaths too. Jen checks her hair in the rearview and lets down her ponytail. She finds a red lipstick in the cup holder and puts some on.

The police officer takes forever to get out of his car. He saunters up to the Chevy like a sloth. I can't handle the suspense. The trepidation. I can't believe it's the real police! I screwed up bad. I should have left the party when I had the chance. I should have run. I chickened out. I suck. Stupid. But I'm really a good kid. Really. How did this happen to me? Will he arrest us? Take us downtown? Driving without a license. Attempted vandalism. Breathe. I close my eyes. They stay shut this time! I can't get arrested if I'm sleeping, right?

"Hello, officer, can I help you?" Jen says in a slow and even tone.

"Out pretty late, aren't we, sweetie?" the cop says. The beam from his flashlight shines right through my eyelids. I groan and pretend to almost wake up. I peek out one eye.

"We were at the movies," Jen lies like a pro.

"Little late for that, isn't it, sugar?" The cop takes a long look at Jen, slowly moving his eyes up, down, and side to side.

"No, not at the Lindo, sir, at the Sky-View. The drive-in. The double feature."

"Ah, that's right, the old drive-in. What'd you see?"

"*The Sandlot* and *Jurassic Park*."

"Hmm. Any good?" he grins.

"Yep," Jen smiles, "I think. But I accidentally fell asleep for some of it."

"Not me," Nate adds, "They were both quality films, officer sir."

"Is that so?" the cop says, "License and registration please."

Jen pulls an ID from her pocket and hands it over. Then she opens the glove compartment and a mess of audiotapes, maps and tampons spill out.

"Sorry, my car is a mess."

"Sure is, honey," the cop chuckles, "That's fine though. Forget the registration. I'll just call your plates in to dispatch." The officer saunters away and sits in his car.

I take a deep breath and hear Jen and Nate do the same. That actually wasn't so bad. The cop bought the alibi. He didn't even ask many questions.

"Marvelous," Nate coos, "An Oscar-worthy performance."

"Shut up, Nate," Jen rolls her eyes.

"Have you even seen Jurassic Park for real?" Nate asks.

"Yes, I have," Jen says, "It's really good. The dinosaurs look so real."

As she speaks, Jen keeps her eyes on the rearview mirror. She's not nervous anymore. She looks pissed. Nate seems completely at ease. I'm pretty calm too, I guess. I'm not getting arrested. Pretty sure, anyway. A car door slams and the cop approaches the Chevy. He hands Jen the ID and an orange slip of paper.

"Gave you a warning, Rachel. You have a brake light out, passenger side. Have your daddy fix that ASAP, okay?"

"Yes, sir," Jen nods.

"Listen, sugar," the cop pauses to scratch his double chin. "Freeport is... Freeport. It's a small town. There's only three things to do here. Watch a movie, go to a friend's house and watch a movie, or get arrested. Catch my drift? Go straight home, alright, Rachel? And be careful."

"Yes, officer," Jen says, "Thank you, officer."

Jen waits until the cop sits back down in his car, then she applies her blinker and slowly merges onto the road. I am very happy. We're free. And Jen was incredible. With her sister's ID! For the second time tonight a swell of laughter rises in me. I can't stop giggling. Freeport is an emotional rollercoaster. These people are insane.

"Sweetie? Sugar?" Jen grumbles to herself, "Stupid old pig. I can change my own goddamn taillight." She sees me laughing in the back seat and grins, "What's so funny, Eric?"

Nate says in a grandpa voice, "Kids, there's only three things to do in Freeport," he laughs, "Actually that cop's a genius! He's totally right!"

Finally, a wide smile covers Jen's face. A deep-down smile. It took her some time to get there, but she found it. Jen eyes me in the mirror and giggles some more. I must look like the happiest fool on the planet. I'm so relieved. It feels great. Jen turns the wheel and follows the side roads home.

When we get back, more cars than ever line the street. Jen has to park two blocks away and we can hear the chaos. Rachel's party is completely out of control.

Chapter 7: Party Busters

People spill across the driveway and all over the property. A foursome of idiots pound beers in the middle of the street. Cigarette butts and empty plastic cups cover the lawn. Somewhere, a yappy little dog barks like crazy. A grown man with a thick gut and heavy beard revs his motorcycle. He grabs a girl and they motor down the street. Their pop-wheely almost crashes and the crowd cheers. This is nuts. Some kids here look younger than me, and others look forty.

On the back porch, the Smurf Piss supply is long gone, replaced by a keg of beer, with a crowd gathered around to fill their cups. There's a crowd of at least fifty people in the backyard too. Jen spots Rachel, who looks sober and stressed out.

"Where have you been, Jenny?" Rachel yells.

Jen hands over the car keys and ID as somebody screams about a fight in the basement. There's a crashing sound like broken glass. Rachel runs inside the house and leaves the cordless phone on the patio table. Jen picks up the phone. She looks around. One boy boosts another onto the roof of the garage.

Jen shakes her head and presses three buttons on the phone. 9-1-1. She listens to make sure it's ringing, sets the phone down, and walks away.

"What?" Nate says, "I thought you promised not to tell? That's how you got the car keys, right? Wasn't that the deal?"

"Deal's off, Nate," Jen says, "This party went nuts."

I nod in agreement. She had to do it.

Jen leads Nate and me back to the Chevy. We grab the toilet paper from the trunk and walk to Melissa's. Jen sneaks back inside the house through the basement door, leaving Nate and me to wait outside.

"Jen is awesome, huh, Eric?" Nate says.

I shrug and nod.

"But stay away from her, okay? She's all mine."

Jen reappears. She stands by the basement door with Melissa at her side.

"Well, look who's awake," Nate announces.

Melissa's eyes are swollen from sleep, and her long brown hair is a twisted mess. Melissa crosses her arms and shivers like it's 17 degrees instead of 75. Compared to Jen's genuine personality, Melissa loves acting.

"So chilly!" Melissa squeals, "What's in the bag?"

"Butt wipe," Nate says. He tosses her a roll.

"Ooh! Good! Let's TP my house!" Melissa grins.

"What?" Jen says, "What fun is that?"

"Please," Melissa says, "Please, please, pretty please? Nate, you and Matt TP'd my house like a month ago, right? My dad was so angry! It was hilarious. I've never seen him so mad."

"Your own house? Seriously?" Jen scoffs, "Please, Melissa. You're just scared of getting caught."

"You've got too many trees anyways," Nate says, "We don't have much ammo. We gotta do somebody with, like, two trees."

"Like your house, Nate!" Melissa suggests.

"Nope. Lame again," Jen smiles, "But I know who to get!" she pauses, "Billy!"

"Oh god, that dork?" Nate says. "I hate that dude."

"Then let's get him!" Jen smiles. "Come on!" she chants, "Billy, Billy, Billy!"

"Nah," Nate argues, "I only TP girls."

"Bullshit!" Jen says, "What's the difference? It'll be fun! He'll never suspect you."

"He'll suspect me!" Melissa says, "Billy loves me."

"That's because you flirt with him," Nate says, "You flirt with everybody."

"Shut up," Melissa says.

"Billy is the perfect target," Jen insists, "The right amount of trees, and he's across the street from Nate's. Right? If the cops come, we run to Nate's garage. We'll see the headlights before they see us. Totally safe! Does that work for you, Mel? How about you Eric? I know you're afraid of cops. You almost shit your pants earlier."

"What?" Melissa grins.

"It's true," I admit with a grin, "Let's get Billy."

"That's the spirit!" Jen smiles, "Let's go!"

Chapter 8: Jail Time

Melissa insists on changing before we go anywhere. She returns wearing black pants, and a black long-sleeved t-shirt, like a cartoon burglar. She also brought out two more TP rolls.

We walk down the street and Nate tells Melissa all about Rachel's huge party, and the nasty donut lady. Then he really exaggerates the part with the cop and me pooping my pants. It's almost true. They all laugh at me, but I'm okay with it. I laugh too.

"I love your laugh, Eric," Melissa grins and touches my shoulder. "You guys had a legendary night! I missed it."

"It probably would have sucked if you were there," Jen teases.

"Totally!" Nate laughs.

The four of us arrive at Billy's brick ranch, across from Nate's little yellow house. Billy's house is small too, built low against a hill. There are manicured bushes and shrubs out front, but Nate says to focus all of our ammo on the two giant maples in the side yard. We each grab a roll from the bag. Nate instructs us to unstick the first TP sheet, and roll out a couple feet of slack.

"This tail here helps the paper release when you throw it," Nate whispers, "Cheers!" He holds up his roll and we tap our TP together.

"Ladies first," Nate bows.

Jen stoops low, arches her back, and sends her TP flying. The TP soars through the air and leaves a long trail behind. Then the roll bounces off a branch, pinballs down the trunk, and hits the ground. Jen runs, picks it up, and sends it skyward again.

After she looks for cops, Melissa throws hers. She has a strong arm too and pitches her roll high into the moonlight. It snags a branch or two and drops down. Melissa runs after her roll while my shot hits the highest branch yet.

Nate takes the opposite approach and douses the tree with a mini-throw method. He plays catch with himself and quickly makes a mess of the lower branches. Jen complements his technique and joins him.

My second throw pinballs down some branches and actually bounces off Melissa's head. She looks to see if the others notice, but they didn't. Then she pulls me close to her. What is happening? Does she want to make-out? I can't. I don't know how.

Melissa looks up and our lips nearly touch. Our eyes meet. She laughs and skips away.

I'm frozen like a mannequin. Melissa glances back and grins. Am I supposed to chase her? I'm sure that's what she wants. But I can't move. I'm chicken. I don't know what to say or do or anything.

I take a breath, grab my TP roll, and throw. I pretend I'm the most devoted TP worker in the country. Pick it up and throw. Forget her. Pick it up and throw.

Before long, multiple strands of toilet paper sway down from every limb. The maple trees turned into giant mops. It looks pretty cool.

Our bag of ammo goes empty just as white light flashes across the yard.

"Car!" Jen yells.

The four of us sprint over to Nate's driveway and kneel behind Dad's pickup truck. First, we see a rusty green Toyota, then a Ford races by, and a Buick.

"The party is busted for sure," Jen says, "They're bailing."

"You sure?" Nate says, "Wouldn't that have happened a while ago?"

"First everybody runs when the cops come," Jen explains, "They come back later for their cars."

More cars pass and we count them. Over two dozen. Then a white Chrysler New Yorker zooms down the hill, clips the curb, and barely misses Nate's mailbox. The car wobbles along with the floppy sound of a flat tire.

"That's Declan," Jen says.

"Your sister's boyfriend?" Melissa asks.

"Duh," Jen says, "How many Declans are there?"

Without slowing, Declan cruises down the hill, past the stop sign, through the intersection, and into an empty lot, where it sinks into some mud. Declan hops out. He looks down at his muddy soccer shoes, cusses a few times, and kicks the flat tire. He jumps behind the wheel, revs the engine, and tries to break the car free from the mud. He gets nowhere. He's stuck. Another car full of kids drives by. They laugh, point, honk and speed away.

"Thanks so very much!" Declan yells with his middle finger in the air. "Daft sons of bitches."

"Let's give him a hand," Nate says.

"Not me," Melissa says, "It's way too muddy, and way too late. I need to get home, you guys. Come on, Jen. The sun's almost up."

"Okay," Jen says, "You two can handle it without us?"

"No problem," Nate smiles, "Come on, Eric."

The girls head uphill while Nate and I run down to Declan.

"Hey!" Declan slurs, "I love you guys! Help pushy, mates. Ready?"

Wow, this dude is drunk. It might be safer for him to be stuck.

"Go, go, go!" Declan yells.

Nate and I lean all our weight into the back bumper. It's impossible to find traction in the mud. Declan spins the wheels and the car goes nowhere. Blue lights flash across the sky.

"Cops!" Declan yells.

"Run!" Nate says.

My shoes are so muddy I can barely move. I drag my feet to the sidewalk, stomp the cement, and run. Nate is right beside me, but Declan stays with his car. He revs the engine one last time. The police car butts up to Declan's bumper, blocking any chance of escape. Nate and I catch our breath and watch from behind Dad's truck.

It's the same cop that pulled over Jen. His flashlight scours Declan's eyes and then lights up the Smurf Piss stain across his chest.

"He's screwed," Nate whispers.

The cop and Declan exchange a few words, and then Declan gets out of his car. Declan stands and touches his nose with his fingertip while the cop watches and laughs. Another police car arrives with a breathalyzer. The dawn sky fades from grey to pink as Declan gets handcuffed and taken away.

Chapter 9: The Green Popsicle

The sunlight wakes me up again and I'm lying on a basement couch. I fell asleep so fast. Haven't moved a muscle in hours. My muddy shoes are still on. What a night.

I head upstairs, and it's hot already. The sunflower shaped clock on the kitchen wall reads 1:35. From the kitchen window, I see the vacant lot covered in tire marks. Declan's car is gone. Is he still in jail? Probably. Poor guy. He was being an idiot though. I grab some OJ from the fridge and wander into the living room.

From the picture window, I see the neighbor's maple trees covered in white tissue. Our TP job looks more impressive in the daylight. That's a ton of TP to clean up. I feel bad now. Two kids clean up the yard. That must be Billy and his little brother. I duck so they don't see me watching.

Nate emerges from his bedroom in plaid boxer shorts and nothing else. He's so skinny.

"Thought I heard somebody," Nate smiles, "Last night was ba-ba-bonkers! Huh?! What a great first day for you." Nate scratches his chest and yawns. "Wasn't Jen the best? So calm with the cops, and the sister ID trick? Damn." He smiles, "I love her. So how's Billy's house looking? I gotta see."

Nate crawls into the living room and peeks out the picture window. "Holy shit. Not bad!" he grins, "Look at Billy. He's such a tool."

Nate walks back to the kitchen and opens the fridge. He finds two pieces of leftover Pizza Hut pizza and offers me one. We eat it cold and finish off the orange juice. Then Nate leads me to his bedroom.

The tiny room is barely big enough for a dresser and a queen-size bed. Nate has pinstriped sheets, a Mickey Mouse pillowcase, and a fuzzy navy comforter, which is shoved in a pile on the floor. A Doors poster and a Lamborghini poster cover his airplane wallpaper. A school picture of Jen is tacked up on his wall, right next to his pillow. That seems weird but I don't say anything.

Nate's closet overflows with Patti's winter clothes. There's also a couple board games, some G.I. Joes, and a few Halloween masks. Nate pulls down a pile of t-shirts from the top shelf and throws them onto his bed.

"Mom said you should borrow some shirts," Nate says, "Take whatever. I'm jumping in the shower."

What an odd selection of clothing. All Nate's t-shirts have a picture, a font, or both. Where are the plain ones? There's a red shirt with Snoopy eating pizza. A black shirt with gold letters reads, 'God is Dead -- Nietzsche' and 'Nietzsche is Dead -- God.' Who the hell is Nietzsche? A light blue shirt with a smiley yellow sun reads, 'Freeport Pool and Spa.' That's Manny's business.

Finally, a Chicago Cubs shirt. Reminds me of the one I had. I'll wear this. I love the Cubs. Bulls are way better, but the Cubs are my baseball team.

I get dressed and the doorbell rings. I head for the door.

"Don't answer it!" Nate yells. He's showered and dressed in a Green Lantern t-shirt and black shorts. He nearly tackles me in the living room.

"Get down!" Nate yells.

It rings again.

Nate dives behind the couch like somebody threw a hand grenade into the living room.

The doorbell rings for the third time.

"Hey, Nate! Are you home?!" The screen door rattles, "It's me, Billy!"

"Why are we hiding?" I whisper.

Nate shushes me and shakes his head. Not cool. I don't like hiding. It's rude. He's letting Billy rot on the front stoop. But Nate really seems to enjoy it. He's grinning like mad.

Again, I whisper, "Why don't you talk to him?"

"Don't do it!" Nate hisses, "Shh!"

Billy leaves the front stoop and walks back home.

From out on the street, another voice says, "What's up, Billy?"

"Hey, Matt! Check out my house! It got TP'd so hard last night! Isn't it awesome!" Billy laughs.

Billy's laughs is a long, grating honk that ranks somewhere between a seal and a goose. I don't hear Matt laughing at all.

Nate whispers, "Billy stops by unannounced all the time. I hate it."

"And you hide?" I ask.

"Yeah," Nate grins, "But now my buddy Matt is stuck with Bill, so we need to rescue Matt."

Nate leads me through the backdoor, across the backyard, through the neighbor's yard, and around the block. We circle back to his own house. Oh my god. This is ridiculous.

"Oh, hey, Matt!" Nate calls from the top of the hill like he's surprised to see him.

"Hey!" Matt says, "You at Jen's?"

"Yup," Nate lies, "Nobody was home."

Matt sits alone on Billy's front stoop. Matt has short brown hair, spiked with gel. He wears flip flops, khaki cargo shorts, and a purple t-shirt that reads, 'FAST, Freeport Aquatic Swim Team.' His pale chin is dimpled, and his eyes squint.

"I was just at your house," Matt says, "Billy was banging on your door like usual. Man, he's stoked about this TP job," he whispers, "You do it?"

"Oh yeah. With Jen. And Melissa, and Eric," Nate grins, "Meet Eric, an old friend from Iowa. Eric, Matt."

"Hi, Matt," I say.

"'Sup," Matt nods, "I told Billy to get me a popsicle. He's taking his sweet ass time."

Billy appears in the doorway with two frozen pops, one red and one green. He offers Matt the green, but Matt grabs the red instead.

"Hey! It's Nate!" Billy says, "Where have you been, amigo? Who's your friend here?"

"This is Eric," Nate says.

"Hello, Eric. It's great to meet you. I'm William Garrett, but most people call me Billy. Welcome to my house!" he smiles, "That's my little bro, Ronnie, over there cleaning up TP. You see him? We just moved here last summer. Well, not moved to Freeport. I used to live on the east side, that's where mostly black folks like me live, but Greenfield Street is a way nicer neighborhood. No thugs, no drugs, and my good friend Nate's across the street, so that's even better. He's my locker neighbor from school. Garcia and Garrett. Cool, right? And now we're house neighbors too! It's been great living here so far. The trees aren't usually this messy, but this super hot girl I know, named Melissa, I think she TP'd me last night. She likes me," Billy nods at me with a huge grin, "Uh-huh. Real bad. So, do you guys want a popsicle too? Hey, Ronnie, you want one?"

"Nah!" Ronnie yells.

Billy runs inside and returns with a purple, a red, and the green one again. I take the green one. There's nothing wrong with lime. The hot sun bathes us, and the popsicles drip like crazy. Billy sucks his down with some extra loud slurps.

We sit on the front stoop and Ronnie joins us. He gives me a brisk hello and then spins a basketball on his finger.

Ronnie is the handsome brother of the two and he knows it. They look nothing alike. Billy is tall and lanky, with a veiny neck, wide set eyes, and long teeth. Ronnie is shorter with small features and a perfect smile.

"New kid, you play b-ball or what?" Ronnie asks.

"Sure," I say.

"Play some Two on Two then," Ronnie says.

"One too many for that game," Matt says, looking at me like I'm diseased.

"You play, Eric," Billy says, "If ya want. I don't mind. I'll clean up some more of this TP of love. "

"Okay," I say, "Thanks."

The four of us stand on the driveway under the hoop. It's a wide flat surface, much nicer than the alley in Iowa. I had to watch for broken glass there. And every once in a while a shot banged off the rim and hit the dumpster.

Ronnie says he'll be on my team, since "Matt and Nate suck." Talking trash already. Ronnie starts with the ball, shoots, and swishes. He's pretty good. Matt seems to be more into defense and rebounding. Nate misses two shots, then makes one. He's slow, but not bad. I shoot a layup and three jumpers. Haven't missed yet. Ronnie and I are killing these guys. This is great!

At one point, Ronnie feeds me the ball under the hoop. I jump and so does Matt. I double-pump, mid-air, and then lay the ball in.

"Oh, hell no!" Ronnie says, "Double-pump was fresh!"

"Nice shot!" Melissa yells from the street.

Whoa, when did she get here? The game stops as we watch her walk by. Melissa holds hands with an older boy who has light blond hair and towers over her. The dude's neck is giant and so are his shoulders. He nods our way and Matt and Nate wave back. The couple continues walking up the hill to Melissa's house.

"Who was that?" I ask.

"Greg Kingman," Matt smiles, "He just graduated. Melissa's boyfriend, usually."

"She has a boyfriend?" I say.

"Doesn't act like it, huh?" Nate winks at me.

"Are we still playing or what?" Ronnie asks.

"Melissa, wait!" Billy yells, "Thanks for decorating my trees! I love it so much!"

"I don't think she heard you," Matt teases.

"Thanks, Melissa!" Billy yells so loud the whole town can hear, "You're the best! And the hottest too! You are a wonderful person in many ways!"

Melissa pauses. She hears but does not look back. I can't stop laughing. Billy has no filter whatsoever.

"You are awesome too, Greg! A big, wonderful man!" Billy turns to us and whispers, "Don't wanna get my ass kicked."

The Melissa distraction dissolves the ball game. It's too hot to play anyway, and we're sweating through our shirts. We take turns drinking from Billy's garden hose while Ronnie challenges us to video games in the basement. We pass, and he disappears into the house.

Billy, Nate, Matt, and I sit at a wooden picnic table in the shade. There's still some toilet paper blowing in the breeze, but not much. Billy cleaned up fast.

"Get this," Matt begins, "I worked yesterday at the photoshop."

"You're sixteen?" I ask.

"No," Matt says like I'm an idiot. "Got my worker's permit. Working for my dad's friend, downtown. Ken Starks, pro photographer. He does senior pics, weddings, and stuff, and I work in the lab developing film. You know, no big deal. But, yesterday, oh man. I'm in the lab and I slide a negative in, put the photo paper down, shoot it with the light, start to focus, and I see a profile. Like I'm trying to figure out what it is. And then I see boobs."

"Whoa!" Billy cracks up, "What??"

"Yeah," Matt nods in total seriousness. "My boss, Ken, gave me the negatives of his naked wife. Can you believe that?"

"Oh my god!" Nate smiles.

"Weird, right? And she's pregnant," Matt says, "Like, huge super pregnant, and she's holding her belly. It's that black-and-white artsy style, like Demi Moore on *Vanity Fair*."

Matt stands up and models the pose. His belly sticks out, and his hands cover his chest and crotch. The sideways look on his face is pretty funny. We all giggle and Billy cries. Billy laughs so hard he falls off his seat and onto the grass. He rolls around on his back and holds his belly.

"Settle down, Billy," Nate says.

"So anyway," Matt continues, "I didn't know what to do. You know? So I just kept developing all these rolls."

"You didn't," Nate laughs.

"I did," Matt nods, "Nearly 60 shots of her, and I developed them, and set them out to dry. And then, like an hour later, Ken walks into the darkroom to check on me. He sees all these five-by-sevens. Of his naked wife! They're hanging up everywhere. And the dude turned green! Like he was gonna barf!"

"Oh my gosh!" Billy laughs, "Too funny! I can't take it!"

Matt continues, "And I'm like, 'Everything okay, Mr. Starks?' And he goes, 'Thanks, Matthew, you can go home now.'"

"Hilarious!" Billy rolls on the ground. "Oh my gosh!"

"Pretty funny," Nate smiles and gives Billy a condescending glance. "But not that funny."

I'm laughing too, and not at Matt, but at Billy. The kid is totally consumed by laughter.

"Matt," Nate asks, "Seen any girls doing senior pics?"

"Oh, yeah," Matt says, "Mandy Hoffman was there last week. Sara Cook. Lindsay Fittipaldi came in. The Rachel Ditmar shots from last year still look the best though. Ken's still got 'em hanging up in the lobby."

"That's Jen's older sis," Nate tells me.

"Oh, oh, speaking of nudies," Billy giggles, "Did I tell you guys I found a dirty movie?"

"What?" Matt says.

"I did," Billy takes a deep breath so he can concentrate on his story, "I was looking through our huge basket full of tapes by the TV, and I found one that said *Dallas*. That TV show's been over for years, so I thought, okay, I'm gonna use this one to tape *Home Improvement* for my dad, since I had a baseball game that he had to go to, so he couldn't watch TV, and that's his favorite show. So I put the tape in the VCR to make sure it truly was *Dallas*, and not something else super important, because one time I did tape over a movie that my mom loved and she was so mad at me. It was her all-time favorite, *Wizard of Oz*. She almost cried. So now I always gotta check first, so I don't tape over something again because that--"

"Jesus Christ!" Matt interrupts, "This story sucks! Get to the point!"

"Okay, okay, fine," Billy says, "So I'm watching this *Dallas* tape, and there's this woman, and she...oh gosh!"

"She what?" Matt asks.

"I can't," Billy laughs so hard he can barely speak. "She, she gets totally naked." He's rolling on the lawn again. I'm laughing too. "And, and then, and then, she..." He can't speak. Billy's laughing so much he cannot complete a sentence, "Then a guy, he starts pumping," Billy laughs, "They're moaning...Aw, man, I can't say it!"

I don't know how Nate and Matt aren't laughing at Billy. They're just staring at him, stone-faced as a funeral. I'm nearly crying over here.

A station wagon pulls into Billy's driveway. That must be Billy's mom, dressed in a silk blouse like she came from work. She waves and honks her horn. Ronnie runs out of the house and hops in the car. "Come on, Billy!" he yells.

"Oh, man," Billy says, "Sorry, you guys, I gotta go. I gotta mow the lawn at my church. Then I have choir practice. See you guys later though. Nice to meet you, Eric."

"You too," I smile.

Billy hops inside and the Winnebago rolls down Greenfield Street. Billy waves goodbye from the backseat window. With an evil grin, Ronnie flips us off.

"Little punk," Matt grins. He sighs, drums his fingers on the picnic table, and then stands up. "Well, time to break into Billy's house again."

"Sounds good to me," Nate smiles.

"What?" I say, "You're kidding, right?"

"Oh, just shut up and follow us," Matt says.

Chapter 10: The Beer Connoisseur

Freeport kids breaking the rules again. This is not cool and it doesn't make any sense. Why go inside Billy's house if he's not home? I should say something. Or stay outside. But these guys seem so casual about it like they do this every day. Billy must be cool with it, right? Maybe. I have no idea.

The front door is unlocked, and Matt walks right in. He struts around like he owns the place, looking down his nose with every step. "What a dump," he says, "Smells like one too."

Matt's a jerk, the house isn't dumpy at all. Billy's spacious living room sits low, like an inverted stage. The green carpet looks old, but it's clean. I can see fresh tracks from the vacuum cleaner. The wicker couches and chairs have brand new cushions. The wall behind the television is covered with expensive picture frames, mostly shots of Billy and Ronnie as toddlers. The TV and stereo system is state-of-the-art. They have a laserdisc and a CD player sitting beside the VCR. Two huge speakers sit on either side of the TV.

Matt kneels and pulls out a large basket of VHS tapes from behind a speaker. "Aw hell," he frowns, "I don't see any pornos. Stupid Billy."

There are at least twenty tapes in the basket, and Matt keeps looking. Meanwhile, Nate fetches three more popsicles from the kitchen.

"What's this, Nate?" Matt scoffs, "Any beer in the fridge?"

"Yeah, you want one?" Nate says.

"No," Matt says, "I'm just asking for no reason. Yeah, of course, I want one. And get this popsicle crap outta here. You drink, Eric?"

I shake my head no.

"Too bad. You just haven't found what you like," Matt says. He sits on the sofa, "I love beer, but it took me a while to acquire the taste. I first got drunk off a whiskey called Southern Comfort. Delicious. Me and my cousins, down in Peoria, we got wasted off that stuff one night. Got laid too."

"Yeah, right!" Nate yells from the kitchen, "You're full of crap, Matt!"

Matt ignores Nate and continues, "You should have seen her, Eric. This girl was my cousin's friend, and she was super hot. And there was a big house party and a sleepover, and everybody split up into separate rooms. I had a room all to myself. So I found this older girl, Nicole. She was eyeing me all night and flirting and stuff, so I whispered in her ear, 'You ready to rock or what?' She just smiled. Didn't say a word. Walks into my room. Takes off her clothes. Boom. Just like that. I'm like, 'Damn, girl.' And she's got a tight body. Redhead, freckles everywhere. We went to town for like five hours, dude. I'm not kidding."

"Hilarious!" Nate laughs, "Missing a few details there, aren't you, champ?"

"What? What else do you want to hear? It felt really good, I remember that."

"Yeah, sure it did," Nate says, "Sounds like a movie I saw once called 'Total Bullshit.'"

"What?" Matt snaps, "Whatever, Nate! What do you know? Stupid ass virgin. Don't listen to him, Eric. He doesn't know what he's talking about."

"Here's your beer, asshole," Nate laughs and sets the cold can on the back of Matt's neck.

"Jesus!" Matt exclaims, "That's cold, you jerk!"

Matt cracks open the can. He looks right at me and takes a big swig. Matt's face goes from cocky to repulsed, back to cocky again. I don't think he likes beer at all. Who's he trying to impress? Matt tells another story, about winning his swim meet. I could care less, but I do believe this one way more than the redhead story. He's almost done bragging when the doorbell rings.

"That you in there, William?" an older voice calls, "Ronald? I know I heard somebody."

"Shit!" Matt says. He springs to his feet. The doorbell rings again. "Who's the old-timer?"

The man wiggles the doorknob and opens the door.

Chapter 11: *The Rich Boy Stare*

"Run!" Nate says, "Go, go, go!"

I run across the room and unlock the sliding glass door. Matt shoves me aside and takes off running. We hurdle some thorny bushes, cut through Nate's lawn, and hide on the far side of his house.

"You think he saw us?" Nate asks, catching his breath.

We creep around the front yard to spy on Billy's house, but the old man is already gone. Or maybe he's inside the house. I feel awful. What were we doing in there?

"Aw man," Nate says, "I left the back door wide open."

"Where's that beer?" I ask.

"Damn it," Matt says, "I spilled it on the couch."

"You dumbass!" Nate frowns.

"Chill!" Matt snaps, "It was an accident!"

The sun is scorching hot. I push the hair off my forehead and rub my eyes. Nate chews on his long bang. Matt rolls up his short sleeves. He glares at Nate's house like it's a torture chamber.

"You guys need AC, a new pool, and like, a new house," Matt grins, "I'm hungry. Let's go to a restaurant."

"Okay," Nate says, "No money though."

"Oh, please," Matt smiles, "I got you. Grab your bike, Nate. Let's go."

There's shade inside Nate's garage, so it's a little cooler. Manny's Toyota Truck takes up most of the space. Leaned up against one wall are two brand new Kmart mattresses. Nate shoves them aside to grab his bike.

"The dads hit Kmart this morning," Nate tells me.

"Cheapest mattress I've ever seen. They make them this thin?" Matt says, inspecting each mattress, "Why would anyone buy this crap?"

"It's my new bed," I say.

"His house burned down," Nate informs Matt, "That's why he's here."

"Oh," Matt says. He smiles, "Then I got an old bike you can have."

"Me too," Nate says, "It's back in the shed."

"No, no, you don't want that antique piece of junk, Eric," Matt says, "Mine's way better."

"No thanks," I say, "I can walk, it's fine."

"Just take it, dude," Nate says. He smiles at me like I've won a contest, "Trust me."

We leave the Garcia garage and Nate rolls his bike while Matt and I walk. We head down Greenfield and hang a right. A couple more turns and we're in one of the nicest cul-de-sacs I've ever seen. I didn't expect to see houses this nice in Freeport. Each home is larger and newer than Melissa's. Every home is brick, and one lawn even has a built-in sprinkler system. Matt points to his giant house. A shiny black van is parked in the driveway. The vehicle is enormous, shorter than a school bus but just as wide.

Matt says they had to remodel his garage door to fit the van inside. In a bored tone, he lists the onboard luxuries, including Corinthian leather captain seats, a mini-fridge, TV, CD player, VCR, Super Nintendo, and a portable phone.

Nate says he went to a waterpark in Wisconsin Dells with Matt last week, and the van ride there was incredible. He felt like a movie star. Matt shrugs like it's no big deal.

Matt leads us inside his three-stall garage. To the far right side, a pair of jet skis rest on a small trailer. Beside them is an empty spot where Matt's dad parks his Porsche 911. Matt says his dad works in Chicago sometimes and stays at a condo on Lake Michigan. Nate says the red Porsche convertible is the prettiest little ride he ever saw.

On the other side of the garage, several shelves stand high against the wall. Every ball from every sport is kept here, along with rackets, sticks, nets, and more. Beside the shelves is a nook filled with scooters, skateboards, rollerblades, and dirt bikes. Matt pulls out a gray seven-speed Trek mountain bike and lets it fall to the floor.

"Take it, Eric. It's yours," Matt doesn't even look at me.

"What? No way!" I say, "It's brand new!"

"No, it isn't. It's all scratched up," Matt wheels out another Trek bike, in purple. "Now this is my new one. Keep that gray piece of shit. Get it out of here."

"You sure?" I say, "This is really nice!"

"This is really nice!" Matt mimics me, "Oh boy, oh boy! That's cute," he laughs, "Eric, get real. Like, seriously. What's your dad do for a living, anyway?"

The look on Matt's face sucks the joy right out of me. I've seen this look before. The rich boy stare. Worse than a bully, smug and pompous. He sees past me like he's above me or better than me. But not because I'm fat this time, because I'm poor. And he's right.

I simmer with shame, but I'm conflicted. I want to punch Matt in the face, but I really want his bike too. It's so nice and Matt's throwing it away.

"Hello?" Matt mocks me, "Your dad? Is he, like, a garbage man or something?" Matt laughs.

"He owns--" I stop, "Well, he owned a pizzeria. On the first floor of my house that burned down."

"He works for my dad now," Nate adds.

"Ha! Working for Manny? Building swimming pools?" Matt chuckles, "Your dad usually hires high school kids for that! Hilarious. And your mom, Eric? She must be a gem."

I hate this guy. How insulting can he be? I put up with a lot of crap in Iowa, I won't do it here too. I've gotta hit him. My face gets hot and my heart beats faster. I don't even know how to fight.

"His mom took off," Nate says, "Left town. Years ago."

"Hmm, I see," Matt gloats, "Oh, yeah, you can definitely keep the bike, buddy. My dad's the richest, most successful lawyer in the state. I can get a new bike, or anything else I want, whenever I want, with a snap of my fingers."

"You know what," my voice shakes, "I don't want the bike. Keep it."

Matt must feel the tension too and he stares me down, "Bullshit, Eric. You want it. Don't lie. I said keep it."

Our bodies are drawn toward each other for all the wrong reasons. I can barely breathe. Here we go.

Chapter 12: Ms. Lyons

I size up Matt and realize one advantage, my weight. If I tackle him first, I could sit on him, and punch him until he cries. I've been beaten up a couple times so I kinda know what to do, and maybe Matt hasn't. Maybe this pampered rich boy is more scared than I am. I square up my body with his and get ready to charge.

"Whoa, whoa! Wait a minute you guys," Nate jumps in between us, "Eric, I know how to settle this. Okay? When's your birthday?"

"Huh?" I stammer, "Last month."

"Okay," Nate smiles, "Easy. Consider this a belated gift. Okay? Voila!"

"Exactly," Matt grins, "Happy Birthday, you poor son of a bitch."

I surge toward Matt, but Nate holds me back. He pats my chest and backs me away from Matt.

Nate whispers, "Eric, chill. Accept the damn bike, okay? It means nothing to him. You know what? I got a CD player once from Matt. He had an extra. An extra! You think my dad can afford one CD player? And guess what? I use it all the time. I love it! This kid is like Santa Claus, alright? Free stuff galore. Just be nice."

"I thought I heard boys out here," a woman says, "What's going on?"

She leans against the doorway that leads into the house. Her sudden presence catches us off guard and cuts the tension in half. This must be Matt's mom. She's tall, like Matt, and their dark hair and sloped noses match. She wears turquoise stirrup leggings and a sweaty orange tank top. A workout video plays from somewhere behind her.

She introduces herself as Ms. Lyons. Ms. and not Mrs.? Matt tells her about the gray bike. Ms. Lyons also insists that I take the gift but in a much nicer tone. She asks me where I'm from and by the end of our conversation, she insists that I call her Johanna. I'm not mad anymore. Johanna saved the day. And this awesome bike is all mine.

"Now give me some money, Mom," Matt demands, "We're going out for lunch."

I haven't ridden a bike in weeks, and riding this Trek is so much better than my second-hand Huffy. The wheels don't wobble, the brakes don't squeak, and the gears actually shift. I take off like a shot. The cool wind feels wonderful on my face.

"Slow it down, Eric!" Nate calls, "God damn!"

I do slow down since I don't know where I'm going. Matt wants Burger King, and Nate leads us down the winding streets. We pass Greenfield Street, go up a hill, and coast past Lincoln-Douglas Elementary School.

Nate recites the town history of the Abraham Lincoln and Stephen Douglas debates. Back in the day, Honest Abe ran for Senate against a short fat dude, who wanted slavery to be a state law. Lincoln lost the Senate race that year but beat Douglas two years later when they both ran for president.

Then Nate explains how Freeport was once a booming German town, with several breweries and bakeries. That's why the high school mascot is The Pretzels. Then World War One brought anti-German vibes, plus prohibition hit, and the town's growth stopped overnight.

"What a nerd!" Matt says, "Chill with the history lesson, Nate."

"What? That's like my only A ever. Okay, fine. I'm done."

We cut through a lawn and hide our bikes in some bushes. Then we climb a chain-link fence and arrive in the Burger King parking lot.

Nate opens the door and sighs, "Yes! Air conditioning! Free refills!"

We order three classic chicken sandwiches, fries, and drinks. Matt pays. The middle-aged woman behind the counter moves slowly but gets the order right.

Nate sets his tray on a table and rushes to the soda fountain. He fills his cup with a squirt of every flavor. "The suicide!" he sips and smiles.

The greasy chicken sandwich tastes salty but good since I'm way hungrier than I thought. Jazz plays in the background of the nearly empty restaurant, and two elderly guys in the corner chat loudly. They complain about the black woman working here, call her dumb, and spit some racial slurs.

The insults grate at me, and I remember my mom. One vivid memory I have of her is from years ago when she got really pissed off. She screamed at my grandpa for being a racist. He said one word and Mom snapped. It was Easter dinner and she threw her plate full of food onto the linoleum floor. It shattered into a hundred pieces. Then she stormed out of the house taking Dad and me with her, and during the long drive home, she preached.

She warned me about hate. For some reason, Grandpa's generation had embraced many prejudices, but Mom refused to let him pass it along. I was way too young to understand, and I cried the whole ride home.

"Something wrong, Eric?" Nate asks.

"Nah," I realize I'm staring at the old dudes and I quickly look away.

"The ancient assholes talking trash over there bugging ya?" Nate asks.

"Shut up!" Matt whispers.

"What?" Nate smiles, "Those old farts can't hear me. They're old, so that means they're deaf. And they'll be dead soon."

"True," Matt laughs, "Old farts!"

insults, lies, and bragging. That's all these boys do. Matt and Nate are a bad combo, constantly trying to out-cool each other. It's exhausting. I tune their conversations out and finish my sandwich.

Chapter 13: The Party Cave

After we eat, Matt heads to swim camp, and Nate and I ride bikes home. I'm happy Matt's gone. I'm relieved.

When we get back to Greenfield Street, I ask Nate for a bucket, a rag, and some dish soap to wash my new bike. I clean the handlebars, chainstay, front fork, and tubes. I save the dirty water at the end for the tires and see the tiny rubber hairs are still on them. This bike is barely used, it was just dirty. Now it's more silver than gray. Nate is impressed.

Thunder booms in the sky. Damn, I can't get my new bike wet. I look for a place to park it inside the garage but there's no room. These mattresses need to go.

I move a mattress to make room for my bike. Then Nate gives me a hand and we carry the mattresses inside, one at a time, down the basement steps and into the cavelike backroom. We set the beds a few feet apart, parallel against one wall.

"Still looks boring in here," Nate says.

He finds some old floral sheets and pillows, and I make the beds. Then Nate grabs a milk crate from the shed and sets it between the beds with a bandana as a tablecloth. He finds a floor lamp too. We search for more stuff while the rain begins to pour. Nate finds a clock radio and a rolled-up poster in his closet. The poster shows James Dean smoking a cigarette and riding a motorcycle in the sunset with Marilyn Monroe riding along, clutching his waist. Nate finds duct tape, and we hang the poster above the milk crate table. Then we raid the kitchen and stash a couple Cokes and a bag of potato chips in the crate.

"Looks pretty good in here now," Nate smiles.

Nate lies down on a mattress and I take the other. I stretch my legs and get comfortable. The mattresses have that new, clean smell, way better than the musty couches. I'm ready for a nap.

"Wait! We need some music," Nate says.

He turns on the clock radio, and tunes in a station. Eric Clapton sings 'After Midnight.' The classic rock song has a bright beat, and Nate sings along. The music is blaring so loudly that I don't hear the footsteps coming down the stairs.

"We having a party back here?" Dad smiles. He's drenched from the rain. "You found the mattresses. Excellent! Looks good down here. The party cave!" Dad pops open a can of Bud Light and sips. "Guess what? Tomorrow is Saturday. No work. And me and Manny have a surprise for you guys. So don't stay up too late, because we're leaving early in the morning. We're going camping!" Dad grins, "And I'm stealing your room, Nate. You guys look way too comfy. And the mildew down here absolutely kills me. Have fun, roomies!"

"What?" Nate says, "No way! You can't take my room!"

"Watch me," Dad laughs like a cartoon villain and runs upstairs.

"Is he for real?" Nate says, "That's bullshit."

"Actually, Nate," I say, "I'm glad he's gone. My dad snores like crazy and his farts stink real bad."

"But he can't take my room. What the hell?"

"You should stay," I say, "Why not? No morning sun in your eyes, and a much cooler temperature. That's good sleeping there."

"Yeah, I guess," Nate smiles, "Like our sleepovers. Back in the day."

He lies down, stretches out, and we stare at the ceiling tiles.

Chapter 14: Dad Jokes

The next morning, Dad's signature whistle wakes me up. He does this stupid noise, like a bird call. His whistle starts low, then swoops up to a high note, and then back down again. Over and over again.

"Rise and shine boys!" Dad says, "Time to get dressed! Big day."

I rub my eyes, while Nate claims the bathroom. I get dressed and run upstairs to the kitchen. Patti stands in her bathrobe, cooking eggs and bacon, while she's also making lunches. She fills a small cooler with ham sandwiches and hands it to me.

"Put this in your Dad's truck," Patti says, "Have fun camping. I'm staying home. Going shopping with my friend Johanna. You guys try to have fun without me, okay?"

After breakfast, Dad drives his truck, and Manny sits shotgun. Nate and I sit in the truck bed amongst the fishing rods, sleeping bags, and other gear.

Manny gives directions as Dad heads west, out of town, and deep into the country. Route 20 passes several farmhouses, barns, silos, and a dog food factory. Near the town of Stockton, we turn onto a dirt road which then becomes a grassy trail. Dad hits a big bump and Nate and I bounce in the air. I land hard on my butt and laugh, even though it hurts. The truck arrives at a small pond, and we park under a shady tree.

I hop out of the truck and walk towards the water. We're in a green valley surrounded by corn, and there's a pretty little kidney-shaped pond that's just bigger than a baseball diamond. Cattails and algae grow along the water's edge. I kneel down and lift up handfuls of baby tadpoles. The little black dots squirm between my fingers. Nate grabs a tin bucket from the truck and tells me to drop them in for bait.

"Pretty spot, huh?" Nate says, "My uncle owns this land. We come here a lot."

There's an aluminum fishing boat resting upside-down in the reeds. Nate and I flip it over and set the wooden oars inside. Then we run to the truck and grab fishing rods and nightcrawlers.

I kick off my socks and shoes, and Nate and I load the boat. I board first and Nate pushes off. He climbs in before his shorts get wet. The boat wobbles for a minute and we laugh. "Don't fall in!" I yell. Nate sits and we're sitting face to face.

"It's all you, Eric," Nate smiles, "Start rowing!"

I grab the oars, and my first stroke barely stirs the water. Then an oar falls out of its lock. I reset it and try again, this time churning deep under the surface.

"Okay, stop! We're centered!" Nate says.

"That was quick!" I laugh.

Nate drops the anchor and hands me a rod. "Thanks." This is gonna be fun. I've always loved fishing. Dad and I used to fish almost every Monday in the summer.

I reach in the can and grab a big juicy worm. I stab the hook through him, wrap his body around the hook, and stab him through again. The little devil poops all over my fingers. I always forget how gross this part is.

"Keeping the hook hidden," Nate nods, "Good work."

My first cast flies high and lands in a shady spot under a tree branch. I take a breath, flip the bail, and watch the bobber float.

"I went fishing on my last normal day in Iowa," I tell Nate, "On that night, while we were driving home, my house burned down."

"Really? That sucks," Nate says, "Just forget it, man. Let's fish." He puts a tadpole on his hook and casts. Then he points at the dads. They sit at a wooden picnic table and drink beers.

"Drinking already," Nate says.

My bobber dips under the water and I softly jerk the line. I feel an unmistakable tension pulling back.

"Fish on!" Nate smiles, "Looks big, Eric!" Nate reels in his line and grabs the net.

Dad yells from the shore, "Bring her in Eric! You got it!"

The fish puts up a fight and I stand up. Then the boat rocks hard and I sit right back down.

"When you fall in, hang on to the rod!" Dad teases. Manny laughs.

The tip of my pole bends and I reel faster. This fish is heavy. A strong swimmer too. My heartbeat races. I keep reeling and the fish gets closer and closer. Then Nate plunges his net into the water.

"Got him!" Nate yells, "Beautiful! A bass, I think. He's a keeper!"

The fish flops in the net and then drums on the floor of the boat. I untangle my line and press the fish against the floor. He's so big and powerful.

The smallmouth bass is almost two feet long, with orange-tipped fins and brown stripes. He's warm and slippery but somehow I manage to pull the hook off his lip.

Nate applauds and so do the dads. I smile and take a deep breath. We caught one. Fast too. I tie the stringer to a cleat on the stern, pass the line through his gills, and drop the fish into the water. He tries to swim away but it's no use.

"Okay, Eric!" Manny yells, "Now, go ahead and smell your hand."

"What?" I say.

"Your hand! Go on! Sniff it!"

I shrug, look at my fingers, and a warm, pungent odor fills my nostrils.

"You like that smell?" Manny yells, "That's what pussy smells like!"

Dad spits out his beer in shock, and he and Manny whoop with laughter. They tap their beer cans together.

"What?" Nate says. He's as embarrassed as I am. Maybe more. Nate shakes his red face and looks down.

"I don't get it," I whisper, "Is that really what it smells like?"

Nate shrugs, "I hope not."

An awkward silence falls over the boat. The weird comment has cursed us. The fish don't bite and the sun gets hot. Nate pulls up the anchor, and I row ashore. The dads stock the boat with beer and take their turn on the water.

I anchor my stringer to a large rock and let my bass swim a while longer. Then Nate and I explore the woods at the edge of the cornfield. We carry back armfuls of kindling.

There's a cinder block fire pit next to a picnic table. I drop a pile of tiny sticks down first, then make a teepee of larger sticks over top. Nate lights the pile and blows at the smoke until we see orange flames. The wood hisses and pops as we add more wood. The thick smoke reminds me of my house.

I envision that night. Dad drove home to find our street was closed. A hundred people had gathered around. We walked closer. It's a dense downtown area. Plenty of other buildings. Could it be ours? Please, no. It couldn't be.

I recognized a face in the crowd. Bev Beasley, the owner of Scoops, the ice cream shop across the street. She saw us and shook her head knowingly. Dad must have seen her too because he grabbed my hand and pushed us through the people.

The big red door of Star Pizza looked normal, but that was all. The rest of the house had turned into kindling. Two-by-fours became black sticks, like a skeleton in flames. My knees buckled and Dad held me. I thought he was crying, but it was laughter instead. He giggled to himself and mumbled "unreal" at least a dozen times.

Floodlights shined and hoses sprayed, but only to protect the neighboring buildings. Ours was beyond saving. The crowd focused on my attic bedroom, the very peak of the roof, waiting for its collapse. As it did, the crowd gasped in unison. Some took pictures. Then everybody went home and left Dad and me alone with the firefighters and police.

Nate drops another pile of sticks onto the flame. Dad must smell the fire too. I wonder what he's thinking.

"Look out!" Manny yells.

I snap out of my memory and look up at the pond. The fishing boat appears empty as it drifts across the water.

"Oh no! It's the Ghost Boat!" Manny laughs.

"Look out, kids!" Dad plays along, "Ghost Boat! Aaah!"

Oh, my god. The dads are hiding on the floor of the boat and giggling like idiots. I shake my head and Nate rolls his eyes.

"Have another beer, you guys!" Nate yells.

"Aye aye, captain!" Dad salutes and pops open another Bud. Seems like the fire smell had no effect, or was drowned away with suds. Escape? Is that why people drink? It can't be the flavor, beer smells disgusting.

Nate stares at the dads and sucks on his bang, "Are we doomed to do dumb shit like them too?"

"Probably," I nod.

The dads run the boat aground in the reeds. Dad and Manny nearly fall in the water as they stand and push themselves out with the oars. Manny steps knee-deep in the muck and Dad cracks up. Their laughter is contagious and Nate and I giggle too.

The campfire is strong now. Nate pokes the cinders with a stick, exposes the orange coals, and sets an iron skillet over top. He pours in vegetable oil and salt. The heavy pan heats up slowly.

I find a baseball-sized rock and pull in my stringer. This part is no fun at all. I drop the fish onto the grass, let him flop around a bit, then I rap him on the skull with the rock. I lay the bass flat on the picnic table, aim my fillet knife, cut behind his collar, and along his ribs. Two thick fillets are each cut in half. Then I chuck the guts and bones into the pond.

Nate pours pancake mix and beer into a bowl. He sips the brew and makes a sour face, "Gross." He stirs the batter and dips the fillets. The oil in the skillet smokes now. The fillets sizzle as Nate places them in the pan.

"Smells terrific!" Dad yells as he drags the boat onto the shore.

The fish tastes light, flaky, and perfectly sweet, as only a fresh catch can. My stomach is full, and I feel happy and proud. I fed us all, and we ate well. Now we can relax and enjoy the afternoon.

Chapter 15: Barf Kiss

After lunch, Dad and Manny nap on the grass while Nate and I blow up some inner tubes. These are the new plastic ones filled with lung power, not the black rubber bicycle pump kind. Inflating them takes way longer than I expect, and I'm light-headed by the time it's done.

I change into a tight pair of Nate's swim trunks and slip my body inside the yellow inner tube. I carry the tube high to hide my fat chest. My belly sucks too, but if I can only hide one, it's my boobs. The water obscures sight though. Once my body is submerged I feel better.

A refreshing breeze blows across the pond. Nate ties a line to a tree, so we don't drift into the reeds. With the tube on its side, he balances his body through the center hole, like me, with our arms dangling in front of us. The pond is deeper than I thought, and I'm an awful swimmer, but I feel safe in my tube.

"Question," Nate says, "Who's hotter? Jen or Melissa?"

"What? No way."

"Answer the damn question."

"Come on," I say, "I know you're gonna say Jen. You're obsessed with her."

"Pretty much. She's better by far," Nate smiles, "I kissed her, you know."

"No."

"Oh, yeah, it was a long time ago. We were little kids. It was weird. I was eleven, I think. We were at my house watching TV, and she planted one on me. Then something happened. Like, somebody yelled at us from the other room, and we had to go," Nate smiles, "That's back when Jen used to eat cat food."

"Cat food?"

"Yeah, cat food," Nate giggles, "Those soft little morsel things. I was over at her house one time, around the same age, maybe younger, and she dared me to eat some. I said, 'No way,' but then she dug her hand in the bowl and chomped it up like popcorn."

"Oh, that's just dumb little kid stuff though."

"Yeah, maybe," Nate nods, "But you know what? I kissed her again for real. And this was recent, like two months ago."

"Really?"

"Yeah," Nate grins, "Last May. She was drunk. Super drunk. She drank brandy slush at one of Rachel's parties. So hammered! Probably the first time Jen ever got wasted. She showed up at my house and barfed in the backyard. Then she slipped and fell in it. Barf all over her. So she whipped off her shirt and threw it in a crabapple tree. She was running around my backyard in her bra. I took my shirt off so she could wear it. Then she got sick again. She started crying. I held her. We laid down in the grass. She kissed me then. With tongue."

"A barf kiss?"

"Oh, no, man. I mean, I gave her a Coke to drink before the kiss. I forgot that part."

"A Coke?"

"Yeah. A nice cold one," Nate says, "It was a good kiss, trust me. Her lips were soft and sweet. She kinda moaned a little bit too."

"Then what?"

"That was it."

"No, I mean, did Jen ever say anything about it the next day?"

"Nope, nothing."

"Did she even remember it?"

"Oh, yeah," Nate says, "She was sobered up pretty good after she barfed. I should have said something to her back then. Or asked her out or something. But now it's been a while, and it kinda got weird. I missed my chance."

"No, it was only last May. That's nothing," I say, "You could still talk to her about it. She seems pretty cool."

"Yeah. Maybe. I don't know. I'll figure it out though. I'll get her back. It's my life's mission," Nate says with a determined look in his eyes. Then he asks, "Hey, but what about you and Melissa, huh? What were you guys doing at the TP session? I saw you hugging under the trees. What the hell was that?"

"I don't know," I shrug, "She started it."

"That girl flirts, doesn't she?" Nate grins, "Better watch out."

Chapter 16: Making The Big Bucks

The evening nears and the air cools off. Nate and I get dressed and spray each other with mosquito repellent. After a few tries, we manage to pitch the tent. The dads wake up from their naps, find more kindling, and stoke the fire. Manny cooks a large can of beans that we eat with Patti's ham sandwiches and potato chips. Dad and Manny drink beer and Nate and I sip Cokes. Food always tastes better outside. After supper, Nate and I roast marshmallows while the dads skip dessert and smoke cigarettes instead.

"Well, boys," Manny announces, "Having fun? Because we brought you here today to tell you something special."

"Oh, no," Nate shudders, "What?"

"You guys are big and strong now, so you are officially hired. I landed a contract for an inground pool. That's a big job. Can't do it without you two."

"Congrats, you guys!" Dad says, "You'll get to earn the big bucks!"

"That's right! Six dollars an hour," Manny smiles, "Cash."

"Are you kidding?" Nate protests, "Can't you just hire somebody else?"

"Oh, come on, Nate," Manny laughs, "This will be good for you guys. Get a tan. Build some muscle."

"Your girlfriends will like that," Dad smiles, "Especially what's her name?"

"Jen or Melissa!" Manny laughs.

"You guys listened to us?" Nate whines, "I thought you were asleep!"

"We tried," Manny smiles, "But you have such a loud voice, Nate. Got your mother's Irish whisper."

"And guess what else?" Dad says, "You'll have money to buy more toilet paper!"

"They did do a pretty good job though, huh?" Manny smiles.

"Oh, yes. Very thorough," Dad nods, "Beautiful craftsmanship. That was like a work audition, really. Now we know you boys are capable."

"What do you think?" Manny asks, "Want to work with us or what? Don't worry. Just a couple weeks, till the inground job is done."

"But what if you sell another inground pool?" Nate asks.

"I'm gonna try," Manny grins, "That's big money!"

"We'll be digging all summer," Nate groans, "Great. There goes my childhood."

The dads laugh and I join them. Nate's groan was way overdramatic. The work sounds good to me. I'll get paid. And it's way better than hanging out with Matt. The dads start another round of beers, and I stuff a delicious, slightly burnt marshmallow in my mouth.

Later that night, Nate and I lay out our sleeping bags. The weather is so nice that we decide to sleep outside the tent, under the stars. We stay up for a while and listen to the dads talk.

I fall asleep, and when I wake up it's pitch dark. The fire is nearly out. The dads sound sober. Maybe they ran out of beer. Their conversation seems serious. Their words are slow, chosen carefully.

"Patti got a hold of Donna last night," Manny says, "Finally."

Donna? Mom's name grabs my attention.

Chapter 17: The Mom Bomb

"What?" Dad says, "Donna? You're kidding me. Where is she now?"

"You should ask Patti. Said she's in Chicago."

"Chicago? In the burbs or what?"

"Not sure," Manny pauses, "Me and Patti were talking about her. Donna has problems, man."

"Oh yeah," Dad says, "I hate talking about it."

"Didn't you find her on the kitchen floor with a bottle of vodka and some pills?"

"I did," Dad says, "Scared the shit out of me. Thankfully the pills stayed in her hand."

"She saw a shrink then?" Manny asks.

"She did see a therapist, and she did okay for a while, but then she got bad again."

"Drinking a ton. Getting plastered."

"Donna couldn't even work, Manny. Couldn't function without booze. It was awful."

"Then she went back to therapy?"

"Well, we talked about it, and that's when she took off," Dad says, "I remember that day. I was downstairs prepping dough and Eric was at school. A Friday morning, busiest day of the week. I was pissed she wasn't helping out. Too drunk again. So I ran upstairs, but she wasn't in bed, or smoking in the back alley, or anywhere. So I called her folks--"

"Called us too."

"Yup, called her cousin, the local bars, and then I called the police. Nobody had seen her, or heard from her, nothing. Then the cops started looking at me like I did something."

"I forgot that part. They found her though."

"Yup," Dad sighs, "Cops found Donna in Des Moines at some cheap trucker motel doing god knows what."

"And she never came back?" Manny asks.

"Nope. Not once. Now and then she lets us know she's alive. Sometimes she'll call and leave a two-second birthday message, like a week late. And she did call after that big tornado hit Fort Dodge. Making sure we were okay."

Somebody stirs the fire and cracks open a beer.

"She stopped through here once," Manny says, "A few years back. Showed up outta nowhere on a Tuesday afternoon or something, and man, she partied hard. Up all night, and then disappeared the next day. That's the last time I saw Donna," Manny says, "I feel for you, Mike. Good riddance. Who needs all that drama bullshit anyway?"

"Remember my wedding, Manny?"

"Sure do. Patti was the maid of honor. Beautiful outdoor wedding."

"It was fun. But you know what?" Dad says, "It wasn't legal. We never filed the marriage license. The business was in my name, the mortgage, and the car loans too. A liberal like Donna didn't want her name on anything. Crazy, huh? Had her finger on the eject button the whole time."

"Well, just because she's gone doesn't mean you guys can't visit," Manny says, "It's good to see you, Mike."

Chapter 18: A Secret Invitation

It's dawn. The sky swirls with blue and gray, and the grass smells sweet as sugar. I forgot that I slept outside. I'm soaked with dew, and my back kills me. A twig snaps and I see a deer. A beautiful doe. She stands stone-still across the pond and stares at me. I sit up on my elbow and stare back. She takes a few steps, eats some buds off a pussywillow, and dashes into the woods. A fawn appears from behind the reeds and follows her.

Inseparable mother and child. The scene reminds me of Mom. She dashed so deep into the woods that she couldn't be found. Chicago. It's so close, but it's huge. Millions of people. Could I find her there? Do I want to? I am curious to meet her. It's been so long. Dad never talks about her. He's never told me exactly what her problem was, but I've heard whispers. It did hurt to hear him say it. Was she that bad? I can't remember. Photos of her spring to mind, but my own image of her is a fuzzy silhouette. Her laugh is a sound I probably made up in my head.

I try to fall back asleep. My stomach growls. I get up, raid the cooler, and find a tube of breakfast sausage. I rinse the frying pan in the pond and gather more kindling. I stoke the coals from last night, and the salty sizzle of sausage wakes up the guys.

"Look at you," Dad grins, "Cheffing it up. Thanks, Eric. Smells like heaven."

After breakfast a black cloud forms on the horizon. Nate and I collapse the tent and toss all the gear into the truck. The wind picks up, and I can smell the rain coming.

We cram four big bodies inside the truck cab, just before rain swoops in and drenches the windshield. We ride down the highway, and the storm fades. Back in Freeport, Greenfield Street looks completely dry. The rain missed town, but something else did strike.

Toilet paper covers every inch of the Garcia's landscaping. This job was done with twenty-times more paper than Billy's. This is nuts. I can hardly make out a green leaf on the branches, and the bushes look like snowdrifts.

Nate nudges me with his elbow, "Somebody likes you, Eric. I lived here my whole life and never got hit once."

I smile at Nate but he's not happy. He's either sad, angry, tired, or jealous. I don't ask.

Dad parks in the driveway and Billy runs across the street to greet us. He looks formal, in leather shoes, khakis, and a pastel green Polo shirt. His Sunday best.

"You got totally nailed, Nate! Oh my gosh! Crazy!" he laughs like a seal again, "They did a major job on you. Major, man! I think I know who it was too. I saw a white car pull up, super late. Kind of like a Cadillac, but smaller."

"The Chrysler New Yorker," Nate nods, "That's Declan, which means Jen and Rachel did it. Maybe Melissa too. Son of a bitch."

"Eric, we had Mrs. Garcia over for dinner last night," Billy says, "She told us all about the fire. That's devastating. And your mom left you? Oh, man, she sounds like a troubled soul. Life's not easy on you, huh? If you ever want to talk about it, just let me know. Oh, and did you guys break into my house?"

Whoa! That question came out of nowhere. And the shocked look on my face probably answers him. I know my cheeks are bright red.

"Of course not," Nate lies.

"Well somebody spilled beer on my couch," Billy says, "And Gramps said he saw somebody inside. If it's you, just tell me, it's no big deal. If it's not you, then yikes! That means a real burglar was in my house. Wasn't it you guys? Just messing around?"

"Nope," Nate says, "Must be a burglar. That's scary stuff."

"Yes, it really is. That stinks," Billy says, "Oh, man. Gotta run. Sunday school. See ya when I get back."

Billy runs across the street and trips on the curb. A grass stain streaks down the front of his knee. He growls at himself and tries to wipe it off. His dad pulls the car out of the driveway. His mom yells at Billy, and he runs inside. Billy reemerges seconds later wearing a pair of tight, white pants that he clearly outgrew. His mom yells again, but the pants stay, and the station wagon rolls down the street. Ronnie smiles at us from the back seat and flashes his middle finger again. Nate smiles and gives it right back.

"Boys!" Manny yells, "How about giving us a hand unpacking?"

Nate and I grab the wet sleeping bags out of the truck and hang them on the clothesline in the backyard. We put the tent in the shed. Then we head inside to the kitchen, where Patti sits in her bathrobe, drinking coffee and reading the newspaper.

"Hey, boys," she smiles, "Have fun? Your vandal girlfriends decorated our house last night."

"That's what Billy said," Nate says.

"You better clean it up," Patti warns, "Oh, and Eric, I bought you some clothes. They're downstairs."

I run down the steps and back to the cave. Four different outfits are spread across my mattress. Jean shorts with a dark purple t-shirt, a gray v-neck with plaid shorts, a striped blue shirt with gray shorts, and a green Polo with brown shorts. I've never had outfits that match like this. Multipacks of socks and underwear are here too. This is so nice.

"Boring shirts, dude," Nate says. I guess he's the one picking out the wild prints.

After microwaving pizza rolls for lunch, Nate and I grab rakes and ladders from the garage. We remove a ton of TP from the trees. It comes off easier than I thought, in big heavy clumps. We fill four huge garbage bags in two hours, and we're done.

We race our bikes up and down Greenfield Street. Then we play catch with a frisbee and I ask about Billy.

Nate assures me that lying is always a good idea. He insists that Billy is an idiot and that nobody in the world is honest with him.

"If Ronnie had asked me, I might have confessed," he says, "But never Billy."

And why should I believe that? He just said 'lying is a good idea.' Nate doesn't make any sense but I don't argue. I do have to live with this guy. We cool off in the basement, shoot a game of pool, and sit at the bar and drink Cokes.

Then we ride our bikes to Jen's. Nobody's home so Nate insists that we try Matt's house. Johanna answers the door and says Matt is sick with a stomach bug. So we ride to Melissa's house and find her in the backyard jumping on her trampoline.

"Hey, guys!" she smiles.

Melissa's nose is sunburned and she brags about going to Wisconsin Dells with her cousins. Melissa swam at Noah's Ark all day, and even braved the scariest, super steep water slide, 'The Plunge.'

Melissa's little brother, Tyler, recognizes Nate and begs him to play catch. They toss a Nerf football around, and Melissa pulls me aside. Her happy smile turns upside down.

"I'm so sad," Melissa whispers.

"Why?"

"Me and my boyfriend, Greg... We broke up."

"Uh, sorry," I say.

"It's not your fault," she grins. "Well maybe, just a little," Melissa presses her body against my arm, "I like you," she whispers, "Come here. Tonight. The basement door. At midnight. Seriously. I'll be waiting."

"Huh?"

Melissa is dead serious. I don't know what to say. I manage to nod my head and she winks at me.

"Tyler!" she yells, "Stop bothering my friend! We gotta go! Come on! Aunt Tori's birthday party, remember?" Melissa glances down at her Mickey Mouse watch and coos, "See you later."

Chapter 19: Kissing Advice

Nate and I ride our bikes up the hill and try Jen's door again, but there's still nobody there. We ride home and park our bikes in the garage. Then Nate says there's a cool place he wants to show me, but we have to walk.

We cut through some yards and Nate leads me past a construction site. At least a half dozen homes are framed up with studs. Plywood roofs with no shingles, no windows, no sidewalks, and no grass.

We keep walking, hike through a patch of woods, and end up on a golf course. We follow along the fairways, past manicured putting greens and giant willow trees. I've never golfed. Not sure why. Too expensive, I guess.

I hear someone swing and a tiny white ball bounces down the hill. Nate and I hide behind some bushes as a golf cart nears us. The brakes clinch and the vehicle skids to a stop. Two men cuss and complain about the large sand trap in front of the green. They wear Polo shirts, ball caps, and sunglasses. One man puffs on a thick cigar. They discuss which iron to use and then, *whack*! Once they leave, we walk the fairway again.

"You gonna tell me what Melissa was whispering or what?" Nate grins.

"She wants me to meet her at midnight. At her house."

"Say what?" Nate laughs and claps his hands, "You're kidding me."

I shake my head.

"Oh, my god. Are you guys gonna have sex?"

"Um, is that what she wants?"

"Totally dude!" Nate laughs, "At midnight? Come on!"

I try to smile but I'm too nervous.

"You've never done it, huh?" Nate says, "Me neither. But you've kissed a girl, right? Like, really kissed her."

I giggle and my face turns red.

"What? You haven't made out before?"

I shake my head.

"Ah, I know why. Fat," Nate says, like he solved a riddle, "Well, don't worry, I know some stuff. Declan gives advice all the time. He says, 'Lick it before you stick it.' Not sure exactly what that means, but he says it's important."

Nate watches me for a response but I have no idea. He continues.

"There is a lot of licking involved, you know. Good kissing is basically licking. Then there's the humping, and you get a little sweaty. It's a workout and then..." Nate stops and stares at my blank face, "Wait. Do you even know what an orgasm is?"

"What? Organism?"

"Oh, man!" Nate howls, "Eric, you poor soul! You haven't lived, my friend. Your life hasn't begun!" he giggles, "You're just messing with me, right?"

"Of course," I totally lie and change the subject, "So who did you make out with?"

"Lindsay Fittipaldi. About a month ago, when school let out. It was fun," Nate smiles, "But then she got with some other dude. Enough about me though, this is all you, Eric. You have to get ready for tonight!"

I sigh, "What if her parents hear us?"

"At Melissa's? That huge house? Trust me, she knows what she's doing."

At the edge of the golf course, Nate and I reach a busy road and wait for traffic to clear. Then we enter a cornfield, pick a row, and follow it. The corn is about as tall as I am and its leaves scratch at my face. After about a quarter-mile, the cornrows fade into prairie grass. We near a creek and the swampy ground squishes under my feet.

"Damn, dude!" Nate smiles, "Melissa's at midnight!"

I am still thinking about Melissa. I'm nervous as hell. I've heard so many warnings about sex. You have to use protection. You could get a girl pregnant. Or get AIDS. And honestly, I barely know this girl. I mean, she's nice and she's pretty, but isn't sex supposed to be with somebody you love? Love. Oh god, I have no idea. Maybe it's all just crap adults preach to slow kids down. Sex has got to be fun. Every song on the radio talks about it. It's either that or getting wasted.

"Hey Eric," Nate asks, "Do you know how to put a condom on?"

"No! I've never even seen one!"

"I got one. You want it? Matt gave it to me. He stole a bunch when his friend Eddie worked at Walgreens."

"Please don't tell Matt about Melissa. Okay?"

"Of course," Nate says.

"I'm serious," I say, "Please. You just lied to Billy's face, but don't lie to me."

"Jesus Christ, Eric. I'm sorry. I just don't like Billy. But you can trust me, okay?" Nate mimes like he zips his lips shut and throws away the key. "Look," he points, "This is what I wanted to show you."

Chapter 20: The Rawson House

A dilapidated two-story farmhouse rises above the open field like a temple. It's obviously stood there for decades and doesn't ever plan on leaving. Painted white, eons ago, it's now a dusty gray. And nearly half the siding fell off, with some held up by ivy. The roof is caved in at one end. The worn shingles look like shriveled scabs. Every window is broken, and the front door is missing. No wires address number or mailbox. No paved road leading up to the home, and any wagon trails have grown over years ago.

An oak tree stands in the front yard, as big around as Melissa's trampoline. It's at least 200 years old. Which was here first, the house or the tree?

"The Rawson House predates the Civil War," Nate says, "The town wants to buy the land and build old folks homes, but the owner refuses to sell or demolish it. And guess what? There's tons of ghosts here. There's a little girl ghost who sings lullabies in German. She tugs on people's clothes. There's a crazy old woman who hacks apart live chickens in the kitchen. And there's a soldier, a deserter from the Civil War, coming home and blowing his head off. Crazy, right?"

"I don't believe it."

"Oh, yeah?" Nate grins and bobs his eyebrows, "Better watch your step."

I smell cat crap as soon as I enter the house. The gamey smell could also be a raccoon, or skunk, who knows, maybe an entire varmint zoo. Ashes of a campfire litter the entryway. Sloppy spray-painted graffiti covers one wall. A fireplace is full of empty beer cans. An ominous pile of bloody denim is wadded up in one corner. A rusty Franklin stove sits on its side in the kitchen.

Nate leads me down the creaky steps into the cobwebbed basement. The support columns are made of logs with the bark still on them. The floor is dirt, with animal droppings in every corner.

"Ancient, right?" Nate says, "How many dudes do you think are buried here? Right under our feet."

"I don't want to know."

We leave the basement and Nate leads me upstairs. It seems like a miracle that the second floor can support our weight. We enter a bedroom, where football-sized holes cover the floor and show through to the kitchen below. Scraps of paper and dust slowly swirl in the air, and the sun shines through a giant hole in the roof. The place is beaten up but somehow beautiful. The old house keeps holding on, refusing to die. It's strange, but I can almost feel the past in here. How did this home manage to survive forever while mine burned away?

Crack! A boom echoes from the kitchen.

"Oh god!" Nate screams.

He runs down the stairs and I'm right behind him. Nate sprints straight across the clearing, past the giant tree, and doesn't stop until we reach the corn.

"What the hell was that?" Nate asks. His eyes are huge and he's out of breath, "It was super loud!"

"I don't know," I laugh at the look of panic on his face, "It was probably a cat."

"Maybe. Or it was a ghost."

"No way," I grin.

"What's so funny? You were running too!"

"I just followed you!"

"Yeah, right. You were scared," Nate says, "We should come back tonight, after dark. Then we'd really get the shit scared out of us. No, wait. Can't. You already have plans."

When we get home, Patti has dinner on the table, hard-shell beef tacos with frozen corn and white rice. I can hardly eat, I'm so nervous about Melissa. Afterward, Dad makes a couple of phone calls, Manny mows the lawn, and Patti watches *Wheel of Fortune* on TV. Nate and I hear Billy and Ronnie shooting hoops. Before we join them, I make Nate promise he won't talk about Melissa.

We play 2-on-2, and then 21 Tip-Out. Ronnie complains because he's too short to get a rebound, but he sinks all his free-throws and wins anyway. We get covered in sweat and drink from the garden hose. Then mosquitos swarm us, and Nate and I head home.

A chemical odor fills the Garcia house as Patti paints her fingernails at the kitchen table. The dads drink beers and watch the Cubs game on TV.

"Cubs are up 4-1, top of the 8th," Manny says, "You guys better get some sleep, big day of work tomorrow."

I almost forgot about work. I'll be so tired. Nate and I take turns in the shower, then we head downstairs, brush teeth, and lie down. Nate wears boxers for pajamas, but I put on one of my brand new outfits that Patti bought me.

"Heads up," Nate says.

He throws me a square foil packet with a serrated edge. A Trojan war helmet is printed on the side with the word 'ribbed.' I squeeze the contents inside and feel a slimy rubber ring beneath.

Nate nods, "That's a condom. You don't have to use it. I'm pretty sure Melissa's on the pill. You might not want to use it. How old is the damn thing?"

Nate shrugs, "I bet it'll still work."

I flip the condom like a coin in the air and catch it. There's no way in hell I'm unwrapping this thing. I'll have a hard enough time just kissing her.

Chapter 21: *Melissa At Midnight*

I lie on my mattress and stare at the ceiling tiles while Nate snores. I need something to do, the minutes are crawling by, and my stomach is sick with worry. Maybe I shouldn't even go see Melissa. But I kinda have to, right? Why? I don't know. I get out of bed, snoop around the basement, and find a closet with a cardboard box full of old paperback books.

I pick up *Tortilla Flat*, by John Steinbeck, and read the first few chapters. It's about these idiot bums who scam people for money to buy wine. Pretty funny stuff. Makes wine seem very appealing. Then the house they're squatting in burns down. Great, I can't read this anymore. I check the clock, and thankfully it's time to leave. I check my hair in the bathroom mirror. Deep breath. Here we go.

I sneak out the basement window. The night air feels fresh and cool. Crickets, frogs, and owls chatter in the darkness. Every house is dead quiet. My footsteps feel loud on the street, so I tiptoe through the grass all the way to Melissa's. Every window in her house is dark. Maybe she forgot or fell asleep. Maybe it was all a tease to make me think about her all day.

Then in the backyard, I see the flickering light of a television. Oh man, my heart is really pounding now. I see Melissa through the window. She's lying on the couch under a blanket. She looks asleep, but when I tap on the door she answers immediately. Melissa swings open the door without making any sound whatsoever.

"Hi," she whispers.

Melissa motions for me to follow her. She flops onto the couch and stares at the TV. It's the only light in the room, so it seems bright. I sit beside her. We're close but not touching.

"Want some of my blanket?" she asks, "My parents have the AC cranked, it's freezing!"

I haven't noticed. Actually, I feel quite warm. I get under the blanket anyway.

An *I Love Lucy* rerun plays on TV. I know this stupid show interests neither of us. We're not laughing at the dumb jokes or Lucy's zany faces. How long do I sit here? This girl is not a conversationalist at all. Usually, I'm the last person to talk. Why won't she say something?

"Didn't that actress just die?" Good one, Eric. Smooth.

"I don't know," Melissa says, "Probably. What's her name?"

"Lucille Ball."

"That's right!" she giggles, "You're so smart!"

I smile and Melissa smiles back. Then her expression changes. Her eyes take command. She leans towards me, and I lean in too.

Her lips feel soft and slippery. Her tongue touches mine and it feels slimy and very weird. Our mouths slide around in chaos. My mouth almost touches her ear at one point. Am I doing this right? Melissa seems okay with it. Her hands touch my back as mine hover around her waist.

"Ouch!" Melissa squeals.

"Sorry. Are you okay?"

"I'm fine," she grins, "My sunburn is scratchy though. Hang on."

Melissa leans back, crosses her arms, and lifts up her shirt. Oh my god, it's her bra. Our lips touch again and Melissa's body slides under mine. I see her flat stomach and her tiny pajama shorts. What do I do now? I'm afraid to get too close. I don't want to stare. I can't move. I'm thinking way too much.

I breathe in. Then Manny's terrible fishing joke invades my mind. Damn it! Why? She definitely doesn't smell like that! Oh my god, my focus is totally blown. I hear Lucille Ball whining on the TV again. I see a potato chip lying on the floor. Everything stalls. What am I doing? Melissa gazes up at the ceiling, licking her lips, and waiting. What do I do?

"Wait!" Melissa says, "Did you hear that?"

"What?"

"My dad!" Melissa says, "Hurry! You gotta go!"

I run for the door and she slams it shut.

I turn to run back to Nate's but then I stop. What's the rush? They can't see me out here in the dark. I watch Melissa through the window. She's in no hurry at all. She slowly folds the blanket and turns off the TV. She walks up the stairs, and the last light in the house goes dark. Her dad was not awake. Melissa lied. She wanted me gone. I screwed something up, didn't I? She knew I was clueless. I blew it.

Lightning flashes in the sky and I walk back to Nate's. I clomp my feet loudly down the middle of the street. Who cares about the noise. I'm so pissed.

I try to focus on the positive. I kissed a very pretty girl. And of course, we didn't go all the way. I don't know her very well. I'm a gentleman taking my time.

Or I'm an idiot. I ruined an extremely rare opportunity. Why is the word coward in my head? I wasn't afraid. Was I? I don't know. This sucks.

Maybe Melissa wanted to slow things down too. I may have another chance. Am I her boyfriend now? Should we hang out tomorrow? That honestly doesn't sound like fun. Do I call her? What's her number? I don't know. What's her last name? Why did I even come over? Why did she invite me? The whole thing is stupid.

As the rain starts to fall, I slide open Nate's basement window and crawl inside. I tiptoe past the pool table and into my cave bedroom. I brush my teeth and lie down. The kissing scene runs over and over again in my head. Melissa on her back, ready to rock. Me, fumbling. What was I thinking? Then Nate stirs under his sheet.

"You fuck her?" Nate asks.

"Nope."

"Lame."

Chapter 22: The Smile Business

Dad's annoying bird-call whistle wakes me up early. I feel like I just closed my eyes and slept for one minute. I blew it with Melissa last night. That did happen, damn it.

"Seven o'clock, let's roll, boys!" Dad yells, "Lots of work to do!"

Manny gives me a 'Freeport Pool and Spa' t-shirt, and Nate lets me borrow an old pair of boots. Patti cooks scrambled eggs, toast, and bacon. She also packs a small cooler full of sandwiches and pop.

"You sure you boys don't want to work at the bank with me instead?" Patti grins.

"Sure, they hiring?" Nate asks.

"No way," Patti laughs, "Hard labor only for you."

Us guys all pile into Dad's Dakota Sport. Nate and I sit in the back. There's no traffic as Dad accelerates east, towards the hot sun. We drive to the edge of town and rumble over a narrow bridge. Dad parks at a warehouse and we hop out. Manny chooses the right key on his keychain and unlocks a steel door.

"Gonna need an 18-foot liner and wall," Manny says.

"Dad!" Nate whines, "I thought we were doing an inground pool!"

"Rained last night. The ground's too wet," Manny says, "We'll start tomorrow."

"You don't need us today then. Can't we go home?"

"Nate, I said you'd start today, so you're starting today."

The warehouse is huge and completely packed. Ladders, hand trucks, and a skid loader crowd the entryway. Along one wall two stacks of hot tubs, four high, pile on top of each other. Giant squares of pool table slates lean against each other like books on a shelf. Everything else is boxed and stacked in cardboard, in piles ten feet high. A tiny varmint scurries by as we follow a narrow path between boxes.

Dad catches my eye, "Chipmunks," he winks.

Dad seems happy and at home here, even though he's only worked a few days. Dad climbs up a pile of boxes and looks back at Manny. "Eighteen-foot liner, right?"

"Yep."

"Lookout below!" Dad pushes a heavy brown box. It falls onto the cement floor with a loud slap and a cloud of dust.

"All right," Manny nods, "The steel walls are back this way."

Manny grabs a dolly and slides it under a tall rectangular box. He wheels it back to the truck and Dad helps lift the box onto the tailgate. Manny throws in some tools and a few more supplies, including a heavy, metal, homemade cage contraption, built low with skateboard sized wheels. Manny locks the warehouse door and we drive away.

The job site is close to Krape Park, which reminds me of my first crazy night in Freeport. Dad parks on a backyard lawn helps unload the supplies and then leaves without us. Manny surveys the land with a laser level on a tripod. Then he hammers a spike into the ground and attaches a cloth measuring tape. With orange spray paint in hand, Manny circles clockwise with the tape, and marks out an 18-foot circle on the lawn. Manny hands me and Nate shovels and shows us how to peel up the sod. If you get the right angle, the grass comes up easily, like peeling frosting off a cake. The soil underneath the grass is black and shiny, for a moment, but the sun quickly dries it to a tan color.

"Can't you hire a backhoe for this, dad?"

"No, Nathan, this is the flattest yard in town, why would we need to do that?"

"My hands already hurt," Nate complains, "Hey, Eric, do you like blisters?"

"Nate, shut up and get to work. Eric, don't listen to him. Pile the sod over here, guys."

The sun beats down as a wide, flat circle forms across the lawn. Dad returns with his truck bed full of sand. Nate and I hop into the truck and shovel the sand into a pile at the center of the circle. Nate shovels slowly on purpose, and it pisses me off. Lazy ass. He thinks he's so clever. I shovel faster to make him look worse. Then I remember what he said last night. "Lame." What a jerk. I shovel faster.

Once the sand is emptied from the truck, we unload twenty flat concrete bricks and space them evenly along the edge of the circle. The laser level is used again, as we test the height of each block, making sure the sensor beeps. Then Manny wheels over his homemade cage contraption, and loads in the heavy wall. His contraption acts like a giant tape dispenser, as the spool of steel is gradually unwound. Above each concrete block, we attach metal columns, which hold the wall in its place. Nate and I screw on the verticals while Dad screws on the horizontal top rails. Manny's cordless drills make the work quick. After the spool runs out, we bolt the ends of the wall together, and the pool stands strong. During lunch, Nate and I spread the latex liner on the lawn so the sun can warm the wrinkles out, while the dads trowel the sand on the bottom of the pool.

"Goddamn," Nate sighs, "Does this job suck or what?"

"Not so bad. I like the exercise." I'm sweaty as hell but feel great.

Soon the pool floor is beautifully flat. We help the dads crawl out of the pool. Then all of us pick up the liner and stretch it up over the top rails. We lower it down evenly and secure it against the wall with long pieces of duct tape. As a garden hose slowly fills the liner, Manny periodically unfastens the tape pieces and lowers the liner a few inches. Manny says this slow method is the only way to avoid wrinkles.

"Good job, boys," Dad smiles, "There it is. Your first pool is almost done."

"Not my first pool. Unfortunately," Nate says.

"Jesus, Nate," Manny frowns, "I thought having a friend here would help you complain less."

"You thought wrong," Nate says. "Can we leave now?"

"Sure," Manny says, "I can do the rest myself. You wanna drop 'em off, Mike?"

Dad gives a thumbs up, and we follow him to the truck. As we're leaving, two children run out of the house. The girl and boy are probably in 2nd or 3rd grade. The kids point at the pool and laugh.

The sister says she wants to jump in first and the brother says the same. They're so happy and excited. I look at Dad and smile.

"See?" Dad says, "Great job, isn't it? We made those kids so happy. Made their whole summer."

Nate and I hop in the truck and Dad heads to Greenfield Street. He drops us off and leaves to help Manny finish up.

Nate and I stand on the driveway and watch a tradesman with a toolbox leave Billy's house. The guy hops into a white cargo van with a logo on the side that reads, 'Safe Security Systems Inc.'

"A security system," I say, "Nate, why didn't you tell Bily it was us?"

"I'm telling you," Nate says, "Don't ever admit to doing dumb shit. Especially to an idiot like Billy. Great. Here he comes now."

"Hey, guys!" Billy waves, "Been working, huh? Make that money, boy, make that, make that money! Make that money boy, make that, make that money!"

"What is that, a song or something?" Nate rolls his eyes.

"Yes! I just wrote it myself," Billy smiles, "Sounds good, right?"

"Please don't ever sing it again," Nate says.

"I work too, you know. At my dad's car wash," Billy smiles, "It's awesome. There's this one old lady who comes in like everyday and gives fat tips. Then there's this other dude, he's, like, from Russia or something, and he yells at everybody like, 'You miss spot! You streak!' What a jerk, right?"

I hear footsteps coming up the street.

"Oh, hey Melissa!" Billy yells, "What's up, girl? Looking good! Hey, Greg! What's going on, big guy?"

Melissa smiles and waves. She holds Greg's hand with their fingers intertwined. He drops her hand, puts his arm around her, and whispers in her ear. She giggles a little louder than usual. They proceed to the top of Greenfield Street towards her house.

"She's with Greg?" I say, "Really? I can't believe that."

"Of course, she is," Nate winks at me and then chuckles to himself.

"I heard they like to, you know, jam," Billy says, "They like to jam, jam. Jam, jam."

"What's with the songs today?" Nate groans.

Billy sings "jam" a few more times while he thrusts his pelvis. Then he lays down like he's doing a push-up and humps the sidewalk. "Jam, jam, ja-jam! Look! The worm, you guys! Check it. New dance move."

"I just can't believe her," I whisper to Nate, still watching Melissa walk away.

"That's how it goes, dude," Nate shrugs.

"Oh, yeah," Billy says, "We be jammin last night, baby. Me and Melissa." Billy laughs, honking like a goose. He jumps up from the sidewalk, and the pelvic thrusts continue. Then he does the worm again.

Billy watches me and keeps dancing until I crack a smile. He knows I'm upset about something. He doesn't ask, he just dances. This dude is hilarious. He's getting into it, like a workout tape. I have to laugh. He's gonna throw his back out.

"What's gotten into you, Billy?" Nate asks.

"Melissa can sing," Billy says, "You know that? Ever hear her? Aw, man. She was in the church choir one year. She had a solo. Amazing. Like Whitney Houston. No joke."

Ronnie yells at us from his driveway. He spins a basketball on his finger, "B-Ball time! Which one of y'all wanna get schooled?"

Later that night, the workday hits me, and I'm tired as hell. My back aches from shoveling and the basketball game didn't help. Nate's exhausted too and nearly falls asleep at the dinner table. Nate and I go to bed early, and just as I'm falling asleep the phone rings.

Patti answers upstairs and gives it to Dad. I hear, "Donna" and sit up. Nate snores as I tiptoe across the basement, and eavesdrop by the stairs.

Chapter 23: Mom's Voice

"No, we're both fine," Dad says into the phone. "Yes, Donna, I know."

His words cut in and out and I can't make sense of the conversation. I remember there's a phone behind the bar, and I gently pick up the receiver. My thumb covers the mouthpiece and I try not to breathe. Her voice sounds deeper than I remember. Is she crying? She sniffles now and then.

"You have no idea how tough this has been," she says.

"No, I know. That makes sense."

"I don't know why. It's just like wow. It's very emotional. All those years."

"I understand. I know."

"I'm sorry, Mike. I just… I don't know what to say," she pauses. "You made it work so long. Star Pizza would have failed if I had stayed. And Eric would have hated me."

"What? No way. Well, maybe. Who knows?" Dad says, "I did miss you, that's for sure. I tried to make your dough. It wasn't half as good. Then I killed the starter. I eventually figured it out. You're a great baker, you know. I'm not sure what your secret is, but you should have told me before you left."

"Magicians never tell," she says and forces a hoarse laugh. "I can't believe it's all gone now. Our beautiful pizzeria. Opening day, remember? I was so proud," she pauses. "What was it, Mike? The exhaust? The grease trap?"

"Electrical, actually. That's what the fire chief concluded. I filed the insurance claim and now we're waiting."

They fall silent for one second and Nate snores louder than ever.

"Eric?" Dad says.

I hang up the phone and jump in bed. A few minutes later Dad comes downstairs. I pretend to sleep as he stands over me. Dad must know I'm faking it. Nate snores again.

"Eric?" Dad says. "Buddy? I'm not sure how much you heard. You want to talk about it? The good news is, your mom is fine. She had heard about the fire. She says hi. She's relatively close by, and wants to see you sometime. Maybe. If you want," Dad touches my shoulder. "I love you, buddy. You're a good kid. We'll talk later, okay? Good night."

Dad leaves and I stare up at the ceiling. I'm mad. Why did she leave? She sounded fine. I still don't get it and I'm too tired to think. I guess it is good that she's nearby. Maybe I'll see her. What did she really look like? I close my eyes and try to picture her face.

Nate snores. He's too damn loud. I grab the *Tortilla Flat* book and chuck it at him.

Chapter 24: *The Faker*

The day begins again with Dad's annoying morning whistle. Can't we just set an alarm? Then Nate starts complaining about his sore legs. Shut up already. Nate says he's strong enough to stand. Give me a break. Manny laughs at him. We leave for work and unfortunately, Nate joins us.

The hot sun scorches us as we ride to the warehouse. We fill the truck with tools and then drive to the job site. The new job is even closer to Krape Park, at a much larger home, with giant oak trees along the property line, and so much land it could fit two football fields. We unload the truck while a backhoe scrapes the sides of a tremendous hole. The opening for the inground pool is a rough kidney shape, at least ten feet down at the deep end. After the backhoe is done and gone, we grab our shovels and climb into the hole.

"See the teeth marks?" Manny points, "Just smooth those out. Don't dig too deep though, the backhoe dug it big already."

The fresh smell of earth fills the cool air inside the hole. Lines of soil go from black to brown, to a light yellow clay color. We scrape the walls and a large pile of discarded dirt soon collects on the pool floor. I fill a wheelbarrow full of discard, and I haul the load up over a plank ramp. Nate stands up high, where the edge of the pool meets the lawn. He helps me lift the load over the bump at the end of the ramp. Then I roll the load across the yard and dump it next to Dad's truck. The wheelbarrow wobbles and my forearms burn after every trip, but I feel myself getting stronger, and tackle another load.

"Get back!" Nate whispers with a devious look in his eye. He stands at the top of the ramp and holds a baseball-sized rock in his hand.

Nate falls on purpose, four feet down, onto the dirt floor of the shallow end. On his way down he bashes the side of my wheelbarrow with his rock. The wheelbarrow and pounds of soil tip over on top of him. He writhes on the ground and cries like a baby.

"What was that?" Manny exclaims, "You guys alright?"

"I fell!" Nate lies, "I banged my ankle on this stupid thing! God, it hurts like hell!"

"I heard something crack," Manny says, "Can you walk? Can you get up?"

"I don't think so."

"Mike!" Manny says, "Run inside. Call 9-1-1!"

"No, no," Nate says, "Maybe I can stand. Yeah. Let me try."

Nate winks at me. What an idiot.

"Okay. Easy," Manny says, "That's good. Try walking a bit more. Walk it off."

"Agh! I can't! It really hurts," Nate falls onto his butt.

"Well, you can put some weight on it, Nate, so it ain't broken," Manny says. "Probably just a bone bruise. Mike, I'll be right back, okay? I'll take Nate home."

"Yep, no problem," Dad yells, "Keys are on the dash."

Manny hoists his son up over the pool wall and then Nate crawls across the lawn. The Dakota Sport drives off. I shovel the spilled dirt back into the wheelbarrow and Dad helps me roll the load over the ramp.

"Walls are looking better already, huh?" Dad says. He wipes the sweat off his brow and hops back into the hole. I grab my shovel and follow him down to the deep end.

"So, what do you think?" Dad asks.

"About what?"

"Nate gonna survive?"

Should I tell Dad? I don't want to betray Nate, but he already screwed me over. Now I'm stuck doing twice the work and that pisses me off.

"Nate faked it," I say, "Don't tell Manny."

"I won't," Dad says, "You can tell me anything, you know. I won't ever tell anybody. I promise you that."

"Nate had a rock in his hand. Cracked it on the side of the wheelbarrow."

"Pretty creative," Dad smiles.

"Pretty terrible. Dishonest as it gets. And lazy."

"Got that right."

My shovel strikes a large rock and I chip at it. Dad steps in, gives it a big whack, and it falls to the floor.

"So how about your mom last night," Dad says, "You want to talk about it?"

"No, do you?" I say.

"Not really, but I know you were eavesdropping."

"Okay, fine," I say, "One simple question. Why did she leave?"

"Well," Dad says, "There's no such thing as simple."

"Oh, my god!"

"Eric, listen. When it comes to people, we're so full of complicated thoughts and emotions that sometimes we don't make any sense at all."

"Dad! Give me a straight answer! Is she a drunk or what?"

"Yes!"

"Why?"

"She was depressed," Dad says, "I'm not sure why or how, but she didn't like her life, or herself. Depression is strong, millionaires feel it too, it doesn't matter who you are. Booze made her feel good, and the next thing you know, she wants more and more. Then she tried to find that fix faster, with other drugs, which were more powerful, more addictive, and the next thing you know she's an addict. An addict, Eric. Sometimes she'll sober up and everything's fine, and other times she's in a very dangerous state of mind, to her and everyone around her. And that's why she left. She didn't want to harm us or put us in harm's way."

"It still doesn't make sense," I say, "Isn't she putting herself in more danger by leaving her family? We could have helped her feel better, and protected her. Or if she totally had to leave so bad, she could have at least visited. She's selfish. She didn't want us anymore."

"I know. I felt the same way. But it's complicated."

"What? You're sticking up for her?"

"No. Well, maybe in a way. I'm just trying to understand her side."

"That's total bull! You have to agree with me a hundred percent. If she loved us she would have come back. Got herself together, and came back. She never even missed us? She hasn't seen me forever!"

"I know," Dad says, "You're right. I do agree. I was angry at her for years, Eric. And I thought your exact same thoughts. And that rage surged up inside of me too. But you gotta see the big picture-- she survived. She's still alive today. And she wants to see us now. She does care. She lives in Chicago, less than two hours away. We could meet her tomorrow if you want. We could drive there tonight."

"What? No way. We gotta track her down? She should come here. She owes us. She's been gone so long she wouldn't even recognize me."

"Eric, listen--"

"No. I don't want to find her. Forget it. Forget her."

"Damn it, Eric, now you're the one being selfish."

"I'm a kid! I'm supposed to be selfish."

"Not anymore. You're a young man. Have some empathy. She nearly killed herself for chrissake."

"So what? She might as well be dead. What do I care? I don't even know her. I'm not wasting my time on somebody who ditched me."

"Have some respect, Eric. She's your mother."

"No, she's not! Since when?"

"You guys doing alright?" Manny says. I never heard the truck pull up. Manny grabs his shovel and jumps into the hole. "Boy, I never heard Eric talk that much."

"We're fine," Dad says, "Having a little chat about Donna."

"Yikes," Manny says, "Sorry to interrupt."

"It's fine. We needed a break," Dad says, "We'll talk about it later."

"Not me," I say. I attack a large stone with my shovel. I hack and hack at it. I'm so mad but I don't care. I'm not even sure what I just said. I'm not sure I believed it. Of course, I'm glad my mom is still alive. Of course, I want to see her. But I'm furious too. I hate her. Why did she leave us? She could have visited. I hate to even think of her. She's so stupid. And why won't this dumb stone fall already? I hack and hack, and the rock finally drops from the wall.

"Good for you, Eric!" Manny says, "Show the wall who's boss. Channel that frustration. I wish Nate would work that hard. Lazy son of a bitch."

"You guys go to the emergency room?" Dad smiles.

"After that fake limp? Please," Manny chuckles, "I played a lot of football in my day, and that is not what an ankle injury looks like. At all."

"Then why'd you let him fake it?" I ask.

"Tired of hearing him complain. Weren't you?" Manny says, "He was slowing us down."

"So now I'm stuck doing his work," I mumble.

"No, Eric, you're not stuck. You should be proud," Manny smiles, "Having a job is a privilege. You do good work, and that feels good at the end of the day. And it pays too."

"Nate basically got fired, then?" Dad says.

"Pretty much," Manny laughs, "What am I gonna do with that kid."

I aim high and skim my shovel across the dirt wall. The spade dives into some clay and comes back up, leaving a shiny, smooth surface behind. The hole looks more like a pool every minute. And I do enjoy seeing the results. The hard work clears my mind. By the end of the day, the deep end is nearly finished. We worked well together.

Chapter 25: The Ditch

When Dad, Manny, and I get back home, I jump in the shower. Dad drinks a beer and reads the newspaper, while Manny changes the oil in his Toyota. Patti is still at work, and Nate is nowhere to be found. I cross the street and knock on Billy's door but nobody's home.

"Nate's probably at that rich prick Matt's house," Manny yells from the garage.

I like that Manny insults Matt in front of me. Maybe we did bond at work today. Manny is confiding in me now. I'm in on his jokes. That confidence makes going to Matt's less dreadful. Matt's just another lazy kid. Why should I worry?

I leave Billy's front stoop and walk down the hill. I easily find Matt's place by myself. I'm getting used to these winding roads. And I followed the sidewalks, never cutting through the yards like a child.

Johanna answers the front door and invites me inside. She leads me past a giant aquarium, at least 100 gallons, with striped angelfish and real coral. Their dining room table is set with fine china and linen. Then she opens a door that leads to a flight of steps.

"Go on downstairs, Eric," she smiles, "I bet they're playing video games."

I find the entertainment room, but the boys aren't here. There's the biggest TV ever with three different gaming systems plugged in and a pile of games. I check inside the bathroom, and then I find a small office. A dusty exercise bike dominates the space. Matching numbered legal books line a shelf on one wall. A large computer monitor, keyboard, and multi-line phone sit on a desk. There's a workshop in the basement too, cluttered with styrofoam balls, a hot glue gun, and a colorful ribbon. I open the basement door and walk outside. A circular brick patio reaches to the edge of the woods.

"Matt?" I yell, "Hey Nate?"

Looking back at the house I see a curtain move in the garage window. Someone must be there. I run through the side yard, up the driveway, and hear a van door shut. The automatic garage door starts closing and I rush inside. Circling the van, I peek through a window and see a leg. Those brand new Air Jordans must be Matt's. I tug at a door handle but the van is locked.

"I see you in there!" I tap on the glass, "Come on you guys!"

There's no response and my temper is rising. I hear their muted laughter inside the van and pound on the glass. This isn't hide-and-seek, this is an insult. Nate hid from Billy and now these jerks are hiding from me. Ditching me! For the second time today, I've caught Nate lying. He's being a dick. A little jerk. I am so sick of his childish games.

I'm so angry that my voice shakes, "Fine then. Bye idiots. Screw you."

I find a side door and leave the garage. I'm walking down the driveway when the automatic garage door opens.

"Hey, Eric! Wait!" Nate yells and runs to catch up. "We're just joking around!"

"No! You guys ditched me. I'm not dealing with this shit."

"What?" Nate smiles, "It was a joke!"

"Chill out, dude," Matt smiles, "We hide from Billy all the time. It's fun."

"No, it's not fun," I say, "You guys treat Billy like crap. But I think he's nice. He's honest at least." I feel outnumbered. I want to leave.

"Eric, settle down, buddy," Nate smiles. He pats my shoulder and I shrug it off.

"Look at you, Nate," I say, "Your ankle's all better now?"

"Jesus Christ, Eric!" Nate says, "Take it easy."

"Why would you ditch me?"

Nate shrugs. He sucks on his hair bang like a baby sucking his thumb.

"Whatever." I turn and walk down the street. My heart is still racing. But I stood my ground. I spoke up. I can't just forgive them and hang out. No way.

"Sensitive Sally, over there," Matt yells.

"Eric," Nate says, "Come back! Come on, man!"

I keep walking and don't look back. I want to get far away from them fast. Then I make a wrong turn, wind up on a dead-end street, and have to double-back past Matt's house again. They don't notice me walking by. The boys are laughing and playing basketball like nothing ever happened. Obviously, they have zero regrets, which makes me even angrier. Now, what do I do? Where can I go? I don't want to go back to Nate's house, but I live there. I'm screwed.

"Hey!" somebody says.

I look up and realize I'm walking by Jen's house.

"Hi, Eric," Jen smiles, "You look pissed. You get in a fight? Where's Nate?"

Jen stands on her driveway beside Rachel's Chevy. She holds a thick auto manual in her hand.

"He's at Matt's," I say, "I was just there."

"What happened?"

"They were being dicks."

"Sounds about right," she nods, "What'd they do?"

I tell Jen about the ditch move. She's seen them ditch Billy before and Melissa too. Jen assumes this time it was Matt's idea since Matt is probably jealous. Nate is one of his best friends and now I'm butting in. Jen thinks I should give Nate a second chance.

I disagree. That was Nate's second chance, if not third. I tell Jen how Nate lied to Billy after breaking into his house. Then I describe how Nate faked an injury to get out of work. That Manny knew about the fake move, but even he didn't want Nate around anymore.

I tell Jen about my new job and the happy little kids who saw their brand new pool. I describe the tremendous depth of the inground hole, with all the different colors of soil and clay.

Jen listens closely to every word, so I keep talking. I've never talked this much to anybody besides Dad, but I don't care. It's easy talking with Jen. I feel relieved somehow, just letting it all out. I even bring up Mom. I talk about how mad she makes me. How selfish she was to leave us behind.

Jen sides with Dad on this one. Maybe Mom's problems could have put me in danger. Jen thinks my mom must have felt so ashamed when she left. A shame beyond anything that either of us can relate to.

Jen says addiction is a real problem in Freeport. Freeport sucks for many reasons. There's nothing to do so people get wasted and blame their problems on minorities or the government. Jen says it's sad that black kids and white kids don't often mix at the high school. She overhears terrible jokes that are racist, sexist, or homophobic all the time. She hates Freeport. Too many old, mean, and dumb idiots. Jen can't wait to move away. She'd love a big city, far away.

Jen dreams of Harvard, the best college in the country, in Cambridge, Massachusetts. The Boston area is full of intelligent people with open minds. Jen visited the Harvard campus a couple years ago. She loved watching the small boats float down the Charles River, with Fenway Park in the background. She wants to study biology and chemistry and ultimately protect the environment. Jen gets straight A's, at the top of her class. Melissa and Matt are pretty smart too, but Nate is not. Jen says she tried teaching him algebra once, and he just couldn't get it.

Then Jen really gets personal. She says her dad died of cancer last winter. They were very close. She loved him more than anything. He was a happy guy, a dentist, who loved to fish, and knew everybody in town. Jen gets depressed when she thinks of him. She hates her memory for leaning towards the sad days, instead of the older, happy times.

Maybe I'm also easy to talk to. She keeps going.

Jen switches topics to her mother. Less than a month after her dad died, her mom started dating. Now her mom is constantly gone, out with a man from Rockford, the next town over. Rachel's gone constantly too, hanging out with Declan, or working at The Garden Deli. Jen is often left alone at the house. I wouldn't mind keeping her company. I like talking to her.

I want to ask Jen about Nate. Does she like him the way he likes her? And if she doesn't, which I think is true, does she like me instead? We've been standing at the end of her driveway, just chatting forever. I want to touch Jen now, for some reason.

Nothing forward. Just to hold her hand, or a high five would be nice. Am I staring at her now? I look away.

I see the Chevy manual and ask if I can help. Jen already found a new bulb in the garage that might fit. She shows me the page about tail light replacement. We find the access panel inside the trunk and remove the old bulb, which is burnt and black and does look the same size as the new one. Jen screws in the new bulb, stands up, and bumps her head on the trunk. She touches her head, and I do too.

It's strange when our hands touch, almost electric. That sounds so stupid, and maybe it's all in my head, but there's a moment when she looks up at me, and something happens.

"You alright?" I ask.

"I'm fine," Jen smiles, "Thanks." She touches my arm and steps away. "Stay right there! I'll test it out."

Jen hops in the driver seat and slams the brakes. I smile as the tail light glows, and I give her a thumbs up. The red glow seems so bright and I realize it's gotten late. The sky is nearly dark. How long have we been talking? It didn't seem like that long.

"Dang," I say, "I gotta go. I'm late for supper."

"Oh," Jen says, " Okay. You can stay if you want. I can make mac and cheese."

"Thanks. That sounds good, but I better run."

"Okay," Jen nods, "Bye, Eric Daniels. I'll see ya soon."

Chapter 26: The Charity Case

I jog to Greenfield Street with the biggest grin on my face. I had a great time with Jen. Just talking, how can that feel so awesome?

I get to Nate's and find a plate of leftover pizza on the kitchen table. I know immediately that Dad cooked it. I recognize his signature brown buttery crust, and the pattern of toppings looks familiar. I take a bite and it's delicious, like I'm back in Iowa.

"There he is," Dad smiles and sips his beer. "How's the pizza? I still got it, right? Even with this measly residential oven," he smiles, "Where ya been?"

"Oh, I was helping Jen," I grin, "We put a new tail light in her sister's car."

"That sounds like fun," Dad winks.

Nate fake-limps into the room. He glares at me and then hobbles downstairs.

"Hmm," Dad says, "Some tension between you two? The novelty has worn off already?"

Dad opens another beer and sits beside me at the kitchen table.

"I have been trying to find us a place, Eric. A full time job, and an apartment somewhere, before school starts. The insurance claim will come very soon. Then we'll have some decisions to make. Don't worry though. You'll be alright here for a little bit longer?"

I shrug and chew my pizza.

"Any more thoughts about the Mom thing?" Dad asks, "No? Okay, good," he quickly squeezes my shoulder and leaves the room. "Hey, Manny, you need a beer? Cubs win today?"

It's a beautiful night, and Dad chats with Patti and Manny on the back porch. After eating, I feel tired. It's been a long day. I yawn, stretch, and head downstairs for bed.

"Jesus Christ," Nate growls as soon as I enter the cave. "One little prank and you try to steal my girlfriend? After everything I've done for you?"

"Whoa, what?"

"Me and Matt spied on you two, you asshole. You didn't even notice us. I walked by and you didn't look up. You and Jen, all caught up in a happy little conversation."

"Dude, relax, we were just talking. I helped fix her tail light."

"Bullshit! I saw you glowing like goddamn sunshine. You know I love her, Eric, and you pursued her, just to get back at me. And now you like her. Fuck you! You're such a prick."

"Nate! Seriously, we were just talking."

"I saw the way she looked at you! And guess what? I talked to Matt. Remember when he was home sick the other day? He wasn't really sick, he was hungover. He did TP my house, and Jen was there too. She couldn't stop talking about you."

"Matt's full of shit, Nate. You said it yourself."

"No! You're full of shit! You come in here like a pathetic charity case, and the girls gobble it up. Poor Eric, he's homeless. Poor Eric, he's so nice."

"What did you say?" I ask. "Charity case? Is that what this is?"

"Oh, please. What are you going to do, Eric? You want to fight me? In my own damn house? Wearing the clothes my mom bought you? Huh, fat boy? After your junkie mom left you, to go fuck every trucker in Iowa."

Without a second thought, I bury my shoulder into Nate's chest. Our bodies slam into the brick basement wall. The back of Nate's head hits hard, and I throw my fist into his stomach. Nate grabs the neck of my shirt and pulls. My shirt rips and I fall, grabbing Nate's arm on the way down. We land on my mattress. I roll on top of him and land a right hand straight into his nose. Blood gushes out. I punch him in the jaw and red splatters across the wall.

"Whoa!" Manny yells, "Hey! Break it up!"

Manny picks me up like a sack of potatoes and stands me in the corner. Dad grabs my arms and holds me back.

"Easy, Eric," Dad whispers, "Easy now."

My heart races in my chest and every muscle fires. Nate stands up, and we're both huffing for air. Nate's nose bleeds heavily and one of his eyes is already swollen. He looks awful. Patti comes down, screams when she sees the blood, and runs back upstairs for ice. I realize there's not a scratch on me and I feel terrible. Tears roll down Nate's cheeks and he buries his face in Manny's shoulder. Dad pulls me out of the way as Manny leads Nate upstairs.

"Eric?" Dad whispers, "You alright?"

I'm still breathing hard, but my heartbeat has slowed almost back to normal. I'm shocked. I'm not sure what happened. The speed of the whole fight... I guess I had enough. I snapped.

"Eric? Where'd you learn to punch like that? Must be your mom's genes. Jesus. Don't worry, Nate will be fine. Guess what? He already quit limping," Dad smiles. "Listen, Eric, whatever just happened between you two, don't worry. Whatever Nate said. Whatever you said. Let it go. It's behind you now. Your feelings are open, so you guys can move forward. Okay?"

"He called me a charity case," I mumble, "He said Mom was a junkie."

"Ah. Well, those are some very hurtful words, and I'm glad you stuck up for yourself, but you should never throw the first punch, okay? Sometimes you really want to, but it doesn't feel good afterwards. You really beat his ass, kid."

I'm an emotional mess, and for some reason, I start to giggle, then tears fill my eyes.

"Oh, Eric. It's okay, buddy, it's okay."

My body shudders. I try to stop crying but I can't. Dad wraps his arms around me and holds me tight.

Chapter 27: Wrong Button

Dad takes Nate's place and sleeps in the basement that night, while Nate sleeps upstairs in his actual bedroom. Nate sleeps through breakfast too, totally avoiding everyone. Dad, Manny, and

I ride the Dakota Sport to the warehouse, grab supplies, and work on the inground pool. We don't talk much at the job. A few words about last night's Cubs game is all.

After three hours of scraping the shallow end, the sky turns dark, and thunder booms. We race to spread tarps across the giant hole.

When we get home, Nate is already gone. I assume he's at Matt's again, and don't even consider going there. I have no idea what to do. I want to see Jen and tell her what happened, but I better not. Nate might be with her too, I'm not sure.

Manny leaves to do some estimates, while Dad calls the insurance company, and then inquires about a job. Dad finds Patti's typewriter and works on his résumé. I eat a turkey sandwich for lunch, and the doorbell rings. Billy stands at the front door and invites me over.

As soon as we enter his house Billy says, "I found the porno."

Billy laughs like a nut and pops the tape in the VCR. The actress appears on the screen. She's pretty, with long brown hair and a low-cut dress. The scene is set in an office. It's a job interview and she really needs the money. Soon she unzips the boss's pants, but she leaves as soon as he says she's hired. "Now what am I supposed to do with this?" the boss yells with his pants around his ankles.

That's obviously an attempt at humor, but I'm way too weirded out to laugh. Billy smiles and we make eye contact, which is even weirder. I look away.

The next scene involves two guys who corner the same woman in a warehouse. Both men have a greedy glimmer in their eyes, and the woman is all sweaty. One man is short with a huge mustache and a potbelly. The other guy is tall and thin with an afro.

After some dumb dialog about new-employee training, the woman takes off her clothes. Soon one man is lying on his back, while the woman is on top kissing him. Then the other man comes over too. What is this? He's getting way too close to the action. And he's not waiting for his turn...

"Oh my god!" I yell.

"Oh, man!" Billy says, "Why? I can't even look!"

"So gross! Why would you do that?"

"I don't know!"

Then the camera zooms in.

"What are you guys watching in here?" Ronnie asks, appearing behind the couch.

"No!" Billy screams, "No, Ronald! No! Don't look!" Billy grabs the remote and violently hits buttons. The screen is now covered in gray fast-forward lines but we can still see two pairs of hairy balls bouncing really fast.

"Dang it! Ronnie! Get out of here now!" Billy finds the power button and the screen goes black. "Oh my gosh. That was sickening," Billy says, shaking his head. "Why?"

"I will never understand," I groan, "I feel kind of nauseous."

"I mean, it was going good for a while, right?" Billy sighs, "And then it really turned."

"It sure did."

We sit there for a second not knowing what to do. I don't want to talk about it anymore. I stare at the floor. Thank goodness the phone rings and Billy gets up to answer it.

"Garrett Residence, William speaking. No, sorry, she's not home right now. May I please take a message?"

I've gotta smile. That's the most polite phone answering I've ever heard.

"What the hell garbage were you guys watching?" Ronnie asks me.

"Nothing," I say, "Really. Don't ever, ever watch that shit."

Ronnie leads me downstairs, while Billy talks on the phone. The Garrets have a nice finished basement, with textured walls and newly carpeted floors. In one corner there's a large TV and a sectional couch. Across the room is a padded weightlifting bench, with several barbells and heavy disks. In the other corner, there's actually a jacuzzi.

"Is that a hot tub?" I say, "I didn't know you could use those inside."

"Sure, why not?" Ronnie shrugs.

I lift the heavy vinyl cover and touch the warm water.

"Don't touch it," Ronnie says, "No kids allowed."

"Sorry," Billy says, coming down the steps, "He's right. No tub. Only when my parents are around. Maybe we could schedule a time in the future, if you'd like to try it out."

"Oh, no," I say, "That's fine. No thanks."

Ronnie sits at the weightlifting bench and lies down, "Yo, Eric. Spot me."

Ronnie does ten 50-pound reps and then sits up. The sump pump goes off, and the rain outside the window continues to pour.

"We lift everyday," Billy grins. He points to a poster on the wall, with several different lifts, stretches, and exercises.

"We're gonna be strong as hell," Ronnie smiles. He flexes his bicep and kisses it.

"You ever work out?" Billy asks, "You look pretty strong."

"Not really," I shrug, "But I'll give it a try."

I lie down and lift the bar off the rack. Fifty-pounds feels much lighter than I expected, and I feel fine after twenty reps.

"That's pretty good!" Billy smiles.

"You gonna be yoked, Eric!" Ronnie smiles.

We take turns on the bench press until my arms ache. Then Ronnie proposes a sit-up contest. He wins. Billy and I do a couple more bench presses and head upstairs for a snack. Ronnie stays downstairs and plays video games.

Billy opens the pantry, which is loaded with tons of chips, fruit-snacks, and granola bars. He insists that I grab at least two snacks, and then we sit at the kitchen table and eat. When we're done, Billy shows off his new camera, and the Frank Thomas home run baseball that he caught at a White Sox game. Then Billy offers me a green popsicle, and it reminds me of the break-in.

"It was us," I say.

"What was us?"

"Nate lied. Me and Matt, and Nate. We broke into your house. Matt drank the beer."

"I know," Billy says, "I know Nate lied. My grandpa saw you guys."

"What? So your mom knows too?"

Billy nods.

"Then why get a security system?"

"My mom was worried about it happening again, especially the beer part. That's not cool. If Matt got in trouble for drinking, he might blame us. I don't know, that sounds like a long shot, but that's the way my mom thinks. We're the only black family in a big white neighborhood. She doesn't trust anybody, and she's always thinking of the worst thing that could happen."

The storm passes, and sunlight shines through the kitchen windows. Like a reflex, Ronnie grabs his basketball and runs outside. Seconds later he comes back into the house.

"Aw hell no!" Ronnie whines, "This ball got flat as hell!"

"Fill it up," Billy says.

"Can't, bro. The needle busted. Does Nate have one?"

"Maybe," I shrug.

Billy, Ronnie, and I walk across the street to Nate's garage. I look around and don't see a needle or a pump. I do notice the silver bike, the Trek Matt gave me, is gone. That sucks. But I'm not surprised.

"What's wrong?" Billy asks.

"Nothing," I say, "No needle. Let's look in the shed out back."

The three of us circle around to the backyard and I open the wooden door. I see the tent, and fishing rods, and then I spot an air pump with a needle already in it. Ronnie spits on the basketball nozzle and inserts the needle. Billy pumps while Ronnie holds the ball still. Once the ball feels firm, Billy puts the pump back where we found it, and I close the shed door.

"What are you guys doing here?" Nate asks.

He totally snuck up on us. And what's that weird grin on his face? Something isn't right, I can tell. My heartbeat quickens and I take a deep breath.

Chapter 28: Retaliation

One of Nate's eyes is black and swollen. And his pupils are glossed over. But that's not from his injury. Is he drunk?

"Damn, Nate! What happened to you?" Ronnie says.

"Eric beat me up," Nate says, "What, he didn't tell you?"

"No," Billy says, "What happened?"

"Yeah, he just went nuts on me."

"Why?" Billy asks.

"I don't know," Nate shrugs, "He's crazy. You guys should be careful."

"Really?" I say, "That's how you're going to play it?"

"It's the truth," Nate says.

"The truth? What about you ditching me? Lying? Insulting me? Insulting my family?"

"Don't believe him, guys," Nate says, "Eric's full of shit."

I feel my adrenaline kicking in. My heartbeat is sprinting and my fists clench.

"You say everybody's full of shit!" I say, "But you're full of shit! I can't believe you, Nate."

"Just shut up, Eric! I'm sick of you guys," Nate says, "The big loser Danielses, mooching off us for way too long. When are you going to fucking leave?"

"I wish I could leave right now!" I yell, "What the hell, Nate?"

"You gonna cry now, Eric?" Nate says, "Oh, poor baby! You want to punch me? Attack me again? Do it, you piece of shit. I dare you."

Matt appears, running across the backyard, followed closely by big Greg Kingman.

"Who's the kid that fucked Melissa?" Greg yells.

"Right here!" Nate points at me.

Greg closes in with lightning speed and pushes me against the shed door.

"I did not--"

Greg's fist explodes into my chest. I can't breathe. He pushes me to the ground and kicks me in the stomach. Twice, three times. I'm curled up in a ball, gasping for air.

"Look out!" Billy yells.

Matt holds a wooden baseball bat behind his back. Billy grabs it, pulls, and Matt struggles to hold on. Ronnie sprints away.

I look up and Nate spits in my face. Then Nate leans down and smacks me.

"Stay away from Jen," Nate says, "You worthless piece of trash, stay the fuck away!"

"What is going on?" Dad yells. I can't see where he is, but I hear his voice.

Nate, Greg, and Matt disappear. Billy won the tug-of-war and still holds the wooden bat. He drops it on the grass and runs over to me.

Dad moves in close and sweeps the hair off my face. His hand hovers across my body, checking for damages. My ribs are on fire. God, I might barf. I finally catch my breath.

"Jesus," Dad says, "You okay, Eric? You alright?"

"No," I say, breathing again as my chest rises high with relief.

"Mr. Daniels, if you guys want to stay at my house you can," Billy says, "I'm really sorry about all this."

"Can you stand up?" Dad asks me, ignoring Billy. Dad helps me up, looks me over again, and pats off some dirt. I notice that Ronnie is back now, standing next to Dad.

"I think I smelled booze on them," Billy says, "Those guys must be drunk or something, because that was crazy."

"Sure was!" Ronnie says.

"I tried to stick up for you, Eric," Billy continues, "Matt had a bat. See? It's a small wooden one, like for pee-wee league, but still, that's no joke. I stopped him though. I grabbed it."

"Thanks, Billy," I say, "I saw."

"I ran and told your Pops," Ronnie says, "Greg is a big old dude."

"You gonna be alright?" Dad asks, "What hurts?"

"My ribs are sore, but I'm good."

"Good," Dad sighs, "I'm not sure what to do now. I'll talk to Manny. I hoped Nate would forgive and forget, but maybe not."

"Forgive us our trespasses," Billy says, "Good advice. That's what the Bible says. Lessons learned there. Important lessons. You guys can come to our church anytime if you want. We go to that really nice church on Kiwanis. They let gay people worship too, and blacks, Mexicans, whatever. God is love, and love is blind. They say that sometimes. I've been going there since I was like, I don't know, a baby. Was I baptized there? Yeah, probably. That's the one that happens when you're like three months old, so I was baptized there for sure, and I just don't remember it. Did my parents get married there? Maybe. I'm trying to remember what their wedding picture looks like that's hanging on the wall in their bed--"

"Who was the other boy?" Dad interrupts.

"Greg Kingman," Billy says, "He plays football at Minnesota State. Well not yet, but he's going to play there pretty soon. He goes to my church. He just graduated from Freeport High, and I heard he got a scholarship for thousands of dollars. He's gonna play safety, or maybe linebacker, I'm not sure. I don't remember. I'm more of a baseball fan. Or basketball. Football isn't really my--"

"Well, thanks for helping," Dad says, "Eric needs some good friends like you guys. Come on, Eric. Let's get some ice on those ribs."

"Bye, Billy," I say, "See you, Ronnie," I slowly follow Dad up the back porch steps.

Dad tells me to lie on the upstairs couch. He lifts my shirt and pushes on my ribs just slightly. Then he balances two bags of frozen peas on my bruises.

"Oh, yeah," he smiles, "You'll be fine."

Manny gets home and sees me laid up in the front room. Dad tells him what happened and his face gets very red. Manny's eyes bulge when he hears about the baseball bat and the spitting. Manny grabs the phone, calls Matt's house, and then hops in his Toyota Truck. After Manny leaves, the phone rings.

"I'll get it," Dad says. Then he hands me the receiver, "For you. A girl."

Chapter 29: The Peace Offering

Dad goes outside for a cigarette, and I'm thankful for the privacy. My side hurts as I bring the receiver up to my ear.

"Hello?"

"Hi, it's Jen," she says, "Are you okay, Eric? I heard what happened."

"Oh. I'll be fine."

"I'm so sorry. I don't know what they were thinking. They came here bragging like I'd be proud of them or something. They're idiots. They're drunk too. I hate them. Why would they attack you like that? It makes no sense. I don't know you that well, Eric, but I know you wouldn't hit Nate unless he said something terrible... I feel like I should have warned you. Nate can turn. He can be unstable. I've seen it before," Jen pauses, "And I know you and Melissa didn't... Nate totally lied to Greg." Jen pauses again, "Listen, do you want to come over? Would tomorrow night be okay? We might go to Sky View. Have you been there yet? It's a drive-in movie place. Real old-fashioned. Like the only drive-in left around here. You should come with us if you want. It'll be fun. No Nate. No Matt. I promise. I yelled at them. I'll be mad at them for a long time."

"Um," I say, "A movie sounds good. I'll see if I can go."

"Great! Then I'll see you soon. Come over around 8, okay? And I'm serious-- Nate is not invited. He loves me, I know. But the feeling is so not mutual."

For supper that night, Patti cooks yellow summer squash with parmesan cheese. Manny grills hamburgers. Dad skips the beer and acts as a security guard between Nate and me. The two of us stay in separate rooms. I watch the Giants slaughter the Cubs, and Nate hides in his room and listens to music.

After dinner, there's a knock at the door. Manny invites everyone to step outside onto the front stoop. Johanna stands next to Matt, and the silver bicycle.

"I believe this belongs to Eric," Johanna says.

"I don't want it."

"Eric," Johanna says, "Let this be a peace offering, okay? It was only days ago when Matt and I gave you this bike, to welcome you into the neighborhood. There is no reason why you shouldn't feel welcome here. Please. Accept this bike as an apology."

"Apology from who?" Dad asks, "You're talking, but as I understand, Matt here was the one with a goddamn baseball bat."

"I never swung it!" Matt says, "I never even got close. I just brought it for show. I'm sorry! Really. It was an awful idea. So stupid. I'm sorry, Eric."

I think Matt is actually telling the truth. I can't believe it. Does he really feel bad?

"Please," Matt says, "Please take the bike that I gave you since--"

"Since what?" I say. Now the pompous Matt is back. He was going to say 'since I'm poor' or something insulting.

"Since you don't have one!" Matt says. And he is still genuine. What? He looks at me like I'm his favorite person on earth. He might cry. I'm so confused. Who is this kid?

"Enough!" I yell, "I don't need your stupid bike. I don't need you. I don't need anything. Just leave, okay. Leave me alone!"

I run inside the house, go downstairs, and collapse onto my mattress. I throw punches into my pillow and then chuck it across the room. What is Matt doing? I can deal with a villain, but a nice guy too? Which one is it? I'm not sure, and I can't stand him either way. And I hate that damn bike. I hate Freeport. I'm so angry that tears well up in my eyes. I want to destroy something. I scream at the top of my lungs. I grab *Tortilla Flat* and rip it into a hundred pieces. Paper flies everywhere.

I hear the others enter the house. Nate still hates me, at least he's consistent. I hear him sneer, "He should have took the dumb bike." Nobody agrees, there's no response at all.

Nobody comes downstairs to bother me either. I'm still pissed. I just want to leave Freeport and forget it ever existed. I wish I wasn't here. My ribs hurt. I want to go home, get a hotel, sleep in a tent, or go anywhere else. Maybe I can sleep until we leave this town forever.

Chapter 30: Iowa Returns

The next day there's no morning whistle from Dad. I get out of bed, pee, and then crawl back in bed, and sleep till one. After sleeping for 14 hours, my ribs feel much better. I can breathe without wincing.

I walk upstairs and find some twenty-dollar bills sitting on the kitchen table. There's a note that reads, 'Eric's payment. Hard worker, Thanks!' in Manny's handwriting. I do the math, and per hour, it looks like I got a raise. A Donuts Plus box also sits on the table, and some poor soul already ate a couple. Dad's talking on the phone in the living room. He hangs up and joins me in the kitchen. I avoid the donuts and eat a bowl of cereal.

"Hey, sleepyhead," Dad smiles, "Made some big money, huh?"

"Yeah. More than I thought."

"You earned it. Full time, hard labor. What's wrong, you don't like donuts?"

"Not from that hell hole."

I tell Dad about the disgusting donut cook.

"Mmm," Dad laughs, "No wonder they're so good."

After I finish my cereal, we sit in the living room and watch *American Gladiators* on TV. The show ends, and the Garcia family is still not home.

"Where is everybody?"

"Remember the pond?" Dad says, "They went camping. Be back tomorrow."

"What about the pool job?"

"Too wet."

"The tarps didn't work?"

"Groundwater. Came up from the bottom."

What a relief. I'm glad I don't even have to look at Nate. I don't ever want to see him again. I walk over to Billy's, but nobody's home. Then I search the garage and am relieved that the silver bike is not here. I find Dad sitting behind the typewriter again. A stack of newspapers clutters the dining room table.

"What sounds better?" Dad asks, "Gourmet Chef, or Restaurant Entrepreneur?"

"The second one. Pizza isn't gourmet, is it?"

"True," Dad nods, "Hey, I can do this later. Why don't we do something fun? Want to go to a movie?"

"Actually, Jen invited me to a movie tonight."

"Oh. Cool. Okay... Wait! I got it, come on. Let's go. I know what we can do."

We hop in the truck and Dad only makes one wrong turn as he drives through downtown Freeport. We still don't know the streets that well, and the one-ways of the business district are confusing. Dad parks near an old brick building with a huge antique neon sign that reads, 'Union Dairy.'

"Always room for ice cream, right?" Dad grins, "Look at this place. What a time capsule."

We walk inside and I shudder in the cold air conditioning. A giant mural of dairy cows covers the walls, and there's a horseshoe-shaped bar, desk height, with spinning red cushioned stools. Dad's right, it's like the 1950s in here. The music plays Buddy Holly and the employees wear pointy paper hats. But the smell of the place is so familiar. That sweet fresh cream reminds me of Iowa. I haven't had ice cream in a long time.

I remember old Bev Beasley smiling behind the counter at Scoops, digging into the cookies and cream before I could even order. I used to cross the street and walk in that shop at least three days a week. Of course, the fire flashes across my mind, but I try to refocus. What about the good times?

On most days Bev's grandson Nick would be there at Scoops. We looked alike, he was blond and chubby too, like we could have been cousins or brothers. We'd finish our homework together, or throw a baseball in the back alley. In the winter we'd hop on our sleds and slide down the hill at Island Park. I can picture the downtown Christmas lights hanging high on the Clock Tower. With Nick and I racing home before it got too dark. Nick and I grew apart, but he was a great friend for a long time. He was honest and we never fought once.

"Cookies and cream?" Dad asks.

Dad's voice brings me out of my daydream. I'm back in Freeport again.

"You know it," I nod.

"Thinking about Scoops, huh?" Dad says, "Me too."

We finish our ice cream and leave the Union Dairy. Next door there's a toy store and in the front window is a large display of stuffed animals. Amongst the teddy bears, unicorns, and elephants, there's a chubby yellow duck who looks just like Dilly. I pause a moment and stare at him. Dad stares too.

How many Iowa memories can I have in one afternoon? That little yellow duck slept by my side for a decade. I'd never seen another one like him anywhere. But here he is, in Freeport, brand spanking new, and waiting for me.

"Dilly lives!" Dad laughs, "Wow! He must have escaped the fire and followed us here. Should we get him? I'm serious, I'll buy him if you want."

A childish grin covers my face. I can't believe it. I thought I'd never see old Dilly again. His cute little orange bill smiles back at me. But I am 15 years old. I don't need a new stuffed animal, do I? And that isn't really *my* Dilly. Maybe he's a close relative, but it's not really him. There's no maple syrup trails on his head or that marinara stain on his foot. This new duck is way too clean and bright. I'm too old to start a Dilly. I slowly walk away, and Dad follows without a word.

We drive back to the Garcia house, Dad jumps in the shower, and I watch a cheesy *Batman* rerun. Pretty soon Dad starts cooking supper, my favorite.

His process of making pizza is like a ritual. First Dad takes the dough ball and flattens its edges with his fingertips. He flips the circle over and repeats. Then he grabs the rolling pin and makes two heavy passes. One swipe forward, and one diagonal. Precision and speed, each movement with purpose. Dad slaps off the loose flour, and then throws the dough, and spins it in the air. He laughs as it nearly hits the ceiling. He kneels on the floor and throws it again.

Star Pizza had much higher ceilings. It was an ancient building, at least a hundred years old. It had been a general store originally, and then a Chinese take-out joint. When Mom and Dad moved in they installed an authentic brick oven. Dad constantly stoked that oven, and it was my job to make sure the woodpile was full. The whole house smelled so good, all the way up to my attic bedroom. They also baked French baguettes and cinnamon rolls. They fried chicken wings too. And nothing was frozen. Everything tasted fresh and delicious.

"Mom loved pizza," Dad says. He spreads the red sauce across the dough with the back of a ladle. "She used to close her eyes when she bit into it. Then she'd slowly shake her head, and smile so big."

"I think I remember that," I say.

"She said she could taste things better with her eyes closed."

"Is that really true?"

"Maybe a little," Dad shrugs. He pinches off bits of raw hamburger and drops them over the pie. "Food was another escape, I guess. The more she focused on food, the less she could focus elsewhere."

"Did you know?" I say as I help drop some sliced green olives.

"Did I know what?"

"Did you know that she might leave?" I ask, "Did you see it coming?"

"Maybe. But I was in denial. I had the most at stake, you know? And I loved your mom. She was an artist. One of those aloof types, but the best at what she did, when she focused. But she had some real demons she was dealing with, and thank god she survived."

I grab a handful of shredded mozzarella, reach up high and let it go.

"There's a mom trick, right there," Dad smiles, "Drop the cheese from up high, so it rains down evenly like snow."

"Really? I learned that from her? That's a cool trick."

"Most of my cool tricks came from her," Dad says.

He places the pizza in the oven and sets the timer. Then Dad looks at me and pats my back. It's a pretty touchy pat, almost a hug. He squeezes me just for a second.

"Yeah... I knew," Dad whispers, "Because I told her to go."

"Why?"

"You were very young, Eric, and fragile. And she agreed, and then she did it her way. But I thought she'd come back, I really did. She was supposed to get help. She promised. I should have known better. I should have chased her down, or something, but it was bad, and I was so tired of it. I just never thought she would leave forever.

Chapter 31: *The Wise Old Sage*

After the last slice of delicious pizza is long gone, I say goodbye to Dad and walk to Jen's house. I'm feeling pretty good. Nate is out of town, thank goodness, and Dad came clean with the most truth about Mom yet. The truth does hurt, but it helps to know what really happened, right or wrong. And I'm fine with it for now. Now I get to hang out with Jen, and this should be fun.

I hear their music from half a block away, and I expect to see another full-blown house party. Instead, it's just Jen, Melissa, Rachel, and Declan hanging out on the back porch. I haven't really spoken to Melissa since our midnight thing and I'm not sure what to say to her. Thankfully Declan leads the conversation.

"There he is!" the Irishman announces, "Eric, the man of the hour! The battle survivor! I heard about Greg Kingman, mate. Brutalized by a collegiate linebacker, and lived to tell the tale! Incredible. Not a scratch on you. Nice to see you again, my friend," Declan shakes my hand. "Happy to have another sausage join the party here, I was getting bogged down by all the estrogen in the air."

"Shut up, Declan," Rachel smiles.

"Hi Eric, sit down," Jen says, "You doing okay?"

"Fine," I smile.

An elderly mini dachshund saunters up to my feet and sniffs my ankle. He gives it a lick with a warm dry tongue.

"That's Pepper," Jen says, "He's fifteen. Moves pretty slow."

"I didn't know you had a dog."

"Yeah," Jen nods, "He's been hiding in my parents' bedroom a lot lately. Getting old."

"Agh, the little shit just sleeps all day," Declan scowls.

"Don't be mean to Pepper!" Rachel says, "He's a sweet little guy."

"You should put him out of his misery, Rach. He can barely see, hardly walk, pisses everywhere. Look at his little back, it's all bent up and knotted like a bloody pretzel. He's probably in pain every moment of every day."

"Declan, shut up," Jen says.

"You see, mate," Declan tells me, "I'm glad you showed up here tonight. The only thing these women say is, 'Shut up, shut up.' We need to form an alliance, Eric. Leave them behind. We must talk about something macho. Something tough, like guns or engines... Oh, and silly me. I never thanked you for giving me that push in my car. Too bad it didn't work, but almost. I do remember."

"The night you got busted?" Rachel says, "Again."

"Yes, my love," Declan grins, "Your heart was in the right place, Eric. Unlike these evil girls here. Add their weight to the physics equation and the outcome could have changed immensely."

"I'm sorry," Melissa smiles, "I had to go to bed."

"I just don't like you," Jen teases.

"Well at least someone's being honest then!" Declan chuckles, "Eric, can I get you a beverage? You look thirsty. You like getting drunk? High? Hammered? Yes? No? Smoking weed? Ludes, dude? What's your pleasure? My job is to corrupt you somehow, some way. You seem like such a stand-up, proper young man. That simply cannot be tolerated."

"Don't listen to him, Eric," Jen says, "I'm just drinking a Pepsi."

"Well, we won't allow Jennifer any alcoholic drinks anymore," Declan explains, "Last time she was so hammered she got lost and peed on the sofa!"

"Shut up!" Jen smiles, "Not true!" She takes an ice cube from her cup, chucks it at Declan, and hits him on the jaw.

"My god!" Declan laughs, "That was a pretty good shot! Nearly knocked me clean onto the floor. You should play softball, Jennifer, get your scholarship to Harvard in that way. I better not mess with you any longer. Or at least wait until the ice cubes melt."

Jen chucks another cube and hits Declan's chest.

"Now don't be getting a stain on my favorite soccer jersey!" Declan smiles.

"I'll get you a drink, Eric," Jen says. She heads inside and Melissa and Pepper follow.

"No, don't you be getting up too, mate," Declan tells me, "You just got here. You just sat down. Relax. Tell me what you're thinking.

You're a quiet kid, but I know you got a lot going on in that head of yours. What are you here for, anyway? You like Jen, do you? Or is it Melissa? You can't have Rachel here, I've already got dibs on her."

"Declan, shut up!" Rachel says.

"See, that's all I've been hearing all night," Declan grins, "No, no, the fact is that you never tell a woman you've got dibs. That's a disrespectful thing to say, you know. I shouldn't even tease this lovely woman about it, but she knows me well enough, and puts up with me." Declan winks at me and takes a long sip from his cup. "So, you got any questions for me, mate? For I am a wise old sage. Ask thee anything. I shall bestow. You don't have to worry about Rachel hearing us either because she can be trusted too, you know. Come on, Eric. Speak up. I probably know the answer to what it is you're wondering. Sex, drugs, philosophy, I don't bloody know, just ask it."

"You don't have to, Eric," Rachel smiles, "He'll ramble on like this all night whether you pay attention to him or not."

"Well, thanks for that!" Declan says, "I've got to try to impress this young man, don't I? He's new in town, I can relate to that. I was the new boy once. I'm just trying to make Eric feel comfortable is all. I'm not annoying you, am I, Eric?"

"A little bit," I grin.

"Aha!" Declan laughs, "You see! He's a good kid! Copping an attitude with me already. See, he knows how it is. Cheers to that!" He taps his cup with Rachel. "So let us see, Eric, dissect the circumstances. You came here tonight to get away from Nathan, right? Your best friend who betrayed you. It was bound to happen, mate. I've known Nate a while, and he's a bit odd that one. Have you seen the hair turd thing? How could you miss it?"

"Nate left town. He's camping tonight," I say.

"Oh, he's gone then is he?" Declan says, "Hmm. Okay, so you're here just to hang out with Jen. Okay. Then I will let you know everything about that girl. To help you out along your mystical coitus quest."

Rachel laughs so hard she nearly spits her drink.

"Jen is a firecracker," Declan says, "She is very strong-willed, very opinionated, very smart. Tough on the outside, but fragile on the inside. You heard that her father, Dr. Thomas Ditmar, passed away? Not more than eight months ago. So sorry to say. Fucking cancer, mate. He was a great man, an honorable man. No joke. I loved him, truly, I did. Still do."

"Thanks, Declan," Rachel smiles.

"Tom was like a father to me," Declan says, "Nicest man you ever met. Loved to laugh, joke around, had a million friends. Line at his funeral was down the block and around the corner. And, Eric, his biggest fan in the world was Jen. Rachel was older, of course, so she and Tommy had a row now and then. Big fights back and forth, like all teens have. But Jenny was younger, so she never had one complaint about her pops. He was her hero, in every way. Sad, right? So her little heart is still ripped open, mate. It'll take years to mend. And until then, she won't love easily. That's the truth, no bullshit," Declan pauses for another sip, "And what about Melissa? How would you describe her, Rach?"

"Hmm," Rachel ponders, "Eager to please."

"Oh ho, nice! That's an accurate way of describing her," Declan smiles knowingly, "That's very true. She should work in retail. She aims to satisfy. Leaves to question though, which smiles are the genuine ones? Deep down inside she could be an evil troll. Hard to say. I can't really get a read on her soul."

"Her soul, Declan? Really?" Rachel rolls her eyes. "Hell no."

"What? I'm talking to Eric, here, okay, lady? Butt out," Declan places his hand beside his eyes so he can only see me, "I did hear the news that Mel is single, mate. She was in tears an hour ago. Greg Kingman had dinner with her tonight. Told her he's leaving for school very soon. And guess what she did? She dumped him. Said it broke her heart, but she knew he wouldn't be loyal to her at college. So, basically, you got beat up for nothing, mate. Or maybe not... At least there was the thrill of it. Some excitement in your life. If you think about it, all we have is those little moments. Those interactions. Some love, some hate. Some memories that are made. But most of those fade into nothing. Lost in the ether. I mean, look at the stars, Eric. All you have to do is look up to realize that we're just a meaningless speck of shit in all of this. The whole planet is a fucking speck."

Declan pauses, waiting for me to speak, but I have no idea what to say. Then the sliding glass door opens.

"Okay," Jen says. She reappears on the porch with Melissa, "I recognize the flabbergasted look on your face, Eric. Whatever goofy bullshit Declan is talking about, just forget it."

"Thanks a whole lot, Jennifer," Declan says, "I happen to be having a private conversation with my best mate, here, okay?"

"Here you go, Eric," Jen says, handing me a Pepsi. "Let's go, you guys. The movie is starting soon."

Jen, Melissa, and I pile into the backseat of Declan's New Yorker. I'm impressed by the blue leather seats and digital speedometer. The car even has a deep, digital voice, which announces, "Please fasten your seatbelts."

"Oh, you've got to tell Eric the joke," Rachel says.

"That's right," Declan smiles, "Eric? When is a door not a door?" I have no idea and I shrug. Declan puts the car in drive and slightly opens his door.

"A door is ajar," the digital car voice announces.

Everyone laughs as the vehicle roars up Alamo Drive. Then we hit the highway, and leave town. I'm totally wedged in between Melissa and Jen. I'm not sure who to talk to, so I look straight ahead.

"How far's the drive?" I ask.

"Twenty minutes," Jen says.

"Not too bad," adds Melissa.

"What movies are showing?" I ask.

"*The Firm* and *Cliffhanger*, I think," Jen says, "Not sure which comes first."

"The good news is, I've got a big trunk," Declan says, "You guys can hide in there so we don't have to pay."

"I've got money," I say.

"Oh, really?" Declan smiles, "You sure you don't want to be locked inside a dark space with two beautiful ladies? Suit yourself."

"They can't all fit," Rachel says.

"Be worth a try," Declan grins.

Declan shoves an audiotape in the stereo and turns it up. The Grateful Dead blasts from the speakers. I'm not a big fan of the jazzy rock guitar, but it's up so loud it kills any small talk, which is a relief. I finish my Pepsi, and Declan pulls over. He pushes a lever by his foot, and the trunk pops open.

"Alright then, who's going in first?" Declan grins.

Chapter 32: Free Admission

The country road is so dark, with no towns in sight. Declan removes a soccer ball, two blankets, and a small cooler. The trunk is large, but not big enough for three people.

"No way," Melissa shudders, "It's way too dirty in there."

"It's a trunk! What did you expect?" Declan says.

I'm left standing with Jen. Seems like a bad idea.

"You sure about this?" I ask, "I got paid today, so I'd be happy to--"

"Live a little," Jen smiles, "You get in first. We'll spoon. No funny business."

I hop in and lie on my side. The floor of the trunk is covered in sand. There are a couple of large pebbles that I sweep into the corner.

"Ready?" Jen smiles.

She climbs into the trunk and we nearly butt heads. Then she puts all of her weight on me, and my sore ribs kill me.

"You okay?"

"Fine," I groan.

Jen resituates herself so her butt juts right into my crotch. That may have felt good elsewhere, but now I'm so cramped I can barely breathe.

"Lift your waist a second," I say and slip one arm underneath her. Now both my arms wrap around her waist and my shoulder isn't crammed into a corner.

"That's way better," she says. Agreed.

"Aw, two peas in a pod," Rachel smiles and slams the trunk shut.

Everything goes completely dark. With my eyes open or shut, it makes no difference. I can see absolutely nothing. My other senses intensify. I smell the sweet shampoo in Jen's hair and feel her smooth curls touch my face. Her body is firmly pressed against me. Her back rises and falls with every breath. Declan hits a bump, and we bounce against the lid.

"Ouch!" Jen laughs.

"Hang on!" Declan calls out, "Here comes another rough patch!"

We bounce around for several seconds. Each time I hold Jen tighter, and she presses my hands against her. She's having way more fun than I am, but I do smile a little. I'm afraid I'm too sweaty. Am I getting her wet? Gross. It's so hot and stuffy in here.

"Is he hitting bumps on purpose?" I ask.

"Probably, that dumbass," Jen giggles, "It's like a ghetto roller coaster in here!"

The car stops and I hear the doorman of the movie entrance mumble something. Then Declan says, "Three, please." My eyes have finally adjusted, and I see cracks of light coming in from the backseat. The parking lot must be well lit. The car crawls forward, onto the bumpiest terrain yet.

"Oh, my god," Jen laughs, "When will it end?"

The car turns sharply. Declan must be parking. The trunk finally pops open. A burst of fresh air feels cool and refreshing. Thank god. Sweet freedom. I sit up and look around. The lights are so bright I have to squint.

"Finally!" Jen gasps.

"How was it?" Melissa asks.

"Fun," Jen smiles, "But I don't think I'll do it again."

My eyes adjust and I take in the drive-in movie theatre, hidden in a forest. The large silver screen looks small beside a cluster of giant pines. Dozens of cars have parked in the gravel lot. The whole place is like a throwback to 1960.

Our parking spot is in the back row. Declan tunes the car radio and finds the movie's own frequency. The speakers blare orchestra music and the film *Cliffhanger* begins.

In the opening scene, a red helicopter flies across a pristine mountaintop. The shot couldn't look any prettier, with real trees and stars shining in the background. Jen spreads blankets on the grass behind the gravel lot, and Declan and Rachel lie down. Rachel opens the cooler and finds a beer. She grabs a Pepsi for Declan.

"What's this shit?" Declan asks.

"You're driving," Rachel says.

"In four hours! One more beer won't hurt me, babe."

Melissa touches my arm, "You been working out? You're so tan. Come on, Eric. Let's go. I'm hungry."

She leads me to a low, square building made of cinder blocks. I can smell the popcorn from outside. We enter and I see the projection room, restrooms, and a concession stand. I don't say a word.

"How do you like the movie so far?" Melissa asks.

She orders a large popcorn and some Junior Mints. Melissa reaches into her pocket to pay, but I insist on buying. It feels good to have money for once. On the way back to Declan's car, Melissa walks slowly. She isn't the most talkative person, but I can tell she has something to say.

"Eric?" Melissa asks, "Do you like Jenny?"

I shrug, "Sure."

"Yeah, but do you like-her, like-her?"

I shrug again. Of course, I do.

"Well if you do like her, that's totally cool with me," Melissa says, "I just wanted you to know that."

Melissa stares at me, but it's different this time. There's no flirting going on. Is this the genuine Melissa? She's way more at ease somehow. She's changed. Is she being my friend?

"Jenny likes you too," Melissa grins, "Don't be shy. I can tell you like her."

I sigh in relief and let a smile bend my lips.

"Yep," she nods, "I know these things."

Melissa playfully slaps my arm and I giggle. I feel so relieved. What began as an awkward conversation somehow feels great. Melissa is a nice girl, she's my friend. And now our meeting in her basement at midnight seems trivial like it happened a million years ago.

When we get back to the car Declan is singing 'Happy Birthday' at the top of his lungs. The Ditmar sisters are begging him to stop.

"Popcorn!" Jen says, "Thanks, guys."

"Eric paid," Melissa says, "Thank him."

"Do you guys know it's Rachel's half-birthday two weeks from today?" Declan says, "We must celebrate this special occasion!"

"Shut up and watch the movie, you idiot," Rachel smiles.

I sit next to Jen, and Melissa lies down in front of us. The movie plays, and every now and then Jen makes a funny comment. She thinks the bad guy is way over-the-top, which is true. And the hero, Sylvester Stallone, should have totally died like fifty times by now. We all laugh at the scariest parts. It is pretty corny.

As it gets later we sink lower in our seats. Declan and Rachel cuddle and Melissa falls asleep. Jen and I lean closer together on our blanket, and then her head gets heavy on my shoulder, so we lie down. By the time the second film begins all the girls are asleep. I look at Declan and he smiles.

"Just you and me, mate. The men. Too much excitement for the ladies. Either that or we're too damn boring for them. Whatcha wanna talk about?"

I shrug.

"How long are you staying here for anyway? Days, weeks, months?"

"Not sure," I say, "We'll have to find a place before school starts, I guess."

"Weeks then. No wonder the girls love you, mate. Zero commitment. They can love you and not have to worry about the awkward glances in the hall after you break up."

"Huh?"

"Think, Eric. They don't know you, and you're leaving. It's perfect. Nobody wants effort or permanence at this age. We all just want to play the field. Test the waters. But on the other hand, sometimes the best thing is right in front of you. If you keep looking for something better, you miss what you've already got. These Ditmar girls are real pearls, you know. I love them to pieces. I'd marry Rachel in a heartbeat. I would. I'm going to Knox College with her this fall, over in Galesburg. Yes, indeed. I'm no student but I'll find a job. I'm serious. I really do truly love her. I've got regrets in my life, but none of them are about Rachel."

"What regrets?" I ask.

"You think I'd tell you? You little shit!" Declan laughs, "No, just joking. You seem like a good kid. And, if you're not, I'll never know, because you'll just move away before I can hate you." He laughs and lights a cigarette, "Want a smoke?"

"No, thanks."

"Boy, you're clean as a whistle, eh? That'll change. Eventually, you'll want to know what all us adults are crazy about. All I do is drink and smoke and for good reason. It makes me feel good. It helps me escape the world." Declan takes a drag, "Slowly kills me too, but that's okay."

Declan reminds me of Mom. Is this how her drinking began? But Dad drinks too and he's fine. And Declan certainly doesn't appear depressed. Constantly cracking jokes and laughing. He points at the screen and giggles. I watch the movie too, and the actor, Tom Cruise, sprints down the street of a suburban neighborhood. Some intense drums echo in the background.

"Look at this twerp," Declan laughs, "So serious!" He puts out his cigarette and sighs, "Can't run forever. Can't run from your past. I do have regrets," Declan continues, "Yup. Been arrested a few times."

"For what?"

"Drunk driving, for one. You witnessed that. Dumber ones though too, like threatening an officer with a deadly weapon."

"What?"

"Oh, it's simple, really. Nothing scary. I was working at a deli in Chicago, just before I moved here. And this cop comes in and he is bossing me around something awful. A true piece of shit that man was. A total turd in every way. So, I'm putting the lettuce on for him, and he says it's brown. I'm putting on tomatoes, but they're not red enough. He says the cheese looks slimy, the meat looks shiny, there's something wrong at every turn, right? So then, I'm finally done, I cut the sandwich in half and he says he wants another one. He says I didn't cut it exactly down the middle. And I've had enough of his ass at that point, and I said, 'Just get the fuck out of here.' Well, the problem is, I still had the knife in my hand. And like I said, the cop was a prick. He arrested me right there in front of all the customers. Put the cuffs on me, threw me in the car. Then I got fired. The charges were dismissed, thank god, but it was humiliating."

Declan pauses to open another beer, and then continues, "It's kind of funny now, looking back on it, but back then I was so angry. The officer abused his power. Bloody cops, I hate them all. But I learned something that day. I did. Always try to hold back. You can't always say exactly what you're thinking. With certain people you can. Like with Rachel, that's why she loves me. I don't sugar coat a damn thing. But with others, I gotta hold back. Especially pigs."

"I'm the opposite. I always hold back."

"That's true. You don't say shit. And that's a good thing."

"Sometimes."

"What do you mean, Eric? Speak up."

"No... this is dumb."

"Oh, come on! Be a man for chrissake!"

"Well, sometimes... I wish I had said something to somebody, but the moment goes past."

"Everybody has that," Declan smiles, "But if you want to speak, then speak. Say it loud. Volume is good for you. Yelling is therapeutic. Really. Don't hold back. You're more capable than you think. I know reality is a mind-fuck. It's hard to wrap your head around it, what other people see you as, because you're always trapped inside of you. A part of you always wonders how you come off, and what people think. To me, Eric, from my standpoint, I see a confident little shit. It's true. You're a bit irresistible, even."

Declan opens a Bud Light and hands it to me, "And if you don't believe me, that's one thing alcohol is good for. Liquid confidence. Here, have a beer with me, Mr. Daniels. We get along well now, don't we? You're a pleasure to talk to, young man."

I grab the beer and tap Declan's can, "Cheers."

The beer tastes sour and bubbly, but it's ice cold. And I'm so thirsty after the popcorn. By the third sip, the beer tastes sweet, and before I know it, the can is empty.

"Sorry, no more," Declan says, "That was my last."

When the movie ends, we wake up the girls and pile into the Chrysler. Rachel insists on driving, and Declan sits shotgun. I take the window seat behind him, and Jen sits in the middle. Her head rests on my shoulder, and Melissa winks at me. I try to fight off sleep for a while, maybe the beer made me sleepy, and when I open my eyes, I'm back in Jen's driveway. It's nearly 2 AM.

I say goodbye and get hugs from the girls. I offer to walk Melissa home, but she's spending the night, and so is Declan. The Irishman gives me a firm handshake and says we'll talk again soon. I walk to Greenfield Street and head down the hill.

And what do I see? Matt's big, black, fully-loaded van is parked in Nate's driveway, right beside Dad's truck. What the hell is this?

Chapter 33: Of All The People

I walk in the house and find Dad sitting at the kitchen table, with Johanna and an empty bottle of red wine. Dad has changed outfits since supper, and now wears a red tie and a white button-down shirt that's two sizes too big. Johanna wears a fancy purple dress with puffy shoulders. Matt was not invited to this party.

"There he is!" Dad smiles with his wine-stained teeth. "How's the movie?"

"Good."

"Hi, Eric," Johanna smiles and her cheeks turn red, "Sorry, I borrowed your dad for the evening. I hope that's okay."

"Yeah," Dad says, "Jo shows up and she's like, 'Where's Patti?' and I'm like, 'She's gone!'"

"I had tickets to the play at Highland," Johanna explains, "Patti must have forgotten, but your father was kind enough to join me."

"I'm surprised to admit it, but I absolutely loved the play," Dad says, "It was very funny. *The Foreigner*, right? Hilarious! The lead guy was great!"

Aren't these two in a good mood? But I'm not smiling. I can't believe this. Whether on purpose or not, this was a date. A successful one too. Is Dad dating my enemy's mom? And she's married! Are you kidding me? They are getting along too well. How is this happening?

"It's late, Mike," Johanna says, "Thank you so much. I should get going. I'll give you a call, okay? We should do this again."

"Sounds wonderful," Dad coos.

"Great," Johanna smiles and squeezes Dad's hand. "Goodnight."

She leaves the house and the van disappears down the street. Dad puts the empty wine bottle in the trash and rinses out the wine glasses.

"What the hell was that?" I ask.

"What?" Dad smiles, "She's a nice woman. What was I supposed to do? She wouldn't take no for an answer. She even raided Manny's closet so I had something to wear."

"Dad! She's married!"

"Nope, not for long. She's in the process of getting a divorce. I heard all about it. Mr. Lyons has lived in Chicago for the better part of the last six months."

"What? Then are you dating Matt's mom?"

"Oh, no. No way! It was a fun night, but nothing like that. Don't worry. We did not kiss, not even close."

"You guys were going to. If I hadn't walked in, you'd be screwing right now."

"Whoa! What?" Dad laughs, "It's not like that at all."

"I'm not a baby, Dad. I know why people date."

"Are you mad at me or something?"

"Yes! I am mad. You went on a date with Matt's mom! Of all the people in the world! Matt is going to kill me when he finds out."

"He doesn't have to know. I talked to Jo about that too. Like I said, this is nothing serious. She knows we're leaving, Eric. Listen, she is a really great person. She's had some hard times too. We have a lot in common."

"Oh, god."

"It's true. She loves pizza."

"Oh, please! Who doesn't?"

"And she loves to cook," Dad continues, "Her brother owns a restaurant, and her parents owned one when she was growing up. And that play, it was so good, a perfect show for a first date. I mean, not a date, but, you know what I mean... it was fun."

"Unbelievable," I groan.

"Hey! Give me a break here, alright Eric? I haven't dated much at all since your mom left. I never had the time. It's not easy raising a kid and running a business by yourself. But we survived, right? And I think we're doing great. Look, you and me? We're doing fine, aren't we?"

Dad pats my back. I can't believe it, but it's hard to stay mad. He seems so happy.

"Listen," Dad says, "I've got some résumés floating around out there. One of them's bound to catch. The insurance check will come in soon. We're almost there, wherever we're going," Dad scowls and sniffs the air, "So, when'd you start drinking beers?"

"Huh?"

"I smell beer on you," Dad nods knowingly, "You're not drunk though, that's good. You should always drink in moderation. You probably had one or two, huh? Tried it out but didn't really like it? Well, that's a good thing. Beer is gross. Take your time. You've got your whole adult life to drink. Drink now, and it only gets in your way. And that's no bullshit. Same with girls. They're only trouble right now. Wait till you're older," Dad pauses, "You know what a prophylactic is, right?"

"You're so weird, Dad," I roll my eyes and walk downstairs.

"What? They're not 100% effective, you know!" Dad yells, "Hey, I'm trying, kid. Get to sleep! Okay, buddy? We can talk in the morning. After you sober up!"

Oh, my god. I lie in bed, stare at the ceiling tiles, and try not to think. What in the hell is a prophylactic? It's gotta be birth control. Probably a condom, but I'm not sure.

Jesus. What if Dad starts dating Johanna? What if they get married, and Matt is my brother? That would so suck. That kid is such an idiot. I'll never get to sleep thinking like this.

So, I think about Jen. How good did it feel when she slept on my shoulder? I wish she was here now. I want to see her. I want to hold her. I squeeze my pillow tight and give it a kiss. Just a little one. I can see Jen, sitting at the drive-in, looking up at the screen and smiling. The light reflecting off her face. I can picture her sitting at her house, at the patio table, drinking Pepsi, laughing at Declan's dumb jokes. I see her light blue tank top, her tan skin, and blonde hair. I feel her body against mine in the trunk. I can almost smell her shampoo.

Chapter 34: Don't Shoot

I sleep in pretty late the next day, and by the time I wake up, Dad is cooking grilled cheese sandwiches for lunch.

"Morning... or afternoon," he smiles, "You missed your girlfriend. Jen, right? She called about an hour ago."

"Did you get her number?"

"No," Dad grimaces, "Sorry."

I chow down my sandwich, tomato soup, and lemonade. Then I shower, get dressed, and run out the door.

I see Jen in the driveway. Rachel's there too, and Melissa. They're wearing their bathing suits and washing Rachel's Chevy. Jen's smile lights up the scene. How am I even here? I'm so lucky. These wonderful people want to hang out with me? I still can't understand it.

Jen sees me, grabs the hose, and fires. I run, but still get sprayed down my back.

I raise my arms high in surrender, "Don't shoot!"

"Not a chance!" Jen smiles.

She sprays me full blast and soaks my chest. I'm sopping wet. My shirt is painted on, clinging, and showing every flab roll I've got. I look awful.

I can feel the water dripping into my shorts and underwear, so I've got to take off my shirt quickly. This sucks. I can't let anybody see me. I jog into the side yard and turn my back to the driveway. I quickly peel off my shirt and wring it out.

"What are you doing over there?" Jen says, "Hiding? Don't be shy. I dropped the hose. I promise."

Jen's heading this way. Shit. I wring the shirt once more. Dry enough. I put it back on just as Jen finds me. That was too close. I try not to blush. Jen smiles, grabs my arm, and drags me back to the driveway.

"Come help us," she says.

"Hi, Eric," Melissa smiles, "Grab a sponge."

"Yeah, get to work, kid," Rachel says.

Pepper sniffs me and licks some cold water off of my ankle. I reach into the soapy bucket and find a rag. We cover the Chevy in suds, and then Jen rinses the car with the hose.

Then Declan shows up. He pulls his car into the driveway and rolls up the windows. Rachel refills the soap bucket, and we scrub the New Yorker.

"Hurry up, my loyal servants!" Declan grins, "I've gotta go to work soon."

"Eric, you want to come too?" Jen asks, "Declan works at the park."

Declan nods and points to the Krape Park logo on his green polo shirt. "Boat docks. I guess I can let you guys ride for free this one time. Since you did wash my car. Did a pretty poor job though. Don't forget the rims."

"Shut up, Declan," Rachel says, "We rent boats for free all the time, Eric. He's teasing, as usual."

Jen rinses off the suds from the New Yorker and Declan polishes the pentagon hood ornament until it sparkles like a diamond. Then the girls throw the towels and bucket in the garage and put on some clothes over their swimsuits.

We pile into Declan's car and head to Krape Park. He takes the back way, past the golf course, and through the country. We cross a high bridge where a wide creek rushes below. Then we coast down a hill and I see the merry-go-round, full of kids. A large family reunion has gathered, picnicking in the shade. Declan parks in a lot beside the water. We wait for a second while he checks in with his boss, and then we walk to the docks.

The boats are baked in sunlight. There are two plastic docks, each about ten feet long, floating along the edge of the creek. Four square paddle-boats are tied on, along with four canoes, and four one-seater kayaks. Declan hands everyone a life jacket and has us pick whichever boat we want. Melissa insists on a paddleboat since it's the best option for sunbathing. Rachel agrees, and they pair up. Jen wants to go fast and explore, so she picks a canoe. I hop on it first and grab an oar.

"Oh my god!" Jen laughs as she steps aboard. "It's so wobbly!"

Declan kneels on the dock and grabs a hold of the canoe. He stabilizes the craft at first, then he shakes it like crazy.

"Declan, stop!" Jen screams.

"Okay, okay," Declan smiles, "Have fun, kids. Be careful. Strong current today."

Declan unties our line and casts us off. Jen and I both face forward and we lean into every stroke.

"We're gonna smoke you guys!" Jen yells to Rachel and Melissa.

"Who cares?" Rachel says.

Declan casts off Melissa and Rachel. The girls pedal slowly, while they rub suntan lotion onto their arms.

"How fast can this thing go?" Jen asks me, "Let's find out."

Chapter 35: River Romance

The narrow canoe easily slices through the current. I look back at the paddleboat that flounders along. Melissa and Rachel already look exhausted from pedaling. Jen and I go way ahead, all alone on the water. I get sweaty from rowing and take off my life jacket. Jen does the same.

"There's the waterfall," Jen points to a high cliff with water trickling down. "It's fake but pretty... just like Melissa."

"Oh, man!" I laugh, "Good one."

The canoe coasts across the murky brown water alongside the grassy green shore. We pass several empty picnic tables and a tiny brick cabin.

"That's the skate house," Jen says, "For ice skating in the winter."

"No summer ice skating?"

"Shut up," Jen smiles.

"Any water skiing?"

"Nope. No engines allowed," Jen says, "My god, it's hot out."

Jen takes off her tank-top, down to her yellow bikini. My t-shirt is soaked with sweat but I leave it on. I dip my hand in the water and get my hair wet. I splash Jen with water and she giggles. Revenge for the hose.

"Stop!" Jen laughs, "That's so cold!"

"Guess what," I say, "My dad went on a date last night."

"With who?"

"You won't believe it. Matt's mom."

"No way! What?! Oh no!" Jen laughs so hard her shoulders shimmy. She smiles at me over her shoulder, "Matt's gonna be pissed! What about his dad?"

"They're getting divorced."

"Really? Okay. Well, you can't blame your dad then. Matt's mom is a saint, and she's gorgeous," Jen pauses, "You know, this feels weird talking like this. I'm facing the damn river. I should be looking at you instead." Jen tries to stand and the boat rocks. "Whoa!" She passes back her oar. "Hold this." Then she raises her legs high and spins on her butt. Now we're face to face.

"Hello there, Eric," Jen grins.

"Hi," I smile.

She's proud of her spin move but then she recoils, "Now I feel so exposed," she mumbles. "Stupid bikinis." Jen puts her arms across her chest. She grabs her tank top off the boat floor, but it's soaked. She attempts to wear it anyway, but her head gets stuck in the armhole. "Damn it!" she giggles. "Whatever," Jen throws her shirt back down, grins, and shakes her head. "I can be myself around you, right?" She stares at me for a second and then asks, "So what are we going to do about you and Nate?"

I shrug and keep rowing, "Camping helps. His folks will lecture him. But he's probably getting home tonight."

"It's crazy," Jen says, "The dude has a fatal crush on me or something. Which is so creepy. Honestly, I think of Nate like a brother. I've known him forever. I've known everybody in this shit-hole town forever," she pauses to adjust her ponytail, "Nate went psycho before, you know? Last year. I went to homecoming with this boy, Barry Woods, and there was a party afterward. Mostly older kids, since I was a Freshman, and Barry was a Junior. Anyway, Nate shows up at this party. Totally uninvited. He's not dressed up or anything. Nate walks up to the keg, buys a cup, fills it to the top, and walks right over to me and Barry. We were sitting on some lawn chairs in the backyard just talking, a pretty boring conversation actually. And then Nate takes his cup, and pours the entire thing on Barry's crotch."

"What?"

"Yes! And Barry was shocked, humiliated, and then super pissed! And Nate took off running like a scared little bunny. He zig-zagged across the yard, hurdled the neighbor's fence, and disappeared into the darkness."

I laugh and picture Nate's panicked face running as fast as he possibly can. Like when he ran for his life from the "ghost" at the Rawson House.

"You have the best laugh, Eric. You should laugh more often."

"I was just picturing Nate. Running for his life."

"Yes," Jen grins, "He's a goofy looking dude. You should see his picture in the yearbook. It's terrifying."

"You know what? Nate has a picture of you in his room. A school photo. It's pinned on the wall. Right next to his bed."

"What? Are you kidding me? Why? That is so gross!"

"Nate told me something, I probably shouldn't tell you," I pause, "He told me in confidence, so..."

"Tell me!" Jen says, "You can't defend a guy who spit in your face!"

"Well, if you put it that way, fine. Nate said he kissed you."

"Really? When?"

"Like a couple months ago. When you were drunk. And you barfed. And you ripped off your shirt, or something, so he gave you his shirt. It was a detailed story."

"Really?"

"Yep."

"Never happened," Jen says.

"Which part? The kiss? The barf? The shirt?"

"Any of it. All of it. None of it. No such thing ever happened. Definitely not. Never. Sure, I've gotten drunk before. I admit that. But never around Nate. You hang around Rachel and Declan long enough and you'll get drunk. But no, I've never considered Nate attractive. Yuck. I'd rather date Billy. In fact, Billy asked me to Homecoming too, but I had already said yes to Barry. That's why Nate hates Billy so much."

"Because he asked you to a dance?"

"That's all it takes," Jen says, "So what else did Nate say about me?"

"You ate cat food."

"What? That is so absurd!" Jen laughs, "Why would I do that?"

"He said you were, like, twelve or something."

"Yuck. I don't like cats. Where's the cat even coming from? I never had a pet cat, neither has Nate. That's insane."

"It is," I say, "I'm not sure why I believed Nate to begin with."

"Of course, you believed him," Jen sighs, "He's your friend. He's my friend too. With so much history. We've both known him forever, Eric. We can't just stop being friends with him. It's not that easy. He's like family. Unfortunately."

I row the canoe upstream, pass a bend, and Jen spots three turtles sunbathing on some rocks. We keep going and duck under a low footbridge, the exit of Krape Park. The murky water looks much clearer now. We coast beside a gravel road, and then under a rusty railroad bridge. As we near a highway, cars roar by, oblivious to our tiny boat floating low beside them. Then a cemetery approaches, and the river veers away from the highway noise. The water gets wider and deeper. Jen spins around and faces the front again, so she can steer us through the flooded woods. We swerve and duck to avoid low branches.

Then we coast into an open stretch and enjoy the peaceful silence in the sun. Floating lazily along the water feels nice. I don't worry about what to say, we're just here. Relaxing. Sometimes people chatter because the silence feels tense, but Jen and I can chill in silence, feeling happy without laughing. And I don't know how, but I can tell Jen is happy too. What is this? A fun canoe ride? Or is it romance? Is it love? No way. Well, maybe. I don't know. Stop thinking and enjoy the moment. I take a breath. The sky is blue. Not a cloud in sight.

We float along as the river narrows, and the current increases to its strongest yet. Cornfields appear on the shore, and then one majestic-shabby rooftop comes into view.

"Isn't that the haunted farmhouse?" I ask.

"It is," Jen says, "Rawson House. You've been here?"

"Once."

"It's kinda cool. Wanna take a break? Let's check it out."

My arms ache as I pick up as much speed as I can. We run the canoe aground against the shore. Jen hops out and pulls the canoe onto land.

"Race ya," she says.

Jen runs fast and reaches the front stoop several steps ahead of me. I'm winded. My ribs are still a little sore. Jen laughs and gives me a high-five. Our hands touch and she holds on for just a second. Our fingers intertwine. Then Jen steps away and pushes open a plywood door, which wasn't here last time. Inside the house, it's cleaner than I remember, like maybe the floor was swept. And there's a couch that wasn't here before either. Everything else looks the same, all cluttered and ancient.

"When's the last time you were here?" I ask.

"Last summer," Jen says, "I came here with Nate and Matt quite a few times. Not sure why. My brief destructive stage, I guess. We threw rocks and broke windows, but after that there wasn't much to do. They started setting fires to the furniture, and I was done. Not a fan. I thought the whole house was going to burn down."

"I'm no fan of fire either. Trust me."

"Oh, sorry," Jen grins. She kneels on the floor beside an old cabinet drawer. She runs her fingertips along the inside corners of the drawer and feels for anything stuck in the cracks. She stops at one point and pulls out a tiny tortoiseshell button that's smaller than a dime.

"Damn," Jen says, "I was hoping for a coin. This button is beautiful though. I wonder what it was for. A shirt maybe? Or a pioneer woman's dress, with that high, frilly collar."

Jen presses the button against her skin, into the little round notch between her collar bones. With her other hand, she gathers her ponytail into a high bun. Sun from the broken window highlights her face. She arches her neck and straightens her back, like a proper antique portrait. Jen glows, and every inch of her is beautiful. Even though she wears a bathing suit, I can almost see a pioneer woman sitting there. Jen gives me a very serious look and raises one eyebrow. Then she cracks up and I do too. Jen tosses the button back into the drawer, stands up, and dusts herself off.

I follow Jen upstairs, where she searches another drawer and finds nothing. I gaze out the bedroom window and spot our canoe. Then a boy walks up to the boat.

"It's Matt," I say.

"Oh, crap. What's he doing here?" Jen runs to the window, "What's that idiot doing to our boat?"

Chapter 36: Float Like A Rock

Jen and I run down the stairs and out of the house but it's still another fifty yards to the shore, Matt, and our canoe.

"Matt!" Jen yells, "Stop! Don't!"

Matt pushes the boat off the shore. The current grabs the canoe and takes it downstream.

"You're such a dick!" Jen yells, "You idiot! Why would you do that?"

"What?" Matt says, "A shitty old canoe. Who cares?"

"It's our canoe, you asshole!" Jen says, "It's a nice boat! It says Krape Park right on the damn side!"

"Nice bikini, Jen. What were you guys doing in there?"

"Nothing. Shut up!"

"Yeah, right," Matt smirks.

"Screw you! Matthew, you suck!" Jen says.

Jen yells at Matt while I run along the shoreline and try to catch up with the canoe. The corn gets in my way, and I can't run fast enough. The boat finds the center of the stream and picks up speed. The water is deep and I jump in.

"Eric, no!" Jen yells, "The current is too strong!"

My body rolls over in the rushing water, and when I come up for air, I'm not sure where I am. Then I see the canoe. I straighten my body flat, and my arms make a few decent strokes, but I'm an awful swimmer and I'm already tired. My ribs ache, and my arm muscles are wrecked from rowing. I point my toes and try to touch the bottom but it's way too deep. I rest for a second and the canoe moves further away. My muscles burn like fire. For an instant, they lock up, and my head dips below the surface.

I come back up with a mouth full of water. It goes up my nose and stings. I wish I had my life jacket on. I picture it sitting worthlessly on the floor of the canoe.

The canoe keeps drifting away. Oh, forget it. I'm failing. I'm exhausted. Just leave the boat and get back to shore. A doggy paddle is the best I can do. I bob along the surface, churning, coughing, and gasping for breath. I touch the bank, but it's too steep. The current pushes me away. I try to pull myself back onto land, but it feels like I weigh a million pounds.

I hear Jen yelling from somewhere in the corn. I try to hoist myself up on land again, and I fall. I grab a root and it breaks. I'm flailing back into the heart of the stream.

Jesus, am I gonna die? I try to calm down. I take a breath, hold it, and try to float. But I can't. I'm too panicked. My heart is demanding air. My muscles are done! I dip underwater. Then I'm back up. I'm back down. I can't think. I can't breathe. I'm so dead. I sink again. This time for good. Swim, damn it! My muscles don't respond.

I see a flash of red. It's coming near. What is it? One last bit of strength hits me and I bob to the surface. Matt swims in red shorts. He's the picture of expert form, with his head down, body planked, kicking and stroking like an Olympian. Matt passes me and chases the canoe. I can barely keep my head up, but I focus on him, watching and hoping. One more minute. Give me one more minute. Matt is almost there.

I'm sunk. I'm under. I gasp for one more breath but get water instead. I choke and cough. Every ounce of me burns for air. My body shakes and sinks. I'm in slow-motion. The light on the surface fades. Then an orange blur floats above me.

Matt grabs my arm and hoists me onto the life jacket. He fastens it around my shoulder and neck. He slaps my back. Adrenaline rushes up and I'm coughing like a maniac. Water and mucus seep from my nose and mouth. Matt pulls a rope, and the canoe comes towards us. This feels like forever. I'm in a daze. My head is killing me.

Matt flips me onto my back, grabs my hands, and directs them, "Hang on!"

I realize I'm being towed off the end of the canoe. I'm aching, but I'm safe now, and I finally get a decent breath. The air feels wonderful.

Soon my feet touch the bottom of the stream. I let go of the life jacket and stand in the shallow water. I fall back down. I'm back at the Rawson House.

Jen runs into the water. "Eric!" she yells, "Are you okay?"

Her body collides with mine. She feels warm and sturdy as stone. Thank god. Now I really get some decent breaths. My throat aches but my lungs aren't on fire anymore.

"You swim like a fucking rock!" Matt says, catching his breath.

My legs wobble up the shore and I collapse onto the grass. Jen presses up against me, hugging and holding me, touching my face and neck. Then she sits me up and rubs my back. I cough a few more times.

"Get a room you two, Christ," Matt smiles, "Where's my massage? I saved his life."

"Thank you," I groan. My voice comes out as a scratchy growl, but Matt seems to understand. He smiles and I'm glad. He should be proud. He saved me.

"Don't give Matt too much credit," Jen says, "This never would have happened if he didn't launch our boat."

"Shut up, Jenny," Matt says, "I saved his goddamn life and you're giving me shit? That's messed up. You got your stupid canoe back. What more do you want from me?"

"What do you want from me?" Jen says, "A damn trophy?"

"Enough!" I mumble, "Matt's right. I was dead. Thank you."

"Of course," Matt shrugs, "You'd do the same for me, right?" He turns and walks towards the Rawson House.

"Where're you going now, Matt?" Jen asks.

"Getting away from you. Then I'm gonna break stuff in this stupid old house," Matt says, "Is that okay, princess?"

Jen rolls her eyes and Matt disappears. Jen grabs my hand and helps me stand. She wraps her arms around me and squeezes. Our bodies push together, closer than ever. My soaked, flabby dead weight doesn't make her cringe one bit. This hug feels absolutely wonderful. I begin to feel good again. My heart did not explode. My lungs are still working.

"You're going to be alright, Eric," Jen whispers, "My god, you scared me."

Her arms loosen but remain tied around my waist. She looks up at me, and I look down. Our eyes meet. We close in, nose to nose, and lips to lips.

"Let's go," Jen says, "Gotta get back to the boat docks before it closes."

"That's right," I whisper, "Almost forgot."

Chapter 37: Nate's Encore

It's a very slow ride, but we arrive at the docks just in time. Declan locks up the boat rental shack and gives Jen and I a ride home. The sunset shines pink and yellow by the time I return to Greenfield Street.

Manny's Toyota Truck is back, and Nate is playing basketball at Billy's. I'm still soaking wet and so exhausted. I wave at the guys then turn and walk inside the house.

Patti washes the camping skillet in the kitchen sink. "What happened to you? You're soaked. Nate's playing basketball," she says, "Go on over, Eric. We had a big talk. He's fine."

I sigh and drink a glass of milk. Then I scarf down a plate of leftover fried fish, broccoli, and mashed potatoes. I really don't want to see Nate again, but I guess it's time to get this over with. I throw on some dry clothes and cross the street.

"Yo, Eric!" Ronnie yells, "Come on, bro, let's play two-on-two!"

"Hey," Billy says, "You survived. We heard all about it. Matt just left."

"He saved your life?" Nate asks.

"It's true," I nod.

"Said you were with Jen too," Nate says, "You guys were making out in the Rawson House?"

"That part is not true. We did not kiss."

"Sure," Nate frowns, "I just don't get it, man. I was done being upset with you. I was. And I felt sorry that I attacked you, and sicked Greg on you like that. I apologized to Billy and Ronnie too. It wasn't cool. But here you are, again, and you're still hitting on my girl. Again. And I'm really pissed at you, dude. So pissed! Can't you find another girl? Come on!"

Nate doesn't sound too upset, but Billy steps in between us, just in case.

"No, Billy," Nate says, "I'm good. I'm not gonna lose my temper. Really. But this piece of shit here keeps hitting on Jen, man. Why? Why are you doing this to me?"

"To you? Nate!" I yell, "Wake up, dude! She doesn't like you! Not that way. At all! You gotta let it go! Get over yourself!"

"What do you know, huh?" Nate says, "You've been here for a couple weeks, and you think you're best friends with everybody? Well you're not! Not even close."

"Nate, listen," I say, "Jen thinks of you like a brother. Honestly. A brother! She told me that herself."

"Bullshit. I used to think of you like a brother. Until you stabbed me in the back."

"Dude! Give me a break! I did no such thing. I never even kissed her. And if I did, who cares? You can't control her, dude. She does whatever she wants."

"Stay away from her," Nate warns.

"No! Fuck that. No way!" I say, "Because you know what else? She called you a liar. You never kissed her, Nate! She never ate cat food."

"What?" Billy says.

"Then you went psycho, Nate," I continue, "You poured a damn beer on her date for no reason?"

"That's not true," Nate says.

"Not true? Bullshit!" I yell, "Who's telling the truth? Who am I supposed to believe, huh? Jen or a dude that fakes an injury? Lies, ditches me, and spits in my face? Tell me the truth, Nate! Did you kiss her, or not? Did you make up the cat food story? Was it a different girl? A dream? Some big dumb fantasy? Why would you lie to me? I've known you my whole life. You don't have to impress me, Nate. Why would you even think that? What is your problem? Huh? What is the deal?"

I stare at Nate and inch towards him. Billy's hand presses against my chest. I thought I was beyond exhausted but now I'm fired up. I'm so sick of dealing with Nate's lies. No more. I've had enough. I'm speaking up.

"Take it easy," Billy whispers.

Nate stares at me and then looks away.

"Nothing to say, huh, Nate?" I say, "You can be honest with me, man. Friends are supposed to be honest. That's the number one rule, isn't it? Right?"

Billy mumbles, "It is a good rule."

"I'm sorry, Ronnie," I say, "But I can't play ball right now. See you guys later."

"Yeah, keep walking!" Nate yells, "Why don't you just walk away forever, Daniels? Huh? Just leave! And don't come back. Nobody wants your fat ass around here anymore!"

I raise my middle finger high and don't look back. I cross the street and march inside the house.

"You guys okay?" Patti asks.

"Fine," I chirp, without looking up.

I go straight downstairs and collapse on my bed. That argument took every last bit of strength I had. My mind hurts. My body aches. Every muscle I have hates me. I'm done. My head hits the pillow and I'm asleep in seconds.

Chapter 38: Running His Mouth

The next morning comes too soon. I hear Dad's morning whistle like I'd been asleep for one second.

"I let ya sleep in a little, kid. So hurry up," Dad says.

I get dressed, eat some cold scrambled eggs, and join Dad in the truck. The tailgate is already piled high with sand.

Dad drives us to the inground job. The groundwater is gone. I'm surprised that the water didn't affect our work that much. The walls still look pretty smooth. I'm also surprised to see Nate here. He scrapes off the last of the shallow end, while Manny fills a divot in the deep end. Dad backs the truck to the edge, and I grab a shovel. My arms ache from yesterday, but I tough it out. After four truckloads of sand, the dads begin to trowel the floor.

Nate and I haven't said a word. The hot sun bakes down on us. I find a shady tree to stand under, and Nate finds another one across the yard.

"Hey boys?" Manny yells from the bottom of the pool, "Me and Mike will be trowelling down here for a while. Go ahead and walk home. Go on. Good work today. Thanks."

Nate and I grab our paper lunch bags from the cooler and cut through Krape Park. We trudge loudly down the quiet street in our heavy work boots. When the birds hear us coming, they chatter and scatter away. I find a picnic table under a shady tree and sit down. Nate sits too.

I open my lunch bag, which is thankfully still cold. I open my can of Mountain Dew and take a swig. Then I bite into my ham sandwich. Nate slams all of his pop at once and then lets out a huge belch. He grins at me, but I'm not impressed.

I chew my sandwich and watch the water rush down the stream. That current nearly killed me, but now it looks beautiful. I glance at the boat docks, but Declan isn't working.

A group of little kids and their moms hop off the merry-go-round and then play on an antique fire engine. The ancient truck is a permanent exhibit now, just a toy for kids to explore. The fire engine is covered by a barn-like enclosure, which includes a fireman's pole to slide down.

"You remember that old fire truck?" Nate asks, "One of my favorite things here growing up. Those antique tires have a distinct odor. You smell it? It brings back memories."

I nod, "You fell off the top of the fire pole and broke your arm."

"I did," Nate nods.

"That's an old memory," I say.

"It sure is. Very old. I think I was seven. And you were in town visiting," Nate pauses. "I remember, I was so glad that you were there with me. You kept telling me I'd be alright. That meant a lot to me. It really did." Nate looks down and speaks slowly, "I did a lot of thinking last night... And I talked with my folks, again. I'm not sure what my problem is, man."

"I do. You want to hear it? I have zero patience anymore."

"Shoot."

"You're obsessed with a girl who doesn't like you," I say, "And you're a compulsive liar."

"And?"

"And you had no right to attack me. You insulted me, insulted my family, told Matt about Melissa, and lied to Greg for no reason. Lied about Jen, lied to Billy's face. What else? Am I missing something? You lost my trust, man. I don't know what else to say."

"Okay. Fair enough," Nate nods. He watches a little boy climb the fire pole. Then he stares at the ground and sighs. "I'm not sure why I do it. I lie all the time. I guess I must enjoy it. It's like my little secret. A weird thing that I do. It doesn't make any sense. I lie about stuff that doesn't even make me look better, you know? Sometimes, I do want to impress people. Like, someone will ask me something, and I act like I know what they're talking about, but I don't. Or I won't know an answer, so I make one up. Stuff like that. Sometimes it's a competition thing. Like Matt will say he did something cool, so I'll say I did it twice. All just stupid, worthless lies. Other times I just make stuff up. For no reason whatsoever. Like that cat food thing. What the hell was that? I don't even know where that came from. A dream? A book maybe? A movie?"

"You sounded so honest when you told me that one."

"I know," Nate says, "That lie was planted in my brain somehow, and it grew roots, man. But it's not true. I guess it's not. Sometimes I can't even tell."

"That's not good, dude. All those details of the kiss story? Such an intense lie."

"Total fantasy. Another movie detail that I confused with reality."

"Maybe you just talk too much," I say, "You start running your mouth and all this crap spills out."

"Don't be mean, dude. Running your mouth? I hate that expression. Be nice, okay? I'm trying to be honest here."

I take a deep breath. He's right, he is trying, which is amazing, but I'm still pissed at him. Maybe my tone was too harsh, but what else am I supposed to say? I don't want to talk anymore.

Nate continues, "It's not all crap that I say. Declan runs his mouth. Billy runs his mouth."

"Billy doesn't make shit up though. Neither does Declan. And if he does, it's obvious that he's just teasing. You don't play obvious. You trick people. Huge difference. And those guys aren't evil, Nate. You tricked Greg into attacking me. A huge linebacker dude could have beaten me senseless! What the hell?"

Nate pauses again. He's thinking harder now. "The anger, the mean stuff, it's just more lies," Nate sighs, "I don't want to hurt you. I don't want you to leave. I really don't. I just got all nuts about Jen. I don't know why."

"You love her," I say, "But not in a healthy, normal way. At all. You gotta let it go."

"Stupid," Nate whispers, "I'm an idiot."

"Yes you are," I agree, "But not always. Not always."

Nate smiles. I guess that settles it. We're silent for a while. I finish my sandwich and a mini bag of Cheetos. Then I throw the empty lunch bag in the garbage barrel, and we start walking home.

Chapter 39: Everybody Has A Thing

It's still a long walk from Krape Park to Greenfield Street and Nate and I don't say much. I'm still mad at him. It's nice that he's trying to be honest, but I still don't trust him. And he's going to start running his mouth again soon, I know it.

Along Park Avenue, amongst the big trees and tiny homes, Nate points to a house. It's Lindsay Fittipaldi's place. She's the girl he swears he made out with once "for real." Man, I wish Nate would obsess over this Lindsay girl instead. That would make everything so much easier. I dare Nate to knock on her door, but he won't. Says he's too dirty and sweaty from work. We keep walking.

Nate points out the middle school and the eye doctor where Billy's mom works. Soon we hit the downtown. Nate tells a little story about every damn store down here. Like Emmert's Drug, with the old fashioned soda fountain. You can buy tomato soup for lunch, and they heat it up inside its can. They cook soup that way at Roy's Fountain too. And Roy's has the best milkshakes. You get the full soda glass plus a half-full mixing cup. It's always too smoky in there though, he says.

Then we pass Messing and Becker Sporting Goods, where Nate bought his mouthguard for his one year of Junior Tackle Football. He burned his mouth after he boiled the guard and bit down too soon. Then there's E & W Clothing Company, where Nate bought his Boy Scouts uniform. He quit Scouts because he hated saluting the flag with two fingers. "Why not use your whole hand?" Nate snaps.

Nate says he got an acoustic guitar at The Music Stand. He begged Patti to buy it for months, played the Fender for a week, it made his fingers hurt, so he sold it in a garage sale. He wishes he still had it though. We pass the Landmark Cafe, but most people call it "The Landfill." He says the chicken and rice soup cooks for so long it turns into salty jello. Speaking of salty, we pass the Mrs. Mikes Potato Chips factory. They're delicious chips but they're so greasy, you can light one on fire. And if you need a lighter, hit Clark's Gas Station across the street. Matt's friend Eddie will also sell you a pack of smokes, a lottery ticket, or a case of beer.

Awesome stories Nate, and at least they're honest ones, but who cares? I try to tune him out. He never shuts up. We walk by the Union Dairy and T&D's Toy Store, but I don't tell him a big dumb story about when I went there. I don't even say a word.

We walk past the beat-up, shut-down Rawleigh Factory. The ancient building, with three brick smokestacks, towers over us. Nate says that eighty years ago, the Rawleigh Company made millions of dollars for Freeport. The factory produced lotions and liniments sold around the world. Fascinating.

We come across a little store called Earwax Records and actually go inside. Nate quickly browses the New Wave section and buys a tape by The Smiths. The guy working behind the counter has blue spiked hair and an earring in his nose. Never seen anybody like that before. I don't like it. Looks stupid. The guy compliments Nate's hair turd. I cannot believe it.

"Sorry, Eric," Nate says, "We totally took the scenic route home. I had to get this Smiths tape. They're the best. They speak to me, you know? Like there's this lyric: 'Shyness is nice but shyness can stop you from doing all the things in life you'd like to.' Isn't that so true? Man, it's like great advice, I can totally relate to it, combined with this awesome guitar in the background that's actually good, almost classical. It's not like some power-chord grunge crap. It's real, highly talented stuff. I just love music, you know? That's totally my thing." Nate looks at me and grins, "Eric, what's your thing? Do you know? Like, what do you love? Matt likes video games. Billy likes church. Ronnie likes sports. Melissa likes boys, right? Um, Jen, she's way into school. Declan and Rach like to party. But what about Eric Daniels? What's your thing, dude?"

I have no idea. Do I not have a thing? Do I need one? This is just another stupid Nate idea.

"I know," Nate says, "I know your thing. You're a hard worker. You are!" he laughs, "My dad kept talking about you. Not stopping one bit, just shovel, shovel, shovel. He was so impressed. And I got jealous. I had to come back and work hard, man. You were showing me up. You are the working man. That's it!"

"Maybe," I shrug.

I have always enjoyed working. I helped out a lot at Star Pizza. Had a paper route too. And I like making pools. I do. And getting paid. Learning new skills. Work can be good exercise too.

"There's the smile I like to see," Nate pats my back as we walk. "Can we actually get along again? Like old times? Yes, indeed. Maybe it is possible."

Then Nate looks up and points to an 80-foot tall limestone obelisk with four life-sized, green copper soldiers standing guard. Nate says it's a Civil War memorial that went up in 1871. I smile again. I think Nate is more of a tour guide than a musician, but I don't say a word.

We finally get home, take turns in the shower, and then change into shorts and t-shirts. Nate plays his new tape in his bedroom while I read a newspaper on the couch. The music is loud and Nate howls along.

I turn on the TV, hoping for a Cubs game, but it's soap operas and talk shows. Work would be better than this. At least I could make some money. The air in the living room is hot and stuffy. I recline on the couch and close my eyes. I picture Jen paddling our canoe, looking over her shoulder at me and smiling.

When I wake up, Dad is sitting next to me reading the newspaper. Patti cooks onions in the kitchen. I feel groggy. I'm always in a daze after a nap. Work and the walk wiped me out. Manny and Nate get home with groceries, and Patti finishes her awesome chicken fajitas.

After supper, Nate and I play pool downstairs. The air feels much cooler down here. Dad and Manny join us for a couple of games of two-on-two eight ball. I'm not sure if the dads really want to play, or if they're just making sure Nate and I get along.

It gets late, and Nate's the first one to call it a night. When he goes to bed, he walks to the basement cave, not his upstairs room.

"That's a good sign, right?" Dad asks.

I shrug.

"Trying, huh?" Manny smiles, "Good man."

Chapter 40: One More

The morning starts with Dad's whistle, and all four of us guys hop in the truck. We stop at the warehouse and fill the truck with several heavy, black plastic wall sections. We get to the inground job, lower the plastic sections into the pool, and screw them together. The wall sections in the deep end sit on a small ledge, and the shallow ones rest on the floor. Then we tap in long carriage bolts that pin the wall to the soil.

Next, we grab some 2x4s and build wood forms around the pool. Nate and I dump large bags of Quikrete into an electric mixer. The sweet dust clouds the air and clings to my sweaty forearms. We add some water, let it stir, and then pour the cement. We fill a sidewalk-style landing that includes footings for a diving board, a large slide, and two ladders. It's heavy, dirty work that takes all day.

"We're done, boys," Manny grins, "Still gotta install the liner, but not till the cement cures," he pauses, "And sorry guys, but I have one more job that needs to get done ASAP."

"What? Are you kidding me?" Nate whines.

It's hard to believe that we'll have time to start another job this late in the day, but Manny insists it's an easy one. We head back to the warehouse, find a wall and liner for a small above-ground pool, hop back in the truck and ride to the next job. I recognize these streets right away.

"Here we go," Manny says, and Dad pulls into Nate's driveway.

"Wait? We get the new pool?" Nate smiles, "Yes! About time!"

It's funny to see how little Manny cares about the details of his own pool. We barely scrape the ground and don't even use the laser level, or sand. By the time we start stretching the liner, the sun is still pretty bright. Patti gets home and watches us work from the porch. She gives us a thumbs up and the biggest smile yet.

"I can finish the rest," Manny says, "Mike, why don't you take the boys to that store we were talking about."

"Sounds good to me," Dad says.

We hop in the truck, hit the highway, and twenty minutes later, we roll up to a red-striped circus tent set up in a grocery store parking lot, just across the Illinois-Wisconsin border. Black Cat posters hang on the walls, and at least twenty wooden tables are piled high with explosives.

Dad says we only have ten minutes to shop before the store closes. Nate and I run to the bottle rockets and fill our arms. Then we grab sparklers and ladyfingers. Dad laughs at how much we want to buy. It's a huge pile of explosives that covers the entire checkout counter. Dad says he'll pay, only if he can light some too. Nate and I happily agree.

When we get home Dad says Nate and I can light one bottle rocket each. We set our fireworks in an empty beer bottle, one at a time. Dad hands me his cigarette to light the wick. The short string sizzles for just a second and then shoots into the sky. At its peak, fifty feet in the air, the rocket pops, and a tiny burst of orange flame flashes across the stars. That feels surprisingly gratifying. Especially for a kid who hates fire. I want to light one more but Dad insists we save the rest for tomorrow.

Chapter 41: Jello Shots

I wake up to the sound of Nate snoring on the mattress beside mine. So loud. Who's the worst roommate, Dad or Nate? I check the clock. Ten-thirty seems early for a holiday morning sleep in, but I'll get up.

I head upstairs and find Patti standing at the kitchen counter. She's wearing red, white, and blue ribbons in her ponytail, a blue tank top with white stars, and red shorts. That's about as USA as it gets. In a glass bowl, she stirs hot water, jello powder, vodka, and milk. It makes a cloudy white solution, like a vat of thick saliva.

"Happy Fourth!" Patti grins, "My favorite day of the year."

"What is that?" I grimace, "Gross."

"Are you kidding me?" Patti says, "These are the prettiest, most patriotic vodka shots in town! Hands off, though. Adults only."

Patti stirs her bowl a couple more times and then pulls a sheet pan out of the fridge. The pan holds dozens of Dixie cups, already partially filled with a thin layer of red jello. Patti spoons in the new layer of white, and then places the shots back in the fridge. Blue must be next.

"You're going to love the Fourth on Greenfield, Eric. Did Nate tell you? We close off the block, and have a party in the street! You hungry? I got some fresh Donuts Plus. Go ahead. Have one."

No way. I pretend not to hear her donut offer and walk outside. What a gorgeous sunny day. And look at this new pool. Beautiful. That makes me smile. All full of water and ready to go. Manny cleans his grill in the shade, and Dad smokes a cig and drinks coffee at the patio table. The fireworks we bought last night are separated into two grocery bags. One is labeled 'Dads' with a magic marker, and the bigger one 'Boys.'

"All sorted out?" I grin.

"Oh yeah!" Dad grins. He hands me a cigarette lighter. "Let's try to wait till it's dark though, okay?"

"Okay, thanks," I smile and put the lighter in my pocket. "The pool looks full."

"The water is still pretty cold, but it'll do," Manny smiles, "Got some good news, Eric," he pumps his eyebrows, "Scored Cubs tickets. For tomorrow."

"Really?" I say, "That's great!"

"Yes!" Manny nods, "One of our customers has season tickets. Good seats too. Should be a fun day. Me and Patti can take you and Nate. You been to Wrigley before?"

"Never," I say, "Only Triple-A at Taylor in Des Moines."

"Welcome to the big leagues!" Manny laughs.

Billy and Ronnie cross the street and run over to the Garcia backyard, "You guys got a new pool! Wonderful!" Billy says, "And did you see? They already closed the street."

Billy shows me the orange traffic cones, and then we wander over to his house. Billy's mom and dad are busy in the kitchen, pressing hamburger patties and boiling brats in beer. Billy is excited to finally introduce me.

Yvonne wears her hair in braids, with a red tank top, and cut-off jean shorts. She's at least an inch taller than her husband. Bob has a bushy mustache, and a clean-shaven head, with a red t-shirt to match his wife. Both parents politely say "Hello," and then get right back to preparing the food. Bob seems very nice but I don't look him in the eyes. I know he bought that nasty porno. Or maybe it was Yvonne?

We walk outside and sit on Billy's front stoop. Then Melissa comes walking down the hill. She's with Greg.

"Hey, Mel-mel!" Billy yells, "The songbird! Looking hot! Happy Fourth! Yo, Big Greg! What's up?"

Melissa wears a bathing suit top and jean shorts. She carries a large bowl of potato salad covered in plastic wrap. Greg wears a Minnesota State football jersey with bulky cargo shorts. His massive arms carry a ridiculous amount of folding chairs.

Nate appears from inside his house and helps Greg set up the chairs. Billy, Ronnie, and I join them.

"Nate, you got a new pool," Greg says.

"Oh, yeah!" Nate nods, "Um, do you remember Eric?"

"Sure," Greg says.

"Well?" Melissa snaps, "You gonna say sorry, or what?"

Greg looks at me again and then realizes who I am. He blushes and extends his hand, "Oh my god, dude. Sorry about the other day. Really. A huge misunderstanding," Greg shoots a look at Nate, shakes his head, and smiles at me, "Happy Fourth."

Neighbors begin to pour out from every home, carrying more furniture and food. An old lady brings some deviled eggs, a thirty-something dad with three little kids starts a charcoal grill, a few middle-school girls jump rope, some elementary school boys throw a plastic football, and a pair of old men light up fat cigars. Melissa's folks arrive with her little brother, Tyler, and a giant plate of chocolate chip cookies. Manny wheels out his gas grill and cooks hot dogs, and the Garretts' burgers and brats. I help Billy carry a long, heavy banquet table onto the street. Billy has several chairs too, all borrowed from his church.

Three coolers are stashed in the shade filled with beer, wine coolers, pop, and juice boxes. Two card tables are pushed together and stacked high with coleslaw, beans, corn on the cob, potato chips, buns, and pasta salad. Somebody brings a halved watermelon full of melon balls. A couple of buckets of fried chicken sit beside a huge platter of grilled meat. Another table has desserts like blueberry pie, rhubarb cobbler, brownies, and a vanilla sheet cake. Then the neighbors line up, fill a plate, and raise a drink. Everything I eat tastes delicious, so I finish and fill a second plate.

Nate runs inside and grabs our radio from the basement. He finds an extension cord in the garage, tunes in some classic rock, and turns it up. 'Hot Blooded' by Foreigner, blares across Greenfield

Street. Nate also grabs the 'Boys' bag of fireworks and proudly sets it at our table like a centerpiece. The "teen" table, as Patti calls it.

The heat of the day reaches its peak as the beers flow and the party gets louder. Manny plays lawn darts with Bob, and Dad plays bocce ball with the cigar guys. Patti, Yvonne, and Johanna sip white wine spritzers in the shade. Some younger kids, including Ronnie, take over the pool and scream with delight. Greg starts a whiffle ball game but it doesn't last long in the heat. I do manage to hit one pitch high over Billy's house, and it feels great.

By three in the afternoon, almost everyone looks sweaty, and the adults look drunk. That's when Patti brings out her patriotic jello shots and yells, "Cheers to the USA!"

Then Jen arrives and I can't stop smiling. Sun-bleached highlights streak her blonde hair and tiny brown freckles spot her cheeks. She looks content, and happy to see me. Rachel and Declan arrive too. All three of them complement the new pool, grab a chair, and sit at our table. Declan peeks in the fireworks bag and laughs.

"Fully loaded, eh? That'll be fun," Declan grins, "So, question: When will the parents be too drunk to notice that we're drunk?"

"They've already passed that mark," Greg says, "Jello shots sealed the deal."

"Ooh, any left?" Rachel asks.

"Tons!" Nate says, and bobs his eyebrows, "I got you covered."

"Want a real drink, Deck?" Greg asks. He reaches into his cargo shorts and pulls out a pint bottle of Grand Marnier. Hiding the flask under the table, Greg pours a healthy dose into his own red plastic cup. Then he pours one for Declan.

"Fancy stuff, Greggy," Declan smiles, "It's a cognac, no?"

"Orange cognac," Greg nods, "My dad loves this stuff."

"Jesus it's strong!" Declan winces, "It'll get the ball rolling, won't it?"

"Let me try," Nate says. He takes a huge gulp and coughs.

Greg has another pint in another pocket and gives Nate another giant shot. Then Nate disappears, returning moments later with at least a dozen stolen vodka shots. Even Melissa and Billy try one, so Jen and I do too. Not too bad really. Tastes like normal jello, with a little heat at the end.

Nate quickly steals another round of jello shots for everyone. He's already getting klutzy and mumbling. Maybe Nate is sneaking extra shots for himself.

Then Matt arrives on his purple bicycle. "Happy Fourth!" he yells and greets everyone with a big grin. He shakes my hand and hugs Greg and Nate. Is he drunk too? Says he already hit a party at Eddie's house. That's the dude who sells to minors, so Matt must be lit.

"Time to light some shit up, Matt!" Nate yells, "Goddamn, I'm drunk."

I watch the parents' table and they look our way. Uh oh, did they hear Nate?

Chapter 42: Way Too Wasted

"Drunker than hell!" Nate announces again.

"Nate!" Jen whispers, "Not so loud!"

"Yes, Nate, shut up!" Rachel says, "Your mom is right over there. Let's move this party to my house before he gets us busted."

There's no argument to that. We all stand up and walk quickly past the adult table, keeping our distance. Nate drops the fireworks bag and I pick it up.

Patti has claimed the radio and 'Lady in Red' blasts from the speakers. She and Johanna sip margaritas now, and the dads drink beers. Manny and Dad giggle over their little stash of fireworks, deciding which to light first.

"We're heading to Jen's," Nate yells, "Adios!"

"Have fun!" Patti waves, "Happy Fourth!"

Our group heads up the hill. Melissa and Greg lag behind and argue about something. The drunken linebacker stumbles and nearly falls. Melissa slaps his arm and he straightens up.

Matt and I look in the fireworks bag while we walk. Matt's actually being pretty nice. He helps count and there's way more here than I thought. Over 200 bottle rockets, 50 packs of ladyfingers, and 100 sparklers. It'll take forever to light all these.

"Save the sparklers for tonight," Matt says, "They look better in the dark."

"We'll do these first," I say, and hold up the ladyfingers, "These aren't pretty at night, right?"

"Yeah, they are... pretty annoying," Rachel laughs.

"What are we waiting for?" Nate slurs, "Give me a goddamn thingy!"

Nate rips open a package of bottle rockets. "Who's got a lighter?"

I'm sure Rachel and Declan both do, but they ignore him. Dad's lighter is in my pocket, but I don't offer it either.

"Oh, come on you fuckers!" Nate whines. He throws the rocket in the air, makes the explosion sound with his mouth, and accidentally spits all over his chin. That's pretty funny and I gotta laugh.

Our group arrives at the Ditmar house. Nate runs inside and cranks up the music. A Bon Jovi song blasts across the backyard.

Pepper, the elderly dachshund, emerges from the house, sniffs everyone's feet, takes a pee, and then rests in the shade.

"Now can we blow some shit up?" Nate asks.

"Wait till it's dark!" Rachel says.

"Yeah," Greg agrees, "Let's go see what else there is to drink!"

"Follow me, boys!" Declan grins. He leads Matt, Nate, Greg, and Rachel into the house.

Jen, Melissa, Billy, and I stay on the wooden porch and sit at the patio table.

"Don't feel like drinking, huh, Melissa?" Billy asks, "If you're worried about your figure you shouldn't be. You are looking beautiful today. Damn!"

"Oh my god," Melissa rolls her eyes, and Jen giggles.

"Wow, Billy," Jen says, "You say what's on your mind, huh? That was actually pretty forward."

"Was it?" Billy blushes, "My bad."

Jen shrugs and smiles at me. It's nice to have Billy and Melissa here, but I wish I could be alone with Jen. I wonder if I'll get that chance at all today. It's already getting late and the sun is setting. A light pink line forms along the horizon.

"How about just one?" I smile.

I empty the bag of fireworks into a big pile on Jen's patio table. A red packet of ladyfingers looks too good to pass up. I find the blue wick, burn the end, and white smoke spews everywhere. I toss the firework onto the lawn and twenty-four ladyfingers explode in two seconds, like a machine gun, echoing across the neighborhood.

"Alright!" I laugh.

Billy lights a few more packs of ladyfingers and laughs like a nut. Jen lights a couple too.

Surprisingly, the sound of explosives doesn't bring Nate and the gang running outside. That makes me worry. Nate is already drunk and who knows what they're doing in there.

"What's taking them so long?" I say.

"Should we go inside and see?" Billy asks.

"No," Melissa says, "I know exactly what they're doing. Greg is acting like a drunk frat boy idiot. Probably pouring shots of tequila, or playing some stupid drinking game."

"Or smoking weed," Jen adds.

"You don't like drinking, Melissa?" Billy asks.

"No way," Melissa says, "Not excessively. I've seen my parents get wasted before. They are so gross."

"Wow, Melissa," Jen smiles, "Judgy, judgy."

"Oh shut up," Melissa says, "Yes, I've been drunk before. And so have you. But honestly, I don't like it. People get violent or sick, or just dead-stupid."

"What do you want to do instead?" Billy asks.

"I don't know," Melissa shrugs, "I hate fireworks too. I might just go home."

The sliding glass door opens. Declan, Rachel, Greg, Matt, and Nate slowly emerge from the house. They all look much drunker than before.

"Who wants a shot?" Greg asks and raises a bottle of vodka high in the air.

"Me!" Nate smiles. He opens his mouth, arches his neck, and Greg pours a splash down his throat. Nate coughs like he's gagging, but he somehow manages to keep it down.

"Ooh, I've got an idea," Greg says, "Body shots! Melissa, come here. Take your top off."

"Excuse me?" Melissa yells, "You are so drunk, Greg. Oh, my god. Billy, walk me home, right now. I'm done."

"What? The black kid?" Greg slurs.

"Shut up, Greg!" Melissa yells.

"You shut up!" Greg smiles.

"Whoa!" Declan says, "That's enough. Just let her go, mate."

"No," Greg says, "Come back here, Mel. Now!"

"Billy. Let's go." Melissa grabs Billy's hand and walks away.

"Go ahead then," Greg yells, "See if I care! Have a good life, skinny little bitch."

Oh god, this dude is toxic. He's prowling, and he's huge. The tension in the air makes me sweat. I'm not sure what to do. Melissa and Billy hustle down the street and out of sight. Smart. Jen looks at me and shrugs. Maybe we should leave too.

I watch Nate. He's on another planet. A minute ago he wanted to light fireworks and now he's forgotten they're even here.

"How about you, Jen?" Greg smiles, "Take your top off?"

Rachel yells, "Oh, hell no!" She punches Greg's arm, hard, but he just giggles.

"What?" Greg grins, "I heard Jen has great boobs. Nate told me all about it."

"Nate did, huh?" Jen scoffs, "Yeah, right."

"Really?" Greg says, "Well, well, well, Nathan. Did you lie to me? Again? Do you just lie and lie about every little thing you ever said?"

Nate stands completely still, burps, and stares at his hand. He never heard a word Greg said.

"Greg, listen, of course, he lies," Declan says, "He's a Freshman. With a turd hairdo."

"I didn't ask you, mick," Greg growls, "I asked Nate."

Greg nudges Nate's shoulder with the vodka bottle and he nearly falls over.

"Huh?" Nate smiles, "Oh, hey. What's up, man?"

Greg laughs, "Oh, shit. You haven't heard any of this? Where have you been, dumb-dumb? You are long gone, huh? Too much drinky, little buddy? Too much wacky tobacky?"

Greg pushes Nate's shoulder, harder this time. Nate stumbles back, falls forward, and his knees bang hard on the wooden patio floor. That had to hurt, but he's drunk and numb.

"Oh, hello. Whatcha gonna do down there, sweetie?" Greg giggles. He looks around like he's expecting applause. He gets silence, which angers him, and he scowls. "Nate! Damn you! Now get up. Look at me! You lying, worthless piece of shit! Get up, boy! I said, get up!"

Chapter 43: Blow Up The Moon

Nate's head wobbles as he looks up at Greg. His eyes are so glossy. He's either going to cry or vomit. He's lost. Somebody has to help him, but I can't fight Greg. The dude is huge and he beat my ass once already. If I say one word right now he'll attack me.

Is this what Nate deserves for getting super drunk? No. Nothing this bad. Greg is the problem, picking on a helpless kid, half his size. I can't stand here and watch.

Matt is too wasted to help. The booze or something else has kicked in and he looks green. Declan slowly paces around with a wine bottle to his lips. Is he paying any attention? Rachel and Jen exchange worried looks.

Greg slaps Nate hard across the face. Nate's nose slowly bleeds and he doesn't even notice.

"Greg!" I say. My voice shakes and all I can hear is my heartbeat.

Greg slowly turns to face me. "What in the fuck," he growls, "do you want?"

Greg squares his massive shoulders even with mine and takes a step forward. He's slightly unsteady on his feet, but my god, he's a giant. Greg stares me down while he unscrews the vodka bottle and takes a long sip.

"Eric just wants a drink," Jen says, "That's all." Her voice is shaking too. Jen looks at me and nervously nods her head.

"He does?" Greg says, "Really?" He thinks a second and then nods, "Okay." Greg puts the cap on the bottle and sets it on the table. "But first, I'm kicking his ass."

Boom! Greg's eyes roll back and his knees buckle. He falls to the floor like a tree. Declan stands over him with his wine bottle gripped like a baseball bat. The bottle did not break.

"Think again, asshole," Declan mumbles.

"Oh my god!" Matt yells, "What did you do?"

Matt collapses over Greg. He pats Greg's cheeks and forehead. Matt checks his head for blood and his neck for a pulse. Greg makes a soft moaning sound like he's having a bad dream.

"Oh, thank god, this idiot's okay," Matt says.

"What happened?" Nate smiles. He lies down on the porch and closes his eyes.

"Eric," Declan says, "Help me drag Greg to my car. I'll take him home. Get him outta here."

"What? Hell no!" Rachel says, "Declan, you're drunk. Stay here! Do not drive!"

"Relax, Rachel," Declan says, "I'm fine."

"Bullshit, you're fine, Declan!" Rachel yells.

"C'mon, mate," Declan whispers to me, "Give me a hand." With all of our strength, we drag the linebacker to the driveway and stuff him into the back seat. Greg moans several more times. He's going to wake up soon.

"I'm coming with," Matt says. He sits shotgun in the Chrysler and waits. "Take me home."

Matt asks me what just happened. How could he forget? Declan says that Greg merely passed out drunk. Matt gives a thumbs up. He's looking greener by the second. I'm afraid the motion of the car ride might make him barf. I grab the car wash bucket from the garage and hand it to him.

"Thanks, Eric. Stay here with Jen," Declan tells me, "I'll be right back."

Jen, Rachel, and I sit at the patio table as the New Yorker disappears down the block. Rachel lights a cigarette, and Jen lets Pepper out. Nate snores on the floor and Pepper snuggles against him for a nap.

Rachel complains about Greg being such a jerk, and Declan drunk driving again. She worries about returning to Knox College in a few weeks and whines about how much she'll miss Declan. Then she runs inside the house and brings Jen and I some "very mild" Zimas. I take a few sips and it tastes like 7-Up. Not bad, but still gross. Before I can finish, Declan's car pulls into the driveway.

"That was quick, thank god, you idiot!" Rachel says. She gives Declan a hug and a kiss.

"Of course," Declan smiles, "Smooth sailing. We dropped Greg in his yard. Laid him there by his hammock. Looks like he fell right out. He'll be fine. Then Matt puked all over Greg's sidewalk. He felt better afterwards, but still wasn't making sense. He apologized several times, for no reason, and then he called me a prick."

"He got too high," Rachel says.

"For sure," Declan nods, "Gotta know how to puff, either switch on, or shit the bed," Declan opens a beer, "I see Nate's napping, eh? He shit the bed for sure," he laughs, "Well, now, Eric, I see you're having a drink, eh? Good for you, mate! You look relaxed. Let's put all that awful violence behind us, shall we? Let's say we have another beer and try to blow up the moon!"

We drink a few Miller Lights and I do get lightheaded. I feel kind of wild. I laugh harder and lose my shyness towards Jen. While Declan and Rachel hold each other at the patio table, Jen and I sit just as close. Jen puts her hand on my thigh and I put my arm around her shoulders. Soon the sky turns completely black. Declan fetches yet another round of beers. Empty bottles cover the table and surround the fireworks pile.

"I've got an idea," Jen grins.

Jen stuffs as many bottle rockets and sparklers into one empty beer bottle as she can. We follow her lead, and every bottle gets crammed full. We place the stuffed bottles on the patio railing, and Rachel hands out lit cigarettes.

"Ready?" Jen grins.

"Hold up. Nate! Wake up!" Declan yells but Nate sleeps away. "He'll be fine. Ready?"

"No, wait!" Rachel lets Pepper inside the house. "Okay, now we're ready."

Jen counts down, "Okay, three, two, one!"

I start the sparklers with my lighter, and light bottle rocket wicks with the cigarette. Everyone is burning everything they can reach. Within seconds, the bottles light up. The sparklers spray, and the rockets fly into the air. But soon the bottles heat up too hot. The sparklers glow blue and one bottle implodes. Then another! Other bottles fall over and rockets shoot everywhere. We're covering our heads and dodging fire. The back porch is a total war zone. My heartbeat is racing, but I'm not afraid. It must be the alcohol.

"Hit the deck!" Declan laughs.

I grab Jen and we lie flat on the floor. I cover her head with my hand and she giggles. Declan and Rachel retreat and watch from the far end of the backyard.

The chaos wakes up Nate. "Hey!" he says, "What's going on?"

Nate stands up in a cloud of smoke and panics. He runs blindly, at full speed, and collides with the sliding glass door. "God damn!" Nate yells. His body ricochets off the glass like a rubber ball. Nate lands flat on his back and squirms on the floor. He glances around, trying to figure out what happened. The confused look on his face is pure comedy. Funniest thing I've ever seen.

I laugh so hard I can barely breathe. Jen laughs too and Rachel and Declan howl from the backyard. The collision did knock some sense into Nate, and he forces a laugh.

"Watch out," Nate grins, "That glass door is closed."

"No shit!" Declan yells and we're laughing again.

The firecracker bottle bombs fizzle out and the smoke clears. One bottle is still melty hot, and Declan sprays it with the garden hose. The porch is covered with ripped paper bits, broken glass, and spent bottle rocket sticks.

Nate finds Greg's vodka bottle and chugs it down. Then he falls onto the grass and curls up. Crazy. Did he pass out again? I think so. Declan and Rachel check on him and then disappear inside the house.

"Let's get out of here," Jen smiles.

Jen grabs my hand and leads me through the woods beyond her backyard. We come to a grassy clearing under a giant tree. Jen flops down onto the ground and lies on her back. I lie down beside her. The grass feels cool and clean after all of the firecracker smoke. I take a deep breath. Fireflies blink in the distance. I gaze up at healthy branches of wide green leaves. The crescent moonlight barely peeks through the foliage.

"Beautiful night," Jen says. She pulls my hand close. Our fingers intertwine.

Chapter 44: Diving In

Jen and I turn our bodies towards each other and stare. I love her freckles. The moonlight flatters every feature on her face, every little curve on her cheek. Her eyes shine like stars and she smiles.

I lean in, close my eyes and our lips near. I keep my eyes closed and hear her breathing. I feel comfort like I've never known. There's anticipation, and welcome, and longing, and joy, and we kiss. Then I lie back down, look up at the leaves, and Jen says, "I don't ever want you to leave." We lie still, in complete peace. I'm not sure how long we stay. When she stands up, I do too. Then we leave the giant tree behind.

We walk to the top of Greenfield Street. I hear soft-rock music and water splashing. It's Nate's pool. I recognize Dad's deep voice and Patti's "tee-hee-hee" laughter. Jen and I walk downhill and steal a kiss under the street light. Then we sneak into Nate's backyard, hide behind the bushes, and spy on the pool.

"They do have suits on," Jen says, "Thank god."

There are two couples in the pool, Patti and Manny, and Dad and Johanna. A peaceful green light reflects off of the water. I mostly see silhouettes but every once in a while a face comes into view. They're playing chicken-fight. Johanna balances on Dad's shoulders and tries to knock Patti off of Manny's. Patti has a sturdier seat on Manny's wide shoulders and the match is hardly fair. Johanna falls, splashes into the pool, and comes up a second later.

"You all right?" Dad asks.

"Damn you, Patti!" Johanna laughs, "Best three out of four!"

The dads take a moment to swig their beers and then another figure comes into view. It's Nate, wearing nothing but his boxer shorts.

"Geronimo!" he slurs and dives into the pool, head first.

"Jesus!" Manny yells. He lunges across the pool and lifts Nate out of the water, "What is the matter with you?"

"He's wasted," Dad says.

"Get him out of my pool, Manny!" Patti screams, "My god, he could have broken his neck! Nathan! You know better than that!"

Nate spits up water, "Momma, I'm sorry." He coughs like he might vomit.

Manny hoists Nate onto the porch and helps him inside the house. Patti hops out of the pool, waves goodbye to Dad and Johanna, and runs inside.

"Oh, Nate," Jen whispers.

"Yeah, that was bad," I say, "But I can't watch this either."

Dad and Johnna are left alone in the pool. I cover my eyes with my hand.

"Oh, stop," Jen smiles.

Jen turns my chin towards hers and kisses me. We're getting better at this.

When I look up at the pool again, Dad and Johanna have climbed out. They don't seem affectionate at all. Johanna towels off and puts on her shorts, while Dad finds his t-shirt.

"Party's over," Jen grins, "Is it our turn now?"

Dad walks Johanna down the block to her van. Then Dad hops in and they drive off.

"Whoa," I say, "You see that?"

"Don't worry about them," Jen smiles, "Come on, let's swim."

"It'll be loud," I say.

"We'll be super sneaky. No splashing. Come on!"

Chapter 45: Making Waves

Jen and I creep up to the side of the pool. Inside the Garcia house, every light is still on. Manny yells at Nate, while Patti shoves a piece of toast in his face. Nobody's watching the pool.

Maybe this will work. I dread taking off my shirt, but it is pretty dark here. I dip my hand in the water and the temperature feels perfect.

"Hold it right there!" a voice calls. Then we realize it's just Declan crossing the street with Rachel.

"Yes! We got here in time for the skinny dip!" Declan smiles, "Sorry to interrupt, but we have urgent news. Is Nate here?"

"Yeah," I point to the kitchen. Nate is slumped over the table. Patti drinks a glass of water, while Manny scowls and shakes his head.

"Oh boy," Rachel says, "He's so screwed."

"Speaking of screwed," Declan grins and pumps his eyebrows.

"Oh, my god," Rachel grins, "You've got to hear this."

"So we were looking for Nate, right?" Declan begins, "You guys took off, but Nate woke up and wanted another drink."

"You should not have given him one," Rachel says.

"Whatever," Declan shrugs, "He seemed okay."

"Not even close," Rachel says.

"Can I tell my story or what?" Declan smiles, "So we hung out with Nate for a little while, and he wasn't making any sense, at all, which was hilarious, and then me and Rach went inside for a sec. But when we came back out, Nate was gone. So Rachel starts freaking out."

"He was very drunk," Rachel says.

"Yes, and so I'm like, 'Let's go find the little guy.' So we walk, and we're tracking him, like he's a fox or something, right? First, there's a puddle of vomit in the driveway. We assume it's his. Red, white, and blue. Then we find his Nietzsche shirt, hanging on the neighbor's tomato plant. We keep walking that line, until we see a light coming from a house, from a basement window. The window is wide open with an odd mist coming out. There's no odor, so it's not smoke. But it's strange. Then Rachel says, 'Oh, that's Billy's house.' Okay then, Nate found his friend, and they're hanging out, no problem, right? But we better make sure. Then we peek into the window and see Melissa! Bouncing up and down on a sweaty afro. Riding the hell out of Billy!"

"What?" Jen smiles.

"Yes, exactly!" Declan laughs, "She's in the hot tub, sitting on his lap, making waves, baby! Splashing all over. Then Billy lets out this groan, 'Ooaahr!' Sounds like a broken tuba, mate! Loud as thunder! Then all the lights come on upstairs. He woke up the whole bloody house!"

"Oh, no," I grin.

"Did they get caught?" Jen asks.

"Don't know," Rachel says, "When the lights came on we ran."

"This just happened like two minutes ago," Declan says.

"Melissa might still be there," Jen smiles, "Come on."

Jen leads Declan, Rachel, and I up the hill at a steady pace. We wait on the corner of Greenfield and Alamo, right under the street light.

"Here she comes," Jen says.

With her hair soaking wet, Melissa speed-walks up Greenfield Street. When she sees us on the corner she slows down.

"Don't be scared, Mel," Jen calls, "It's us. What's up?"

"Oh, hi," Melissa says, sounding relieved, "What are you guys doing?"

"About to ask you the same thing," Declan grins.

"Why's your hair wet?" Jen asks.

"Oh," Melissa says, "Um, I don't know.

"Did you slip and fall into a hot tub, by chance?" Declan grins.

"What?" Melissa says.

"Declan!" Rachel laughs.

"I'm sorry, sweetie," Declan smiles, "But I just saw you two making love in the jacuzzi."

"Oh, my god," Rachel laughs.

"You should laugh, Rach!" Declan howls, "You saw 'em too."

Melissa turns red, "I can't believe this."

"Is it true?" Jen asks.

"Of course not."

"Melissa?" Jen says, "Truly?"

"No! But so what if it is!" Melissa yells, "I can do whatever I want, and fuck you for laughing!" Tears wet her cheeks and she runs towards home. Jen follows.

"Melissa, wait," Jen says.

"What? What do you want from me? You knew all along, didn't you? And you came after me? Why? So you could laugh at me? That's bullshit!"

"Melissa--"

"Why are you such a bitch, Jenny? Why couldn't you just leave me alone? You wanted to question me. To humiliate me. Well good job, you did it."

"I'm sorry, Mel."

"Really? Do you really feel bad? No. You don't care at all."

"I'm sorry. I didn't think it through."

"Billy's a nice guy, Jen. He really is. I've known him for years. And he worships me. He's sweet. He's really a good person."

"Okay. That's good then. Good for--"

"And I've never had sex. You know that! I'm not sure what Declan saw through the window, but Billy and I wore bathing suits. Declan is full of shit. But that doesn't matter. You humiliated me, Jenny," Melissa says, "Friends don't pull shit like that. They don't."

Jen slumps her shoulders and stares at the ground as Melissa walks away.

"I'm sorry, Melissa, really!" she calls, but Melissa keeps walking.

Jen looks up at me and a tear rolls down her face. I put my arm around her.

"Why did I do that?" Jen asks, "That was none of my business. And I know Billy is nice. Probably the nicest guy she ever liked."

"It's late," I say, "You're tired. Everyone is. It'll be okay. You'll see her soon. You guys have been friends forever, right? Friends fight sometimes. It happens."

"You sound like my dad."

"I sound like my dad too," I smile.

"Walk me home," Jen says.

"Sure thing."

I look around but Declan and Rachel are gone. A quiet calm blankets the neighborhood. A few partiers are awake somewhere though, because one last firework bursts orange in the sky. When Jen and I arrive on her front stoop, she pulls me close. She gives me a single kiss on the lips and then hugs me tight like she really does want me to stay forever.

Chapter 46: The Friendly Confines

Dad wakes me up with his damn bird whistle noise again. He says, "Morning. Um, there's been a change of plans."

Nate sleeps in the mattress beside mine. Even in his sleep, he looks like a complete disaster. He's sweaty, smelly and his skin is kinda gray.

"Remember the Cubs game today?" Dad asks, "Well, Nate and Manny are not going. Not anymore. Long story short, Nate got super drunk and dived headfirst into the pool. So, he's grounded. Matt got really drunk too. I stopped by his house last night and he was barfing his guts out. I'm not sure what you were up to, but judging by your normal breath and sparkling eyes, you didn't drink anywhere near as much. Good for you, Eric. Seriously. What happened to those guys? Jello shots? Well, you can tell me later. Good news is I'm going to the game now, and we've got a spare ticket, so you can bring a friend. Would Billy want to go? Go ask him quick."

"Okay. What about the other ticket?"

"Oh, it's for Patti. She suddenly decided she's a Cubs fan. Hurry up, Eric. We've got to leave soon."

I shower, get dressed, and run to Billy's house. His mom answers the door, calls Billy over but keeps standing there while we talk. It's kind of tense.

"Sorry, Eric, I'm afraid I can't attend the baseball game with you," Billy says, "I've been grounded. Two weeks. For using the jacuzzi."

"And?" Yvonne says.

"Having a white girl in the basement. Without permission."

"Oh," I say, "No problem."

Before Billy shuts the door, I mouth, 'Melissa.' Billy looks shocked at first, wondering how I know. But then a massive smile covers his face, and he pumps his fist. I'm sure he'd happily be grounded a year for last night.

I must admit I'm kind of happy that Billy can't go. Now Jen is my only option. And Dad won't mind me bringing a girl, I hope.

The birds are still chirping in the morning sunshine. I'm not sure what time it is, but it's early. I knock on Jen's door and nobody answers. She must be asleep. I walk around the house and try to figure out which window is hers. I have no clue. All the shades are drawn. I hate to be rude, but this is kind of an emergency. I return to the front door and press the doorbell five times. There's motion inside the house. I really hope it's not the mom I've never met.

Jen answers the door. Her eyes are all puffy from sleep. She's half-awake in her fuzzy pink bathrobe, and the girl still glows.

"Eric? What the hell?! It's barely eight o'clock."

"I'm sorry, but I've got an extra ticket to the Cubs game today. Can you come?"

"Hell no!" she groans, "I'm a White Sox fan."

Jen slams the door. A moment later she opens it again.

"Just kidding! Your face!" she laughs, "Give me a sec. I'll be right out."

Jen totally fooled me. I can't stop smiling while I sit on her front stoop and wait. Five minutes later Jen reappears in the doorway. She wears tennis shoes, jean shorts, and a blue Cubs t-shirt. Her hair is pulled back in a high ponytail and dark sunglasses rest on her pointy little nose.

"Let's Go Cubbies!" she grins.

I lean in for a kiss and smell toothpaste.

"This is gonna be fun," she smiles.

We get back to Nate's house and Dad flinches when he sees a girl by my side. He gives me a look like, 'That's not Billy,' and I shrug. Dad grins, but he doesn't say a word. Patti does though.

"Oh, boy!" Patti yells, "Bringing Jenny Ditmar along? Hi, sweetie. You guys an item now or something? Look at them, Mike. So cute."

Jen rolls her eyes and we're both blushing.

Jen and I hop in the backseat of Patti's little brown Oldsmobile. The beige upholstery is worn and soft. The car smells like cigarettes and perfume. Dad cranks up the AC and tunes in the radio. He drives, while Patti sits shotgun. We cruise through Freeport and hit the highway.

"Jenny," Patti says, "Did Eric tell you what happened to Nate last night? Jumping in my pool, drunk as a skunk?"

"Uh-huh," Jen nods.

"Turns out he wasn't the only drunken fool in my pool. Your sister and that Declan boy went skinny dipping."

"What?" Jen and I laugh.

"Yes. They were stripped down to their birthday suits having a good old time."

Jen smiles, "Sounds fun."

"Oh, yeah. Manny opened the door and screamed at them, and they went running bare-assed down the street. Very funny, indeed."

Dad laughs too, "Bare-assed?"

"Quite a sight to see," Patti giggles, "So how's your mother doing, Jen? Heard she's dating a man from Rockford? That was quick."

Patti and Jen gossip while I stare out the car window. We drive past a few country towns, then hit Winnebago, Rockford, Huntley, and Elgin. Soon we're deep in the Chicago suburbs. I read signs for Barrington, Hoffman Estates, and Schaumburg. Tall buildings and billboards cover the skyline.

"You mind if I have a beer?" Dad asks.

"Ready for a roadie, huh?" Patti laughs, "Sure. I'll join ya."

"Don't ever do this, Eric," Dad says.

Patti pours some Budweisers into red plastic cups and then chucks the empty cans out the window.

"Interesting," Jen says, "Looks like I might be driving home."

"No kidding?" Patti says, "You got your permit already, girl? You should've driven us in too then."

It's all Chicago exits now, and skyscrapers loom on the horizon. Dad exits on Irving Park Road and we stop in bumper-to-bumper traffic. Patti unfolds her roadmap and estimates another hour to get to Wrigley.

"Stay on this street till we hit Clark," Patti directs, "Then take a right."

"Clark? Okay," Dad grins. He tries to play it cool, but he hates big city driving. His fingers are clenched around the wheel, and a bead of sweat rolls down his forehead.

Meanwhile, Jen and I get comfortable in the back seat. She holds my hand and rests her head on my shoulder.

We're still crawling down Irving Park Road. The storefronts look dirty and crowded compared to Freeport. Dad finds Clark and then circles Wrigley for parking. We get lucky and find a spot on Southport, about five blocks away from the stadium. Dad grabs another beer and locks the Oldsmobile. Patti hands us our tickets and we start walking.

More fans appear the closer we get to Wrigley. Soon Cubbie-blue and white pin-striped shirts crowd the streets. The smell of hot dogs, onions, pizza, and beer fills the air. A 20-foot high wooden stand sells T-shirts with the name and number of every player on the team. A McDonald's has sold off every parking spot to fans. Loud men stand on milk crates and hawk programs for a buck. Scalpers whisper "Tickets" and bums beg for handouts. Wrigley Field rises twelve stories above it all.

I stare up at the famous red marquee and bump into a couple of fans. I hear an organ, and the PA system welcomes everyone to "The Friendly Confines." A line forms at the gate and I watch through a chain-link fence, as thousands of fans march up cement ramps to find their seats.

"Meet you inside," Dad yells, "Patti has to make a phone call."

Dad waves goodbye and disappears into the heavy crowd. He and Patti walk towards a bar called The Cubby Bear across the street. The place looks totally packed.

As soon as Dad leaves I kiss Jen. Just a quick little peck on the lips. She smiles. I hold her hand and we wait in line. Slowly, we file into the ancient stadium. The lower concourse feels dark and smells like rain. There's electricity in the air though as thousands of happy fans hurry by. We stop at a food stand and buy nachos and hotdogs.

We wander along, reading the numbered signs that hang from the ceiling. Jen spots our section, which is way closer than I imagined. We actually march down a cement ramp that leads to the seats.

Then I stop and stare at the prettiest field I've ever seen.

This grass is greener than green, and it just oozes summer. The sand on the infield is as fine as sugar, combed, damp, and perfectly flat. Against the brown sand, the bases look impossibly white. A colossal green scoreboard towers over the bleachers and the famous ivy wall, which looks thick and lush, covering every brick. Several players stroll around the field and chat, play catch or swing a bat. A television reporter interviews the Reds coach and security escorts a lucky little boy into the Cubs dugout.

The crowd in the stands is all smiles. Beer vendors roam the aisles with giant trays full of tall cans. A peanut guy and a cotton candy salesman also yell to sell.

An elderly usher stops Jen and me to check our tickets. She points to our seats, which are so close to the field. We're in the eighth row, third base side, behind the Cubs dugout. My green metal folding chair is more comfortable than it looks. I take a deep breath. There's so much to see and the game hasn't even started.

"Your first game?" Jen asks.

"Oh, yeah."

"I came here a few times with my dad. Pretty cool, huh?"

"Way better than I thought. Way better."

An actor Jen and I have never heard of throws the first pitch, and then a talented 5th grader sings the national anthem. The crowd cheers as the Cubs jog onto the field. Organ music plays 'Sweet Home Chicago,' and the game begins.

The Reds bat first while I finish my hotdog. It's greasy, salty, and not very warm, but somehow still tastes delicious. I dip a chip into my nacho cheese and then duck as a foul ball whizzes over my head. I actually hear the thing whiff by. Man, I've got to pay closer attention down here. I wish I had my mitt.

The first inning goes scoreless. Then in the second, the Reds center-fielder comes up to bat and crushes one. The ball sails high into the sun, and lands in the wire basket above the wall in left field. Home run. A Cubs fan immediately grabs the ball and throws it back onto the grass. We cheer him on. Then for a second, the whole place feels kind of sad. Wrigley amplifies everyone's emotions, it's intense.

At the bottom of the second, the Cubs left fielder, Derrick May, bashes one. The ball flies up, up, and out of the park. That's a homer! I stand up and high-five Jen, and then we high-five the couple sitting behind us. Everyone is ecstatic. The organ plays a happy tune. Tie game, 1 to 1.

At the top of the third, the Reds score again, with a leadoff single and a two-out double. But the Cubs answer in the bottom half, when Willie Wilson walks, and Jose Vizcaino hits him in. Then with two outs, my favorite player, the all-star second baseman, Ryne Sandberg steps up. He singles! Line drive right up the middle. Vizcaino scores and the Cubs go up 3-2. At the end of the inning, Dad and Patti finally show up.

"Having fun?" Dad says, "Great seats or what?"

"You missed it!" I say, "Ryno just hit in the go-ahead run."

"That's great! We were watching in the concession line," Dad smiles, "Man, I love this place."

Patti yells, "Go Cubbies!"

The fourth inning goes scoreless, and Dad buys a round of beers. The money and the beverages are passed down the row from fan to fan. I buy some peanuts and the guy chucks the bag at me. I love eating the nuts and tossing the empty shells onto the cement floor.

The fifth, sixth, and top of the seventh go scoreless. Then the PA announces the Seventh Inning Stretch. Everybody stands and looks to the press booth, high above home plate. Harry Caray, the TV announcer, leans out over the crowd. He says, "Ah-one, Ah-two, Ah-three!" Then Harry and thousands of fans sing 'Take Me Out To The Ball Game' at the top of our lungs. I put my arm around Jen and we sway back and forth to the rhythm. Dad puts his arm around Patti and they sway too. I laugh and yell, "One, Two, Three, strikes you're out!" The energy in the crowd is irresistible. Jen, Dad, Patti, and I all crack up when the song is over.

A couple scoreless innings later and Jose Bautista comes in for the save. The first batter strikes out, then the second batter walks. The third batter hits a grounder to Sandberg at second, and it's an easy double-play. The game's over. Cubs win! A white flag with a blue W is raised up high atop the giant green scoreboard.

"That's forty wins," Dad says, "We're at 500. Not bad."

"Want another drink, Mike?" Patti asks.

"How about something to eat," I say, "I'm starving."

"Me too," Jen says.

Patti looks at her watch and nods. The four of us slowly file out of the stadium and onto Clark Street. Every bar and restaurant along the way is mobbed. We keep walking and the crowd thins. At Southport, Patti takes a right. We're near the car now, and there are several bars and restaurants that look busy, but not overcrowded.

"There it is," Patti says.

She points to a restaurant called Chicago's Pizza. We step inside and the bell on the door jingles open. The AC hits me. The cool air feels wonderful.

Cubs and Bears memorabilia covers the walls of this place. Twenty or so tables with red checkered cloth sit beside a bar, with two TVs and several large windows. A few seats are open, and the blonde waiter sits us down in the large corner booth. I scoot in close to Jen. The walk felt good, but I'm tired after sitting in the sun. I feel a sunburn on my neck, and Jen's face looks pretty red too.

"I'll take a Budweiser," Dad says.

"White Zin," Patti orders.

"Coke for me," Jen says.

"Me too," I mumble, and read the one-sheet, laminated menu.

"What do you guys want on your pizza?" Dad asks, "Oh, Jen, when do you need to be home?"

"You're asking that now?" she grins, "Don't worry about it."

Dad orders two large pizzas. One meat lovers', and one mushroom and onion. Then the waiter warns us that each super-thick stuffed pie takes 45 minutes to cook. Looks like we'll be here for a while. The waiter brings out a sliced baguette and some butter, and Jen and I devour it. Dad and Patti suck down their drinks and order more. Patti keeps checking her watch.

At 5 PM the front door jingles open. Other customers have come and gone, but this one catches my eye. She's skin and bones with slightly hunched shoulders and wavy blonde hair. She wears jean shorts, a red plaid button-down shirt, and thick, black-framed glasses. The edge of a tattoo comes up from under her collar.

She walks up to the bar and slams a shot. Then she approaches our table and stands over us. At closer look, I think it's my mom. No way, I cannot believe it. My whole body tenses up. I'm frozen.

"Patti," she says, "Hi."

"No way," Patti says, "Is that you? Donna?! Holy shit!"

Chapter 47: Memory Update

Patti stands and gives Donna a hug. Then Dad slides out of the booth and hugs her too. It's an awkward handshake/pat on the back hug. I've never seen such a forced smile on Dad's face.

"Eric? Hi... Wow...You got so big. I don't know what to say."

I don't say a word. Is this happening? Is this really my mom? I still cannot believe it.

There's a large tattoo of a whisk on her forearm. On her thumb is a tiny black star tattoo, the size of a quarter. That's Mom's star, for Star Pizza. I totally remember that tattoo. Mom had tattoos when nobody else did. I sit completely still and I stare. Everybody is quiet.

"Sit," Patti says, "Please, Donna. Sit down."

Mom remains standing. I'm still not sure how to address her. Mom or Donna? I glance at Jen, and she forces a smile. Dad fidgets like his seat is on fire.

"Hello," the waiter says, "We doing alright here? Another round? And how about you? Can I get you a drink?"

"Gin. Double. On the rocks," Mom remains standing.

"Okie Dokie," the waiter says.

I catch Jen's eye again. She shrugs. I look down at the table and find an itch in my sock. I play with the straw in my Coke glass. Any distraction is welcome.

Then an older image of Mom pops into my head. She's not as thin, with longer blonde hair. There's flour on her wrists, and she's rolling out dough at the shop. She's angelic. Who is this person? This is Mom? But now she's so old. And so am I. It's her, I know it, but it's a shock. What am I supposed to say? I can't believe Dad sprang this on me. I blame Patti too. She arranged this for sure.

Or, maybe I shouldn't blame anybody. This reunion isn't bad. It had to be done. If anyone's to blame, it's Mom. Remember, she left us. And now she's back. But why now? My head is spinning.

The house fire, that must be it. Mom thought she had lost us forever. But why would she care? She didn't care what happened to us for years. She dropped that responsibility entirely. Anger rises inside of me. My heart rate quickens. My stomach growls.

"I'm Jen," she says, "You're Eric's mom, right? I see the resemblance."

"Nice to meet you, Jen. I'm Donna."

"Nice to meet you," Jen says.

Donna. It's Donna now. I'll call her that because she sure as hell isn't my mom. But she is. She was. That is my mom. I stare. I see it now. I see my mom in her eyes.

"Mom?" I say. My voice barely comes out. My mouth is suddenly dry as chalk.

Donna removes her glasses and wipes the sweat from her eyes. "I look different, I know. So do you. Last time you were just a little boy."

"That was a long time ago," my voice shakes, "When you left. And we never heard back. And now you're here. You showed up out of nowhere. Why? Why now? Why ever?"

"Easy, Eric," Dad says.

"Eric," Donna says, "I thought now you'd be old enough to understand."
"To understand what?" I say, "You could have seen me years ago. I needed a mom then too! Even more then! But you weren't around. Because you're selfish. You didn't want me. You didn't care! You should have visited. But you didn't. Not once!"

Tears roll down my face and it pisses me off. My whole body is trembling. I can't sit here for another second. I stand up and walk out the door.

The hot summer air hits me when I step outside. Jesus Christ, where am I? I look up. I almost forgot. I'm in Chicago. I want to run, but I have nowhere to go. Two Cubs fans walk by and stare at me. My face must be all red and soaking wet. Tears roll down my cheeks. I walk down the block as fast as I can. I hear footsteps and Jen catches me.

Jen holds me and squeezes tight. I shudder and tears drench my face. Her hand strokes the back of my head. I feel her heartbeat, pressed up against mine. I remember drowning. It's like the same helpless feeling. Again, I focus on Jen. My rock. I feel her arms, her shirt, the smell of her hair. I'm coming back down now. I can catch my breath.

Dad watches from a distance. He stands at the restaurant doorway. He sees that Jen has found me and goes back inside. Jen squeezes me tighter.

I take another breath and squeeze her back. Her body is warm and we're starting to sweat. Oh no, do I stink? Did I forget deodorant this morning? Everything seems silly, and I giggle. My emotions are so scrambled. Jen steps back and looks at me. She smiles even though she's crying too.

"You," Jen says, "Are the toughest son of a bitch I ever met."

I laugh and cry at the same time. Jen holds my face in her hands.

"You haven't seen your mom in years! She walks in, and you tell her off? That's insane!"

"I didn't mean to."

"I know. I know, but you did. It just happened. And that's good. It's the best thing you could have done. Get it out. Out in the open. If anyone respects how hard that is, it's your mom," Jen says, "But don't stop now. You can't run away like her. You've gotta come back. Spend some time together. It's been so long. No matter what she did, that is your mom in there," Jen pauses and her tears flow, "Eric, listen, I miss my dad so much. I think of him, and I miss him every single day. And I wish, I dream, more than anything, that if I could see him again, for just five minutes, oh my god. All the things I would ask him. Or maybe I would just hold him. See him. Be there with him. I'd give anything for that. I really would. And your mom is here. Right now. She came back. Don't miss this opportunity, Eric. Don't pass her by."

I hold Jen close to me and kiss her cheek. Then I see Donna. She walks towards us, sheepishly, dreading every single step. I sniffle and wipe my face on my sleeve. God damn it, I've got to get a hold of myself.

"It's okay," Jen says, "Just say hi. Start over."

I take a deep breath and Jen holds my hand. This is the last place I want to be. God this sucks. But I sense that Donna is also dreading this. We do have that in common.

"Eric," Donna says, "I know you're upset... so am I. I was afraid to come here today. I knew it would be too difficult."

Donna wipes the tears off her face and looks at me. Eye contact is too much. Her gaze drops to the sidewalk. She can't look in my direction at all. She's weak. And she reminds me of me. I squeeze Jen's hand. I can look at Donna. I can face her.

Then I realize that I'm literally looking down on my mother for the first time. She was so tall before, a giant when I last saw her. I was a little boy. Now I'm grown, and towering over a short, skinny old lady. Do I ignore her and try to remember the old mom? The faint memory who left me? Do I forgive her, and give Donna a second chance?

I stare into Donna's glossy eyes. There's nothing there. She's hiding behind a wall. This is harder for her. But I can handle this. I'm the one who needs to lead.

I let go of Jen's hand and wrap my arms around Donna. I squeeze her and she trembles. I hold her as she cries, and I cry too. Her hands land on my back, and then there's a familiar pat. We let go, and Donna wipes a tear from her eye.

"Your dad raised you good," Donna says, "You were better off without me, trust me. I'm no good. Every crisis, every counselor, every drug. I've been there. I was a wreck. I still am."

"It's okay," I say. I hold Donna again, longer this time, and I do feel a connection. That instinctive parent-child familiarity is totally there. It has faded. But that's okay.

"Come on, let's go, you guys," Jen says, "I'm starving. And you can't have an emotional reunion on an empty stomach."

"No, no," Donna says, "You guys go. I gotta leave. I do. It's fine."

Donna seems content. She has reached her limit. This feels final. And why shouldn't it be?

We saw each other. The images in our minds have been updated. What else is there to say? Donna won't be in my life. She never was. She tried for a moment, which took all the strength she had.

Part of me wants this to be over too. And part of me wants this moment to be happy. Temporary is easy. Another minute and she's gone. Then we can both move on, alone just like before.

Jen and Donna both wait for me to speak. I clear my throat.

"Okay," I nod, "Nice to see you. Take care of yourself, Mom."

I reach out and hug her one more time.

"Be good," Mom says, "And tell Mike and Patti bye for me."

Donna leaves quickly. Another wave of emotion is about to hit, and she needs to run before she gets knocked down. I watch the stranger scurry away, turn the corner, and disappear into the streets of Chicago.

"That's it," Jen says softly, "Let's go."

Both huge pizzas are served as Jen and I return. Each slice must weigh at least two pounds. Thick buttery crust lines the bottom, then a layer of meat, then cheese, and chunky tomato sauce on top.

Something is reassuring about eating a meal. For a moment we all chew and swallow and that's all that matters. I devour my first piece but hit a wall halfway through my second. Dad and Patti look stuffed too. Beers, sun, plus pizza equals naptime. Add an emotional reunion, and we're all exhausted.

Patti boxes up several pieces to go, pays the bill, and leads us back to the Oldsmobile. Dad drives, but he stops at a 7-11 for coffee. We hit the freeway, the sun sets, and Jen and I snuggle in the back seat.

When I wake up, we're back in Freeport. Jen tells Dad where she lives, and he pulls into her driveway.

"See you later, Jen," Dad says.

"See ya. Thanks!" Jen says, "Um, Mr. Daniels, is it okay if Eric stays a while?"

"What time is it?" Dad says, "Okay. Let's see. Eric, you can stay till 11:30. Your parents are home, right, Jen?"

Jen nods.

"Thanks, Dad," I say.

"No prob," Dad sighs, "Sorry I sprang Donna on you. Patti and I weren't sure if she'd show up or not. So I didn't want to get your hopes up, or down, you know? But I'm proud of you, Eric. That was tough and you did well, in the end. And Jen, thank you. I'm glad you were there for him. Sorry again, that was a surprise from hell."

"I know," I say, "I survived."

The Oldsmobile rolls up the street. Then Jen plants one of the best kisses on me yet. I feel an energy that rushes over my body.

"Come on in," Jen smiles. She opens the front door and yells, "Hello? Anybody home?"

Pepper greets us with a few ferocious barks. He sniffs my shoes and licks my ankle. Jen lets him out, and we find a note from her mom on the kitchen counter. 'Out with Charles, be home at 9.' It's already ten. Below the mom message, Rachel wrote, 'Where are you, Jen? You suck!' This is underlined several times.

"Well... we're alone," Jen smiles and pulls me closer. "What do you want to do?"

Chapter 48: That Crazy Witch

My heartbeat accelerates. Jen kisses me and her fingertips flutter down my arms. Jen leads me down the stairs to the basement. We hold each other tight and there's so much energy, so much attraction. I squeeze her and can feel her smile. I smile too and we kiss again. Then she takes my hand and leads me to the couch. She sits, grabs the remote, and turns on the TV.

"Let's watch a movie," Jen says.

It's a large finished basement, much like Nate's. There's a yellow brick fireplace in one corner beside a pile of dusty logs. Another corner holds a shrine to the Chicago Bears, with pennants, mugs, and framed autographed photos. A signed Walter Payton football card reminds me of my baseball card collection. Jen's dad surely collected this memorabilia for many years.

In front of the couch, a large television stands on a black stand, with a VCR, cable box, phone, and cassette stereo. A picture of Rachel and Jen as toddlers hangs in a large frame on the wall. Rachel's senior picture hangs as well, and it's stunning like Matt had said on the day I met him.

"I know the HBO code," Jen winks.

She presses a series of buttons on the remote. Kevin Costner appears on the screen. With a wooden staff, he duels a large man in a shallow stream.

"Robin Hood: Prince of Thieves," Jen bobs her eyebrows, "You seen it? That's Robin Hood and Little John. They just met. It's a pretty good flick, except there's this witch lady who is super creepy. She's got, like, a nasty eyeball or something."

"What?" I laugh.

"Yeah, it's gross. She's scary."

Jen looks at me and licks her lips. I lick mine too.

"I'm worried they feel chapped," Jen says, "Do my lips feel chapped when you kiss me?"

"Not at all."

We kiss, slowly at first, and then something happens. We absolutely smother each other. I can't kiss her enough, and she loves it. The couch gets in our way and we roll onto the floor. Then our hair gets in our way. I swipe it back and gasp for air. The basement is cool, but I'm sweating. We make eye contact and she laughs.

"Whoa," she says, "You're an animal."

We kiss again. Our entire bodies pulse in rhythm. It feels so amazing, so connected. This feels way better than anything ever. There's something uncontrollable here, and I can't get enough of it.

"Jen! Jenny! Are you home?"

"Shit!" Jen whispers, "Rachel!"

Our trance is broken, but the adrenaline is still here. We shoot around the room like ninjas. Wiping our faces, sitting properly on the couch, and pretending to look normal. Jen tries to loosen the tangled nest of her hair that formed on the back of her head. We sit close together, still catching our breath. I smile. Her face is red, and I'm sure mine is too.

"Jenny!" Rachel says, "Whoa, Jesus, you guys! Hardcore makeout session, or what?"

"What do you want?" Jen asks.

"It's Declan," Rachel says, "I can't find him anywhere. He got pulled over last night, at like 2 AM, another DUI, of course, and then he disappeared. He's such an idiot."

"Disappeared?" Jen says, "Are you sure?"

"Yes, I'm sure," Rachel says, "I have to find him."

"Why would he disappear?" I ask.

"Three DUI's, duh!" Rachel says, "That means jail time. He must be devastated!"

"Just try to relax, Rach. Are you drunk or something?"

"No, I'm not drunk!" Rachel glances at the TV, "Oh god, is this the movie with that gross witch? I hate that bitch. I can't watch."

The phone rings. "This better be Deck," Rachel says and answers the phone, "Hello? Hey, Tina. What? Where? Oh, my god... Yeah, that's totally it ... Okay, I'll drive there right now... Thanks... Yeah, we should... Okay... Bye."

"Let me guess," Jen says, "He's fine."

"No, he's not fine," Rachel says, "He's getting drunk, hanging out in the ghetto. Probably buying drugs or something stupid."

"There's a ghetto in Freeport?" I ask.

"Yes, there's a ghetto, dumbass. The east side is a total mess," Rachel says, "Listen, I don't have time for this. I'm gonna find Declan. If the phone rings, stop sucking face and answer it."

Rachel marches up the stairs. "Hi Pepper!" Rachel coos, "How's my little sweetie pie? So cute. Oh, I love you too, sweetie." Then the front door slams shut.

"Intense," I say.

"You mean annoying?"

We smile and kiss, but it's much more controlled. Things begin to heat up again, and we hear footsteps upstairs.

"Jenny?"

"My mom," Jen whispers, "I'll be right back."

So the mom really does exist. I wonder what she's like. I listen at the foot of the stairs, but I'm afraid she might see me. Jen hasn't mentioned that I'm down here.

I sit on the couch and watch Robin Hood battle an army of barbarians. They set his wooden fortress on fire, and steal Maid Marian.

Soon Jen reappears with a smile. She has changed into some silky green pajamas. Her hair is up in a loose ponytail.

"You're getting into the movie, huh?" Jen nods.

"It's not bad."

Jen grabs a blanket and snuggles next to me. I hold her tight.

"Does your mom know I'm here?"

"No," Jen whispers, "Don't worry. She's going to bed."

We kiss and cuddle under the blanket. Jen yawns and I do too. Meanwhile, Robin Hood grabs a pile of horse shit so he can pretend he's a smelly bum.

"Gross," Jen says, "Oh, no! It's the witch!"

"She's creepy, alright."

We watch till the end of the movie and quietly cheer when Robin's buddy, Azeem, throws his giant sword and impales the witch against a wall. The credits roll and Jen sings along: "There's no love, like your love. And no other, could give more love. There's nowhere, unless you're there. All the time! All the way, yeah!" Jen holds the remote like a microphone.

"Again, again!" I laugh.

"Shut up," Jen laughs, "It's a good song."

The HBO previews come on next, and Jen turns down the volume. I lie down, and Jen lies next to me with her back against my chest.

"We're spooning," Jen says, "Like we did in Declan's trunk."

"That's right," I say, "The couch is way better."

I settle into the cushions and Jen nestles into my arms.

"This feels so good," Jen whispers, "I never want it to end. Don't you wish we could do this, like, all the time? All day?"

"I do," I smile, "What a day it was."

"You wanna talk about it? Your mom, I mean?"

"No, I think I'm okay," I say, "Some heavy-duty drama, but there was lots of fun stuff too."

"Like those awesome seats? Ryno's RBI?" Jen says, "Making out with your hot girlfriend?"

"That part was my favorite," I smile. I am so happy. Jen just said, girlfriend. She totally did.

Chapter 49: The Hunt

I hear footsteps upstairs. Slippers drag across the kitchen floor above me. I feel Jen's warm body against mine. I open my eyes. I totally fell asleep. Oh, no! The VCR clock reads 6:30. I slept all night!

Jen's pretty little blonde head is inches from my face. Neither one of us have moved in hours. The TV is still on. I've got to get out of here fast. Is Dad up yet? I'm sure he is. Damn it.

I jump off the couch and gently shake Jen's shoulder.

"Jen," I whisper, "It's morning! I gotta go!"

"Hi," Jen smiles.

"Hi. I gotta go, but your mom's upstairs. What do I do? There's no window down here. How do I escape?"

Jen listens to the shuffling upstairs, "Yeah, that's my mom," she says, "Come here."

Jen walks me over to the Chicago Bears shrine. "Listen, right here," she says, "The bathroom is directly above us. When my mom goes in, you take off. Got it?"

"Nice!" I smile, "Is it that easy?"

Jen nods and wraps her arms around me. She's still very sleepy. We listen. I hear the slippers above, and a door latches shut. Then there's a pretty loud fart noise up there.

"Oh my," Jen laughs, "Go, go, go!"

I run up the stairs, open the sliding glass door, and keep running.

I am so late when I get back to the Garcia house. Nate already sits at the kitchen table, sipping orange juice. He's wearing his blue pool t-shirt, work jeans, and boots. Patti cooks eggs and doesn't notice me. I don't see Dad or Manny. I run downstairs and get dressed.

The guys don't say much in the truck, or at the warehouse. We grab the liner for the inground pool and clip it in. Manny installs the diving board, ladders, and the slide. We turn the garden hose on, and the job is basically done.

We drive back to the warehouse and grab materials for a 24-foot above-ground pool. Then we drive to the new job site on the north edge of town.

The spacious, country property has a large second-story deck, and the owners want the pool to be a safe distance from any jumping stunts. With bright orange paint, Manny sprays a circle onto a subtle hill. Then he and Nate leave to check the inground liner for wrinkles. Dad and I stay and wait.

Ten minutes later, a backhoe arrives to dig the pool area flat. He removes a foot or two of black dirt as Dad and I watch. The machine spews black exhaust and screeches like a car wreck. Man, this thing is powerful. It rips into the ground like a kid playing in the sand.

"Eric," Dad says, "When I--"

"I'm really sorry, Dad. I totally fell asleep. Me and Jen were watching a movie, and we were both super tired. That was a crazy day yesterday. We accidentally passed out. Honest. It was a total accident."

Dad stares at me, trying to detect a lie. Then he watches the excavator and takes a deep breath, "What about sex?" he pauses, never looking at me, only the digger. "Did you have sex?"

"No."

"Ever?"

"Nope."

"Good. You're only 15. But I know you're probably curious. And I can't stop you. But don't do it. It can be dangerous. Diseases, or having a baby? That's life-changing. You're too young. It'll only get in your way."

Dad leaves to talk to the machine operator. Dad points at a high spot and then walks back to me. That wasn't so bad.

"Get any sleep?" Dad asks.

"Yeah. Like the best sleep ever. I feel great."

"Good. You like Jen, huh? I was pretty surprised you brought her. But she's a nice girl. You two get along well," He pauses, "What'd you think of Mom?"

"I don't know."

Dad smiles, "Certainly did provide some closure. Especially before we go."

The excavator guy yells something and Dad runs over to talk to him. He gives a thumbs up and the massive machine slowly drives away. Dad hands me a shovel and grabs the laser level. We slice thin layers of clay and smooth the teeth marks.

Manny and Nate return. They've brought a load of sand and a dozen flat cement blocks. We spread the blocks, test each one to level, and the laser beeps its approval. We roll out the steel wall and screw on the tops and footers. Then the dads start trowelling the bottom of the pool, while Nate and I eat lunch together under a tree.

"Get this," Nate says, "Billy is so full of shit. I saw him yesterday. He said he made out with Melissa in his mom's jacuzzi. What an idiot."

"It's true," I smile.

"What?"

"That night you got wasted? Declan and Rachel saw them in the hot tub. Then we found Melissa, and she admitted it."

"No way! That's... amazing," Nate unwraps his sandwich as he shakes his head in disbelief, "So, what about Jen last night? No sex? Nothing at all?"

"Nope."

"Really?"

"We just passed out," I grin, "Are you still hungover?"

"Goddamn, I let loose for one day and now everybody thinks I'm an alcoholic."

"You got pretty messed up though. Do you remember when Declan knocked Greg out?"

"No. He did?"

"Yes, big time. He saved us all. Greg went psycho and almost killed everybody."

"I kind of remember now. Declan punched him in the nose, right?"

"Not quite," I say, "Do you remember jumping in the pool?"

"No. But I do totally remember getting out of it. I was freezing. I think my body knew that a pool was the only way to sober up. I did feel like complete shit all day yesterday. And I missed the Cubs game at Wrigley. And my dad walked in with a vodka bottle and shoved it under my nose, laughing at me. I took one whiff and nearly barfed."

"Why did you drink so much?"

"I don't know," Nate sips his can of Squirt and tucks his turd bang behind his ear. "I screw up everything. So I said, 'Fuck the world,' you know?"

"I don't know what to tell ya," I say, "I'm happy. I can't stop thinking about Jen."

"Well, you know what? I used to be mad about all that, obviously, and then I guess I had a sad stage, and now things are clearing up, and I'm feeling protective. For her. You'll break her heart, dude. You're leaving. Your whole summer has been temporary, and guess what? I heard my dad talking yesterday, dude. He interviewed a guy for a job-- your dad's job. Your days are numbered. Your dad has something lined up."

"Man," I mumble, "'Closure, before we go.' My dad just said it. And I ignored him. I wasn't thinking."

After work, Nate and I get home, change into swim trunks, and jump in the pool. Dad and Manny grab a beer and jump in too. I stare at Dad. I want to ask, but I don't. A part of me doesn't want to know. I think about Jen and I don't want to leave.

When Patti comes home, she also jumps in the pool and then orders takeout. Chinese food for supper, since it's too hot to cook. Jimmy Lee's delivery rings the doorbell with some of the greasiest egg rolls I've ever seen. The entrees look gross too, and I stick to the fried rice. After supper, Manny reminds Nate that he's still grounded. Nate complains and goes to his room to play music.

I stare at Dad again. I want to talk, but he's too busy talking on the phone instead. Is Dad talking to the job people? I overhear a date:

July 8th. That's only a few days away. Would we be leaving that soon? I pick up the phone in the living room and accidentally drop it. Dad hears me right away, "Patti? Sorry, I'm on the line," he says, and I hang up. I've got to tell Jen about this.

I leave the house, walk to Jen's place, ring the doorbell, and an older woman answers. She's dressed in office clothes, a blouse and a long skirt. The woman looks like Rachel, but with wrinkles, a thick layer of orange makeup, and a bleached perm. She frowns like she ate a lemon. Pepper barks, sniffs my shoe and retreats to the kitchen.

"Hello. Who are you?" she asks.

"Hi, I'm Eric."

"That's what I thought," she says, "The little homeless boy the Garcia family took in. What do you want?"

"Um, is Jen home?"

"Jennifer and Rachel left. I don't know where they went, or when they'll get back. They don't care to tell me much. But I have a feeling that will change very soon. It better."

Did I do something wrong? Besides being homeless? Jesus, I know Rachel can be pretty sassy, but that comment was lethal. I'm not sure what to say. She's about to slam the door in my face. Then I remember her loud fart from this morning and I smile.

"What's so funny?" she asks.

Just then Rachel's Chevy pulls into the driveway.

"Nice to meet you!" I turn and run.

"Eric!" Jen yells. She steps out of the car, grabs my wrist, and pulls me into the back seat. Rachel runs past her mom and disappears inside the house.

"What's going on?" I ask.

"It's Declan. He's still missing. Rachel went to see if anyone called."

"Does your mom even take messages?"

"You finally met her, huh? Sorry, she's pissed off," Jen says, "Her boyfriend dumped her."

"What happened?"

"He sobered up after a month-long bender?" Jen shrugs, "Came to his senses? I don't know. The guy was an idiot."

"But your mom loved him, right? I mean, she was always there."

"Loved him? I don't think so. She smothered him. Probably why he left her. Or the guy realized he was a rebound. No comparison."

I squeeze Jen's hand, "You'll be rebounding soon."

"Oh, shut up! Nope. Don't say it. You're staying forever."

Jen kisses me and smiles. Forget July 8th. That could mean anything. And if it is true, then I want to enjoy these last moments. I want to make her laugh.

"Jen, your mom called me the 'little homeless boy.'"

Jen giggles, "Really? That's not bad! Declan's been called much worse."

Rachel hops back in the driver's seat, "Oh my god, mom is such a bitch! She told us to stay home and I was like, 'Are you fucking kidding me?' And she was like, 'You can't talk to me like that.' And I'm like 'Ha! The hell I can't!' and walked out. Who does she think she is? She's been gone for weeks and thinks she's in charge? As if."

Rachel lights a cigarette, reverses the car out of the drive and speeds down the street. I've never seen her so tense. She's fired up like she drank three pots of coffee.

"So did anyone call or what?" Jen asks.

"No!" Rachel says, "I'm freaking out. I don't know what to do. We went to Tina's, Ben's, Steve's, Adam's, Andy's... "

"What about Stacey?" Jen asks.

"His ex? No way. He hates her."

"Maybe he's camping somewhere," Jen suggests.

"What about that super old house by the river," I say, "Did you look there?"

"The Rawson House!" Jen says.

"Let's go!" Rachel makes a tire-screeching U-turn. She races down Stephenson Street and turns a sharp right at the golf course parking lot. We hop out of the car.

"How long until it gets dark?" Rachel asks.

"At least an hour," I say.

"Good. I'm not setting foot in this haunted dump past dark," Rachel says, "Oh my god, are you guys holding hands? That's so cute. Gag me."

Jen smiles and squeezes my hand.

"How do we even find this shit hole?" Rachel asks.

"This way," Jen says.

The corn is taller now, and the sunbaked leaves aren't nearly as sharp. We hustle down a row of the cornfield and reach the grassy clearing that surrounds the house.

"What? Oh, man. Do you smell that?" Rachel laughs, "Somebody's smoking weed, big time!"

Rachel sprints ahead. She storms up the front stoop and kicks open the plywood door.

"Declan you son of a bitch!" she yells. Then she screams.

Chapter 50: Not A Ghost

"What the fuck?" Rachel says.

Jen and I catch up as Rachel turns and runs, away from the house and towards us. Her face is bright red as she physically pushes Jen and me to follow her in the opposite direction, back to the cornfield. I look back and see Matt standing in the doorway, but I don't stop to chat. I stick with Jen and Rachel, who doesn't stop running until she reaches her car.

"What the hell was that?" Jen asks, "A ghost?"

"No," Rachel says, "Not a ghost."

"I saw Matt," I say, "What was he doing in there?"

"None of my business," Rachel says, "I am so embarrassed. I should have calmly apologized and left, but it was the total opposite of what I expected I--"

"What happened, Rachel!" Jen says, "Tell us!"

"It was Matt Lyons and Eddie Pearn," Rachel says, "They were kissing. Heavy makeout session. Like you guys last night, but I saw them, like actually kissing, kissing. Not a big deal really. I'm just emotional. I'm sorry. I shouldn't have ran. I'm an idiot."

"Matt?" I mumble.

"And Eddie Pearn," Jen says, "He's the guy at the gas station that sells anything."

"Yeah, I heard about him."

"He's kind of a weird guy," Rachel says, "What is he, a Senior now?"

"Yeah," Jen says, "He's nice. A lot of people already think he's gay."

"Who?" Rachel says.

"It's just what I heard," Jen shrugs, "I don't know."

"So Matt is gay?" I ask.

"Look at Sherlock Holmes over here," Rachel laughs, "You solved the mystery!"

I'm still trying to wrap my head around this. Has this been going on for a while, or what?

"Shocker, huh?" Rachel giggles, "It's not a big deal. Really. Get over it."

"Now what do we do?"

"Nothing," Jen says with a serious tone, "We saw nothing."

I nod. Those boys were hiding for personal reasons. That's their secret. I'm not spreading any rumors.

Rachel says, "Refocus on Declan. He sure as hell wasn't in there. Where else could he be?"

"Shit," Jen says, "I'm having a hard time thinking right now."

"I know, me too," I say.

"Um, maybe Krape Park?" Jen says.

"We went there already," Rachel says.

"I know, but we weren't thinking about camping then," Jen says, "Maybe he's in the woods by the trail, or up on Flagstaff Hill. Or the Skate House? Could he hide in there?"

"Maybe," Rachel says, "Let's go."

Rachel starts the engine and races towards Krape Park.

"He's close," Rachel grins, "I can feel it."

"He's gonna show up," Jen smiles, "He just wants you to find him. It's another stupid hunt. You guys are so weird."

"He's done this before?" I ask.

"Yup," Rachel says, "He skipped school and drove to Omaha to see the Grateful Dead. He didn't tell anybody, and just left. Once he spent the night inside Luecke's Antique Mall. Hiding in some corner, because he's an idiot. Remember that time, before he could drive? He biked to Chicago and back. It took him three days. He got the new Beastie Boys album though. Just in time for my birthday."

"He rode a bicycle to Chicago?" I laugh, "That's nuts."

"Duh," Rachel smiles, "That's why I love him."

Chapter 51: The Door Is Ajar

The sun is setting by the time we reach Krape Park. An orange streak of light seeps into the dark blue horizon. The temperature drops, just slightly, and the air feels calm and perfect. There's still a little bit of daylight. Rachel pulls over at a wooden sign that reads, 'Chestnut Trail.' Jen and I hop out of the car.

"Look closely, please," Rachel says, "I'll check Flagstaff and the skate house, and then come back."

Jen and I saunter down the path. The trail is paved flat, and wider than expected for a forest hike. We leave the trail and walk deeper into the woods. I take a closer look around. I can barely see the river below, reflecting the last red glow of the sun. The forest is dense. Every limb is lush and green.

Where could Declan be? If I went camping where would I hide? I'd be closer to the river, so I could fish. But not too close or the ground would be wet, and at a park, police would see me. I look for the perfect site, something flat and hidden near the shore. Then I see something glimmer. Something is in the water. It couldn't be a rock or a stick, it's way too shiny. Is it glass? I can't quite make it out.

"What's that?" I point.

"The river," Jen says.

"No, not that, look closer. The little sparkly thing."

No trails lead that way, but there are several broken limbs on the forest floor. It's hard to notice at first, but then, I see two lines of damage, inches apart.

"Tire tracks," I point.

"I see it! Let's go!" Jen says.

Jen bounds deeper into the woods like a tiger, and I follow. She weaves under branches and through the brush. We get closer to the sparkly thing. Then we realize what it is and our jaws drop.

The pentagon-shaped Chrysler hood ornament perfectly catches the last sunlight and sparkles like a red diamond. Below, in the murky brown water of the steep shore, the grille, headlights, and long white New Yorker hood leads down into the depths. The windshield is still intact and the doors are shut. Maybe one door is slightly open, I can't tell.

"Declan!" Jen screams, "Oh my god! Is he in there?"

"No," I shrug, "I don't know. I can't see inside at all."

"Should I jump in?" Jen asks.

"No. It's too dangerous."

"But he could be in there."

"Jen, it's dark, and if you touch the car it could sink more."

"But what if he's in there? I could save him."

"Jen, if he's in there, he's dead."

"I've gotta know. I have to look! I have to!"

Jen kicks off her white Keds onto the ground and I realize that the forest floor is unnaturally clear. It looks like the New Yorker spun out before it sank. This was a high-speed accident. Could Declan jump out in time? Why the hell was he driving on a jogging trail? If he was drunk, his swimming skills and survival odds are even worse. I see Jen's socks come off next.

"Jen, stop! Seriously!"

"I'm going in!"

"No!" I grab Jen and hold her body against mine. She struggles and punches but I don't let her go.

"Remember the current? Jen, it's so dark! We can barely see anything now, underwater would be impossible!"

"But he could be in there!" Jen says and falls to her knees.

"We'll call the cops," I whisper, "They'll handle it."

"Jen?" Rachel yells from up on the trail, "Eric? Jenny? Where are you guys?" she says to herself, "Oh, god, they're not making out in the woods, are they?"

Jen looks at me and whispers, "Rachel."

This is the worst. How are we going to tell her? How will she react?

Jen squeezes my hand and takes a breath, "Rachel!" she yells, "Call the police!"

"Jenny?" Rachel yells, "Are you okay? Where are you?"

"I'm fine," Jen's voice shakes, "We're down here."

Rachel holds out her lighter and her face glows.

Then I feel the weight of something massive lurching. I hear the sloshing and gurgle of water and the New Yorker sinks even further into the river.

"Jenny?" Rachel whimpers, "What the hell was that?"

Chapter 52: Tomorrow

It's the middle of the night and I'm up, lying in bed. I can't sleep. My head is too full of worry. I can't stop thinking about Dad's job, or the Declan situation.

Rachel freaked out once she knew the New Yorker was underwater. She screamed "He's dead," went into shock, and wouldn't speak for an hour. Jen and I finally peeled her up off the floor, found a payphone, and called the police. Then we waited for the cops to show up, and when they arrived, they sent us home. They didn't let us watch in case they did find something terrible. We went home without knowing anything. Maybe they found Declan, or maybe not. Would the police call the Ditmars? They said they would, but they would have said anything to get rid of Rachel. They'd surely call Declan's parents. If I sneak over to Jen's now, would she still be up too?

"What time is it? 3:30 AM?" Nate groans, "Why are you up? You alright? Talk to your dad yet?"

"No."

"Matt came by here. He was looking for you."

"Oh, really?" I forgot all about that.

"He was acting weird. Like scared, or something. And he definitely wanted you, not me. Almost like an emergency. Why? Did something happen?"

"No."

"You totally know something! I can tell!"

"It's none of your business, alright?"

"Come on, Eric! I won't tell, I swear. Give me a hint. Come on!"

"No! Ask Matt! He's your best friend. I'm not saying anything, okay?"

"You should talk to your dad, dude," Nate says, "He was on the phone all night making plans. He's got the ball rolling."

"Great. No shit."

I lie still for a while, but I can't sleep. I wonder if I should tell Nate about Declan. Maybe talking about it would help ease my mind. Then Nate starts snoring, so forget that idea. I roll around on my mattress and no position is comfortable.

I close my eyes and see Declan in the New Yorker. He's dead, then comes alive behind the wheel. His eyes are wild. He hits the gas and tries to drive the car out of the river. "Pushy, mates! Push!" The forest is suddenly on fire. I wake up sweating. I watch the hours pass. When dawn breaks, I get out of bed.

I'm up long before everyone. I peek into Nate's old bedroom, and Dad's snoring away. I spot some papers on Nate's old desk. There's a résumé, a few letters, and the insurance settlement. It's worth tens of thousands of dollars, and it's just the stub. The check is cashed. Man, my Freeport days are so done.

I leave the house and keep walking. No humans are awake, but the birds are chirping like crazy. I walk down Greenfield and cut through a lawn. The dew on the grass smells fresh and cleans off my Converse shoes. Jen's place is quiet so I keep walking. I pass the construction sites and end up on the golf course. It's still pretty early, but I'm guessing some old guys have teed off by now.

I cut across a fairway I've never seen, a long Par-5 with a beautiful pond, and some tall, beautiful weeping willow trees. I spot the clubhouse and smell hash browns and bacon. The Chinese food sucked last night, and I'm starving.

The sign reads 'Park Hills, The Nineteenth Hole' and I open the door. The place isn't fancy at all. Grass stains cover the beige carpet and a few cheap golfing posters hang on the walls. There are no waitresses, so I stand at the counter and order the Hole in One: One pancake, one bacon strip, one egg, and one sausage patty. And toast. There's always toast. The pancake is fluffy as a cloud and everything tastes delicious.

I feel much more at ease after eating. Maybe things will get better. They have to. I stop by Jen's house and her mom answers the door. She's already dressed for work, and in a better mood today, but not by much.

"Girls are asleep, Eric, it's early," she pauses, "No sign of Declan."

"Okay, that's good news, right?" I smile.

"Perhaps," she nods and slams the door.

Did she smile back? I think she did, a subtle one. Either way, it's wonderful news. There's still hope for Deck. I feel relieved as I walk to Nate's, and then I see a purple bike pulling up the street.

Matt lingers by Nate's front stoop. He takes a deep breath. He knows it's early and doesn't want to wake people up, but he figures I'm surely home, and he probably didn't sleep much last night either.

"Over here," I yell from the sidewalk.

Matt turns and looks my way. He hesitates, arrogance free. It's the real Matt. Maybe. Then he smiles, nods his head at me, and the arrogance returns.

"Hey, um," Matt says, "Listen, I--"

"Forgot it even happened, Matt. Don't even worry about it."

"But," he pauses, "That was just a--"

"Seriously, dude," I whisper, "I don't care. You don't have to make up excuses or whatever. I'm not telling anybody. The girls aren't either. I'm sure as hell not telling Nate. So forget it."

"Really?" Matt says. He stares into my eyes, looking for honesty.

"Matt," I smile, "Look, I'm serious. It never happened. Okay?"

"Okay," Matt nods, "Thanks, Eric. I mean, if word gets out, I don't--"

"Hello, boys. You're up early," Dad says, "Everything okay?" He lights a Marlboro and sits on the front stoop.

"We're fine, Mr. Daniels," Matt smiles, "Thanks again," he says and rides away. I watch his bike disappear down Greenfield Street. Then I join Dad on the front stoop.

"What was that about?" Dad asks, "You and Matt okay? It's awfully early to be socializing."

"Yeah, great, um, we went out for breakfast, at the golf course. It was good."

"Oh," Dad says. He looks away and doesn't notice my obvious lie. I can tell he's worried about something else. He takes a deep breath and forces a smile. "Eric, listen," he says, "It's time to move."

"Really?" I say, "How about staying here instead?"

"Nope. Not an option."

"Why not?"

"There's reasons," Dad sighs, "You want the short answer or the long one?"

Dad watches the sparrows hop around on the sidewalk. He's collecting his thoughts. I've seen this look before, he's been thinking too much. The long answer is coming for sure.

"I'm trying to look at the big picture, Eric," Dad says, "Freeport is a nice town, I suppose, but listen, it's dead. Just like Fort Dodge, Iowa. I'm trying to be progressive, you know? I'm reading the paper, doing some research. I'm trying to see the future. Our future. What's the best place for us? There's a lot of manufacturing jobs in this town, but most factories are moving overseas. Once those jobs go, there's little here to offer, and the town goes downhill fast. I'm thinking forward, Eric, and I've been thinking really hard. So... What kind of place isn't affected by the economy? What place does not rely on factories or farms?" Dad grins, "And you know what? I figured it out. Want to guess? What do you think?"

"Chicago?"

"Not a bad guess. Big cities are pretty stable overall. But the problem is that some neighborhoods are very bad, and they bleed into the good neighborhoods. Chicago is fun for a ball game, but it's too big. Too many people, too many problems. Crime is constant. Plus, I hate big city traffic. Guess again."

"Antarctica."

"Oh, I didn't think of that," Dad smiles.

"You know," Dad continues, "I was digging a hole for a pool the other day. It was wet, you know, pretty muddy. And I went out, bought the sand, filled the truck, and stopped in for a coffee at Donuts Plus. Don't worry, I didn't eat any donuts. Anyways, I'm just filthy, just all grubby looking, and sweaty, and I'm walking back to the truck, and I look over at this guy. And he's pretty well dressed, you know? Glasses, tie, sitting in a shiny red Mazda convertible. He's got his son with him, who's about your age, sixteen or so, maybe a little older. Well, get this, the dad looks at me, turns to his son, and says, 'Boy, that's why you need to go to college.' Then he starts laughing, and his son starts laughing. I felt like throwing my hot coffee onto their windshield, but I didn't. You know why?... Because he's right. Education, Eric. Education. That is the one industry this country will never lose. We have some of the best schools in the world. And they're expensive. College towns are flooded with a new batch of dumb rich kids every fall. They've got a wallet full of daddy's money, and they can't wait to spend it. So, are you ready? I picked a town."

"Where?"

"Boston. The Mecca of American education. You've got Harvard, MIT, Tufts, and Northeastern, all literally within blocks of each other. It's crazy! If you want to open up a pizza place, that's where you do it."

"You're kidding me."

"No," Dad says, "And get this, Johanna's brother owns two restaurants out there! Primo spots too. One near Harvard Square, and one over by Fenway. He's got a ton of money! He's opening a third place. And he needs a new executive chef to focus the menu on pizza. Well, he calls pizza flatbread, but whatever. I've talked to him a bunch of times on the phone. He's a cool guy. His name is Hugo."

"We're moving to Boston?"

"Here's the best part," Dad grins, "Hugo also owns a property we can rent. It's a duplex type of house, but those are really popular out there, I guess. It's on the first floor, two bedrooms, one bathroom, just our size. It's got a decent backyard, and there's a pretty pond nearby. It's a very short commute, and you can walk to the high school."

"Boston? That's so far! Why can't you find something here?"

"Eric, listen," Dad says, "I've got it all set up. It's a great--"

"I don't want to move!"

"Eric, calm down, you'll wake the whole neighborhood."

"Can I stay here? I can move in with Nate, like, for good. Until I graduate."

"You kidding? You guys fight constantly. And we've bothered this family long enough."

"What about Billy?"

"Eric, come on. You gonna list all of your friends now?"

"What about Johanna, and Matt? We all could live there easy. That house is huge."

"Eric. Listen. I've considered all of the options already."

"What about the east side? We could rent our own place, really cheap, right here in Freeport."

"That's enough, Eric. The decision is made. The insurance is settled. The old Star Pizza lot is pending sale right now. The gears are in motion. I know you love it here, and I'm happy you made friends so quickly, and you can do it again in Boston... Look, I'll give you time to say bye to Jen and everybody, you don't have to work. Manny and Patti already know. Come tomorrow morning, we're gone."

"Tomorrow?! What? No way! I'm not going to Boston. I'll stay with mom."

"Donna?" Dad says, "Right. I was waiting for that one. And it stings too, just a little bit... I loved her, Eric. I did. But that was years ago. She ditched us bad. She left without looking back. Went and did her own thing. She had to. But she never visited us, and never gave a shit. Remember? I know you're still mad about it... Listen, that was our final goodbye because the midwest is history for us. Eric, I don't even have her phone number. She didn't offer it. I have no idea where she lives. Patti reached her by calling the damn bakery she works at."

"You don't even have a phone number?"

"No, I don't," Dad says. "Look, I don't blame you for being mad. I'd be mad too... You love Jen, don't you? And you want to stay close to her, I know. I know this stuff, Eric. I get it. Sometimes I feel like I was 15 yesterday."

"Oh, please."

"What? It's true. Really! Forgive me for being so old, and so honest, and Jen is a great girl, but there are millions of girls out there, and you're only 15! Girls come and go. That's the way it is."

"No. It's not. This is different."

"No, Eric! You're not different! You're not! You're a great kid, and you've grown so much, but you're still naive. You have no perspective. You think you've got it figured out, but you don't. In life, you start over, again, and again and again. You will meet another girl, I promise you that. You don't believe me? That's just fine. I'll tell you what. If Jen is meant to be? It will be. You guys will meet up again later, when you're older and wiser. Trust me, Eric. You've got to let her go for now. It's time to move on."

"I won't. I don't want to."

Dad finishes his cigarette and shakes his head, "Okay, Eric. I'm done talking. Tomorrow morning. We're leaving."

Chapter 53: Forget Freeport

Dad opens the front door and walks into the Garcia house. I'm still sitting on the front stoop and watching the stupid birds. What time is it? How long should I wait before I go to Jen's? Is she up yet? She's gonna be pissed. Tomorrow? What am I going to do? I put my face in my hands and try to think.

"You alright?" Nate asks. He stands in the doorway, in his boxer shorts.

"You're up early."

"You guys woke me up. What's going on?"

"I'm leaving."

"Duh," Nate smiles, "When?"

"Tomorrow."

"Holy shit."

"Dad took a job in Boston."

"Boston? What?" Nate says, "Hang on, I gotta get dressed."

I'm leaving. I said it. But it doesn't seem real. Boston? I try to picture Boston but I can't. I know nothing about it. The Celtics and Larry Bird. 'Cheers.' The Green Monster at Fenway. The Red Sox suck. They're as bad as the Cubs. I take a deep breath.

Forget Nate. What's taking him so long? I've been sitting here for a while now. Maybe Manny canceled Nate's workday too. Did Nate go back to bed? I'll walk to Jen's. Hopefully, she's awake by now.

"Thank god you're here," Jen says.

She hugs me as soon as I walk in the door. Her eyes are puffy and red. She's been crying.

"What's wrong?" I ask.

Jen shakes her head and looks away. She smells like peanut butter and jelly. She's so cute in her Snoopy pajamas, but she's not happy. I hold her tight and she calms down a little. Jen wipes her eyes and forces a smile.

"It's Declan," Jen says, "The police didn't find him, and Rachel is losing her mind."

"But that's good they didn't find him, right? Maybe he's still alive."

"Tell Rachel that. She won't listen to me, or my mom. She's beyond rational thought. My mom is yelling at her to calm down, which totally makes everything worse. My mom finally left for work, and Rachel went back to bed, thank god. And now you're here to cheer me up, right?" She looks up at me and smiles.

I shake my head and smile, "No. I'm sorry."

"Don't say it."

"I have to leave."

"I don't want to talk about it."

"Tomorrow."

"Tomorrow!" Jen's hands cover her face as the tears flow. "Why?"

"My dad--"

"Why did you tell me now?" Jen says, "Can't you tell I'm already upset?"

"You want me to wait?"

"Yes!"

"I have no time to wait! I just found out! What else was I supposed to do?"

"Eric!" Jen paces and Pepper follows her wagging his tail, "No! Just go! Leave! This is too much. It's been an emotional rollercoaster ever since you showed up. I can't handle any more drama. Just go, pack your things, and leave. Forget Freeport! No, don't touch me. Just don't. Forget us. It never happened. It's easier that way."

I try to hold her but she pushes me away. I reach for her hand and she slaps mine. She whirls around, runs to her bedroom, and slams the door.

I'm left standing alone in her kitchen. Pepper stares up at me still wagging his tail, thinking this is a fun game. Or maybe he's staring since I'm standing next to Jen's leftover peanut butter toast and he wants a bite. I grab the toast and throw it on the floor. Pepper gives me an appreciative smile and carries his treasure to somewhere in the living room. I wish I was a dog, only thinking about food. That'd be easy. Instead, I want to cry. I was her boyfriend for like a day and she dumped me. I thought Jen liked me. Maybe she's right. Maybe it is better this way. I take one last look at Jen's bedroom door and leave. Maybe Manny will let me work today after all. I could use the money.

Chapter 54: Total Acceptance

My last evening in Freeport, Illinois, begins with a thunderstorm. After a long, hot day of work, black clouds rush in and pour buckets of rain. Lightning fills the sky and dice-sized hail falls for a minute or two. Then the clouds disappear as fast as they arrived, and the blue sky returns.

I eat dinner with Patti, Manny, Nate, and Dad. It's a special Bon Voyage meal, with baked lobster tails, shrimp cocktail, salad, rolls, wild rice, and grilled steak. We finish with hot fudge sundaes. I'm totally stuffed. Everyone is. We sit at the table for a few extra minutes to chat.

Patti says she heard a rumor about Declan. His car was found in the river at Krape Park. I tell everyone that Jen and I actually found the car and called the police.

"That's crazy!" Nate yells, "Why didn't you tell me?"

"What? I was going to," I say, "But you were sleeping."

"Sleeping?" Nate argues, "Are you insane? Wake me up! It's Declan, man!"

"It's going to seem awfully quiet without you guys around," Patti jokes.

"You already miss us," Dad grins.

After dinner, Dad and I pack a couple of bags and throw them in the truck bed. Nate joins us on the driveway. He looks fresh and dressed up compared to me. I'm still wearing my sweaty work shirt, but I did change out of my boots at least.

"What's up?" I ask.

"Nothing," Nate smiles, "Follow me."

I look at Dad for permission and he winks at me. What does he know?

Nate and I walk to the top of Greenfield Street and then head down the hill towards Melissa's. I remember making this walk a few times. Once, to first meet Melissa, and another to kiss her at midnight. I remember meeting Jen too, and following her to Rachel's party, and TP-ing Billy's trees. That all seems like a decade ago, or maybe just a minute, I can't decide.

Music fills the air as we near Melissa's home. There are a few cars here, and the whole house is lit up.

"Surprise, buddy," Nate says, "This party is for you. I arranged the whole thing."

"Really?"

"Yep," Nate nods and pats my back, "Cheers to your last night in Freeport!" Nate reaches into his pocket and removes a metal flask. "Found this in the bar downstairs," he winks, "Vodka!" He unscrews the lid and hands me the flask.

"But I thought you were grounded?"

"Not for this," Nate says, "It's your last night!"

The vodka hits my lips and instantly burns. Nate sips after me.

"Shit is gross, dude," I mumble.

"Sure is," he says.

We enter Melissa's house through the front door and I scan the crowd. There are about twenty people in the living room and I recognize none of them. At least they look my age.

"Surprise!" Melissa yells, "There you are! Our guest of honor! We're gonna miss you, Eric! Leaving way too soon!"

"Hey, Eric!" Billy says, "We are gonna miss you, man! It's sad to see you go! Can you believe my mom actually let me party tonight? I think my dad helped convince her, I heard them debating it for a while. Oh, and Ronnie says bye. My mom decided he was too young to come here, but he said he'll miss you too."

Billy gives me a big hug and Melissa joins in. Then Nate wraps his arms around all of us and squeezes. The embrace ends and I smile at each one of my friends. Why would I ever want to leave? I'm gonna miss these guys.

"What? He's here? Finally!" Jen smiles.

Jen runs to me and wraps her arms around my shoulders. I guess she's not mad at me anymore.

"I'm sorry," she whispers, "About earlier."

"I'm so glad you're here," I whisper back.

Melissa and Billy dance in the living room and Nate joins a drinking game of cards. Jen leads me upstairs to Melissa's room.

There's a white rug, matching white dresser, and turquoise walls. A framed photo of Jen and Melissa sits on her dresser. A photograph of a rose hangs on one wall, and a poster of a ballerina hangs on another. Melissa's four-post bed looks like something out of a fairy tale, with white lace trim draped across the top bars.

The mattress is covered in light blue sheets, with fluffy lavender pillows. Jen locks the door, switches off the ceiling light, and the room goes dark. Only moonlight shines in through the windows.

Jen kisses me and I fall beside her onto the bed. I unbutton her blouse and kiss every inch of her skin. Jen pulls off my sweaty work shirt and I immediately feel uneasy. I'm fat, I stink, and I prefer my clothes on. But Jen is so smooth and secure. She kisses me without hesitation. I run my hands along her sides, and down her legs. She presses her warm skin against mine. The kissing gets hotter. Our hands wander further. We breathe in unison. She climbs on top of me.

"No," she whispers, "I can't."

Our eyes meet. We recoil for a second, full of doubt, and regret, but still wanting. We kiss again and hold each other close.

"Do we have to go back to the party?" she smiles.

"Nah."

Jen kisses my forehead and lays on top of me. Skin against skin. She's so calm. She's happy. Total confidence, peace, and acceptance like I've never felt.

"Have you ever felt this close with anyone?" Jen asks.

"No."

"No girlfriends in Iowa?"

"No way."

"Why?"

"Because I'm fat."

"Yeah, right. You're not fat."

"What? You don't think so?"

"No! Seriously? A little baby fat maybe, that's all. You've got body issues, dude."

Jen giggles and lays her head on my chest. Is she for real? Have I lost weight? I have been working in the sun and walking all over town. I thought Jen couldn't make me feel any better and she did. She readjusts her body and nestles up against my arm. She smells wonderful. What is that scent? We breathe in unison and enjoy our silence together. But I know she's thinking. Choosing her words carefully. I can't wait to hear what she says next.

"Do you ever miss Iowa?"

"Nope," I grin, "Not now."

"Oh, come on. What about your friends?"

"I don't have any. I'm fat, remember?"

"Shut up! Who's your best friend, Eric. Tell me."

"Hmm. I guess that would be Nick."

"Okay, who's Nick?"

"A kid from across the street. He was cool. But he went to a tiny church school and it sucked. His parents wouldn't let him watch movies, or listen to rock music."

"What?"

"Exactly," I nod, "So, we kind of quit hanging out. My neighborhood sucked. There weren't any kids around. Iowa feels like so long ago. I don't think about it much."

"You don't? I don't like that, that we move on, and forget," Jen says. She watches our fingers intertwine. Jen continues, "So much stuff fades away. But what about people? What about love? ... I miss my dad, but I'm getting used to him being gone. I don't want to forget him. Not one thing. But it's already happening. Pretty soon I'll get used to you being gone too. You never talk about Iowa, Eric. It's already forgotten."

"No, it's totally different," I say, "I hated Iowa. Kids made fun of me. My mom left us. The fire destroyed everything and I wasn't happy, so of course, I wanted to forget that. But when it's a good experience, that's different. And the people, for sure, the ones who really affect you, they never leave you. That's what love is, I think. The important stuff, the people who mean something, you never let go of them. Right? You just don't."

Jen smiles, "I hope so."

I kiss the top of Jen's head and she snuggles in closer.

"So where are you heading next?" Jen asks, "Chicago? Back to Iowa?"

"Boston," I say, "Didn't I tell you?"

"Boston?" she laughs, "Boston? You never told me that! I was such a mess this morning, I totally forgot to ask. Eric, Boston is a wonderful place. When I go to Harvard we can be together again. This is perfect!"

"Seriously?" I smile, "You're really going to Harvard? I thought that was just some crazy dream."

"Of course, it's a dream! And it's my life's mission. It's my goal, and it will happen. I'm so relieved now, Eric. You have no idea. I will see you at Harvard. I might even graduate early."

I close my eyes and laugh. I couldn't be any happier. Jen laughs too. I will see her in Boston. We're both pretty damn sure of that.

Chapter 55: Everyone Runs

When Jen and I rejoin the party, we notice it's gotten much larger. At least fifty more kids showed up. The living room is stuffed with people standing elbow to elbow, smoking, and drinking. A couple kids gossip about Declan's car. Some girls dance to the music in one corner. Melissa's little brother Tyler plays his Gameboy on the couch, oblivious to the couple kissing next to him. Across the room, two boys stand chest to chest, like they might fight. An older girl steps between them, ends the argument, and drags one boy out the door. Inside the kitchen, seven or eight kids play a card game. Hands are shown and shots are taken. I don't recognize any of these people, and some of them look old.

Then I spot Matt, out on the back porch. He has a full case of Budweiser. Billy and Melissa stand beside him. I don't see Nate anywhere.

"Where have you guys been?" Melissa smiles.

"This party got crazy!" Billy says.

Five or six partiers have discovered the trampoline in the backyard, and they're bouncing away.

"How many people can that thing hold?" I ask.

"Should we clear them off?" Jen smiles, "Shoot them with the hose?"

"That would be fun," I grin.

"Let's do it!" Melissa laughs.

As we head down the back steps, blue lights fill the night sky.

"Cops!" Matt yells. He runs back into the house with his full case of beer.

"Damn it!" Melissa says, "Who called the police? You guys better run."

Jen and I race across the backyard, Billy follows right behind us, and Melissa stays behind. Two officers with flashlights come sauntering around the side of the house. Kids pour out of the basement and sprint into the woods. We run beyond the trees and across a neighbor's lawn. I spot Nate with a girl and I wave. Suddenly Matt's not far behind us either. He ditched his beer.

We run until we reach Jen's backyard. Nate and the girl lean up against the garage and catch their breath. Billy and Matt grab a drink from the garden hose.

"Eric Daniels," Nate says, "Meet Lindsay Fittipaldi."

"Nice to meet you," Lindsay nods.

The curly brunette hides her braces when she grins. Her lipstick is slightly smudged. She's actually wearing a Smiths t-shirt, Nate's favorite band. Lindsay nudges Nate with her elbow and they smile. Nate looks a little drunk, but he's happy. I'm so relieved.

We wait twenty minutes at Jen's and then walk back to Melissa's. The cops and kids are all gone. The house is dark, except for one light in the kitchen. Jen leads us around back, and up the porch steps. Melissa sits alone at the kitchen table. Billy taps on the sliding glass door, and she lets us in.

"Everything okay?" Jen asks.

"Yeah, I guess," Melissa sighs, "Who would call the cops on me? The party wasn't that bad."

"What'd the cops say?" Billy asks.

"Nothing, They're coming by tomorrow to tell my parents that I had a party. Pricks. I told them that my folks knew and that it was supposed to be a small going-away party for Eric."

"Word got out," Jen says, "That's Freeport."

"I can't believe they took the booze!" Melissa says, "You see the puddle out front? The cops poured out everything. Even my dad's scotch!"

"What? No more booze?" Nate says, "Aw, damn, we're screwed."

"Party's over," Lindsay groans.

"Have no fear!" Matt says. He runs downstairs and quickly returns with his full case of Budweiser. "Still cold too."

"Where the hell did you get that?" Melissa laughs.

"I threw it in the dryer," Matt smiles.

"The laundry dryer?"

"Duh, cops never look there," he winks.

"Matthew Lyons," Nate grins, "You are a genius."

The party moves outside, onto the porch, and the beers go down quickly. Melissa grabs her camera and takes several pics of us together. We smile, put our arms around each other, stick out our tongues, or raise our middle fingers. It gets late, and we sink into the cushy patio chairs. Lindsay checks out first, and goes inside to crash on the couch. And that's about the time a motorcycle comes roaring down Greenfield Street.

We all sit up in our chairs with confused grimaces and watch the bike stop directly in front of Melissa's house. I remember some Freeport jerk at Rachel's keg party popping wheelies and causing chaos. What's this guy doing here?

"Who the hell is this," Melissa grumbles.

"The party's over!" Billy yells, "Go home!"

The driver of the motorcycle removes their helmet, but we can't quite see who it is.

"Come on, mate! I can't let my friend leave town without saying goodbye!"

Declan, in all of his glory, struts up the back porch steps. We stand up to greet him and hit him with a barrage of questions.

"Alright, alright, good god, you guys! Fucking relax. The DUI is some rumor bullshit. I did get pulled over, but I was sober by then. And I sold the New Yorker to Paul Frankel, that daft bastard crashed it into the river, not me. I took the money and bought this little motorbike, and rented a place in downtown Galesburg, like a block from Knox College. Don't tell Rach that part though, it'll be a surprise when she goes back. And yes, Jen, I just left your dear sister's side, and yes, she's happy to know I'm alive. She likes the bike too. Now Eric, let's have one last beer together, shall we?"

Declan opens the lid of a lunchbox-sized cooler, which is filled with ice, two cans of Miller Lite, and two cans of Bud. I can't decide which kind to grab. Do they taste the same? Is one better than the other?

"For christ's sake, grab a cold one, mate, don't let the penguins out!"

Declan slams his beer and toasts to good luck in Boston, then, "I'll leave you youngsters to it," and he disappears just as suddenly as he came.

Once Declan's gone, Nate prods the conversation along. He talks about that first night when we drove across town and got pulled over. He brags about the big fish I caught at his uncle's pond. Nate also brings up the bike that Matt gave me. Matt shrugs it off and then brags about the time he saved my life.

"It's true!" I say, "I swim like a rock."

The night gets later and Nate switches gears to scary, spooky stories. He retells the legends of the Rawson House and the Civil War Soldier who blew his head off. He insists he's been haunted several times.

Melissa talks about the creepy backrooms of the Masonic Temple. Once, during a dance recital, she explored the forbidden building and found a hidden door that opened up to a cavern filled with ancient black robes and animal skull masks. Then an elderly man appeared from nowhere and scolded her for snooping around. When he led her back through a secret chamber to the dressing rooms, she was positive that he had watched every girl undress.

Billy talks about his uncle, who was a dairy farmer, and one morning his alarm clock didn't go off. When the uncle was brushing his teeth, he looked out the window and watched his entire barn collapse. He should have been inside there by then. Over 100 head of cattle died.

Jen tells a story about her dad. He battled cancer for years. It started in his lungs and moved all around his body. She sewed together a little ragdoll to take to his check-ups, for good luck. One day the doctor said they found cancer in his left leg. When her dad picked up the doll, the left leg fell to the floor.

Then Matt says, "Hey. Did I tell you about Eddie Pearn's senior pics?"

"The dude that sells booze?" Nate says, "Your buddy?"

"Yeah, him," Matt nods, "I was working at the photo studio and Eddie was posing for his senior pics, acting like his normal Eddie self. The dude was smiling, friendly as hell, making jokes, and cracking me up. And then I saw all his proofs come in, and they were great. I put them into the folders and my boss, Ken, loved them too. They were perfect shots. They looked just like Eddie. Weren't forced or phony at all, which is hard to do for most people. But get this. His dad comes in, a few days later, and he's pissed. He was like, 'What is this shit? Why are you making my son look gay?' Then he demanded that Eddie take the shots all over again. Oh, man, it was sad. Eddie came back in for his second shoot. Dude had a suit and tie on, didn't smile once, and looked so depressed. Like he was dead inside. Dead but straight as hell."

"That is sad," Nate says.

I nod in agreement. Jen looks at me, and then back at Matt. Is that the end of Matt's story? I know he has more to say. Matt stares at Nate. There's a whole conversation waiting to happen. Then Nate belches and stands up.

"Gotta piss," Nate says. He walks into the backyard.

Matt takes a breath and shakes his head. He's almost defeated, but not quite. He smiles at me and I shrug.

When Nate gets back, I tell everyone about Donna. I talk about Iowa and the fire. Every little detail spills out. My friends can relate, and they add their own experiences.

As their stories are told, I notice that I'm in less and less of them. These Freeport kids go way back. Even Billy, who just moved into the neighborhood, has been in school and church here forever. I realize my time with these awesome people has just begun, and yet, it's already over. Maybe I don't belong here after all.

Chapter 56: See You Soon

The birds wake up and sing. Dawn breaks and sunlight showers over Melissa's porch. Everyone begins to stir, and I stand, stretch, and groan. Billy and Melissa are cuddled together, asleep on the patio chairs. Matt's asleep as well. Nate and Jen look pretty sleepy, but they lasted the whole night with me.

"Is it time?" Nate asks.

"It is," I say.

Melissa wakes up and says goodbye. She finds a pen and paper and asks me to write down my new address, several times, so everybody has a copy. She promises to send me doubles of the photos she took. Melissa hugs me and then sings a few bars of 'So Long, Farewell' from *The Sound of Music*. Nate joins in, way off-key, and we laugh. Then Melissa waves goodbye and disappears inside the house.

Jen, Nate, Matt, Billy, and I all walk together down Greenfield Street. We stop at the top of the hill. I see Dad in the driveway, pulling a rope, tightening a tarp over the mattress-filled truck bed.

Billy says goodbye with a big hug. He promises he'll write soon, and really wants to visit too. I tell him he's one of the nicest people I've ever met, and I wish him luck with Melissa. I ask him to say bye to Ronnie for me. Billy goes, runs past his front door, and crawls in through the basement window.

Matt's farewell is brief but friendlier than ever. He visits his uncle Hugo in Boston all the time and says he'll see me sooner or later. He shakes my hand, cuts through a neighbor's yard, and he's gone.

"My one regret," Nate smiles, "Is that we didn't TP more houses."

I laugh, "My regret is that you never cut off that turd bang!"

We can't stop laughing for a minute or two, all slap-happy and in need of sleep. Jen laughs too and puts her arms around my waist.

"Uh oh, I'm the third wheel," Nate smiles.

"What's up with you and Lindsay?" Jen asks.

"She's cool," Nate winks, "Eric, I'll let you know the details via our new penpal agreement. I may even illustrate."

"Sounds good," I laugh.

"I'll miss you, brother. I'm sorry if--"

"Nope. No way, it's all good," I smile, "Thanks so much, Nate. My oldest friend. Thanks for having me."

Nate hugs me and pats my back. He waves bye to Jen and walks home.

Jen leans in and squeezes me. A tear runs down her cheek and her face gets red.

"What am I going to do?" she says. She punches my arm.

"Ouch," I smile.

"You can't leave me!" Jen says, "You can't. I need to see you."

"I'll fly back. That's it!" I laugh, "Easy! I'll buy a ticket and fly to Chicago. Soon. Okay?"

"You're crazy," Jen grins, "It's too expensive!"

"I don't care. I'll get another job. I will. I'm serious."

"I know you are," Jen grins, "I love you, Eric."

"I love you."

Jen smiles. "Are you really gonna fly back here?"

"Swear to god."

"Okay. Don't forget," Jen says, "You've got my number. Call me as soon as you get to Boston."

"I will. I'll see you soon!"

"You will."

Jen kisses me. I close my eyes and kiss back. This moment isn't as sad as I thought it would be. I will see Jen again. I know I will.

Our lips part and our eyes lock. I don't look away and neither does she. Jen takes the first step. Backward, up the street. I walk backward too, down the hill. We laugh. A staring contest. Neither one of us breaks eye contact. Finally, Jen waves, and turns toward home. She spins back around and I'm still watching her.

"Work on that Harvard essay!" I yell.

"Already am!" Jen blows me a kiss. She waves once more and disappears over the hill. I wait for her head to pop back into view, but she's gone.

"Eric!" Dad yells, "Get your ass down here! Let's go!"

The Garcia family gathers beside Dad's truck. Patti kisses my cheek. Manny shakes my hand and thanks me for all my hard work. Nate shakes my hand too and says goodbye one more time.

I hop in the truck and Dad starts the engine. The Garcias stay huddled together and wave. Dad turns at the bottom of Greenfield Street, and we head towards the highway.

Even though I haven't slept, the rush of leaving Freeport keeps me awake for a while. Dad talks about his new job, and the school I'll attend. He's heard there are plenty of kids in our new neighborhood, kind of like Greenfield Street. Dad talks and talks. He's so excited about Boston. His voice lulls me to sleep, and I'm out cold before we reach Chicago.

I wake up in Cleveland, where the freeway takes a sharp turn. I read a newspaper for a while, look out the window, and then we stop at a diner in Erie, PA. I eat a greasy hamburger and Dad loads up on coffee. He quickly retightens the tarp over the truck bed, and we're back on the road.

"Dad," I ask, "Was that a silver bicycle I saw in the truck?"

"Maybe," Dad grins.

The sun sets and the sky goes black. We're crossing upstate New York for hours. I fall back to sleep. Then I hear Dad's annoying wake-up whistle.

"This is it," Dad says, "Arlington, Massa-two-shits. We're here, kid. We're home."

The street is dark. The houses look giant and close together. Our boxy home towers above us. There are two front doors, set ten feet apart, and Dad picks the one on the left. He finds the key under the doormat and we walk inside. The place is completely empty and our footsteps echo on the hardwood floors. To my left, there's a living room that leads into the dining room, and then a kitchen. The bedrooms and bathroom run together to my right. The whole place is trimmed with thick white molding that looks fancy and old-fashioned. Kinda reminds me of the Rawson House, in its glory days.

"What do you think!" Dad grins and hugs me, "This is our new place! All ours! Feels good, right?"

"Feels empty."

"Well, let's get our mattresses off the truck, kid. We gotta get some sleep. I gotta work soon. Come on!"

Chapter 57: The Epilogue

The sun hits my face and I hide my eyes under my pillow. Where am I? That's right, Boston. Or a suburb, I guess. I see Dad's mattress is empty. I don't hear him either. He must have left for work already.

I wander into the kitchen and find a box of Dunkin Donuts and a note on the counter. 'At work. Back at 5. Love you, Dad.' I bite into a super sugary chocolate long john and scratch my belly. The wooden floors glow yellow. The sunlight reflects onto the walls and warms the room. I open the windows and grab another donut. What time is it?

I open the front door and step outside. The front porch is huge, but the front yard is tiny. Every house on my street is a huge duplex, and there's not much grass anywhere. Parked cars line the flat street, and fences mark every property line. The trees here look so tall and beat up. There's a piece of newspaper blowing in the breeze. The stop sign on the corner got tagged with a Celtics bumper sticker. An older woman, Dad's age, walks her grey schnauzer down the sidewalk. We make eye contact, and I wave. The woman totally ignores me.

"Friendly," I say to myself.

The sun looks pretty high, so I figure it's about noon. I look inside my mailbox that hangs on the blue siding. There'll be a letter from Jen in here soon, or maybe Billy, or Nate. We need to buy a phone so I can call Jen. It'd be nice to hear her voice right now. I wish I could still walk to her house.

Then I hear the familiar churn of a bicycle chain, and I look up the street. It's a girl, about my age, with curly red hair. She wears a navy Red Sox t-shirt, cut-off jeans, and yellow flip flops. Her bike slows as she nears my corner. We make eye contact and she smiles. I guess I better say hello.

Acknowledgments

Thanks first and foremost to the small yet mighty town of Freeport, Illinois, where I grew up and met so many wonderful people who inspired this book. Go Pretzels! To my wife, mom, and sister who read the many early drafts and offered support, criticism, and encouragement. To my kids who inspire me to improve and keep trying. And to hope, moving on, and the moments you'll never forget.

About the Author

Ryan Standley graduated from the University of Iowa, spent some years in northern California, then started writing for newspapers in Chicago, and now lives a thousand miles east of Freeport, near Boston, Massachusetts. To the Top of Greenfield Street is his debut novel. Find him on social media @RyanPStandley or email him at ryanstandley1[at]gmail.com.